THE HIDDEN RIDER OF ᴅARK MOUNTAIN AND SHADOW OF A GUNMAN

Two Full Length Western Novels

GORDON D. SHIRREFFS

WOLFPACK
PUBLISHING
—— EST 2013 ——

The Hidden Rider of Dark Mountain and Shadow of a Gunman
Paperback Edition
Copyright © 2023 (As Revised) Gordon D. Shirreffs

Wolfpack Publishing
9850 S. Maryland Parkway, Suite A-5 #323
Las Vegas, Nevada 89183

wolfpackpublishing.com

Paperback ISBN 978-1-63977-321-3
eBook ISBN 978-1-63977-320-6

THE HIDDEN RIDER OF DARK MOUNTAIN AND SHADOW OF A GUNMAN

THE HIDDEN RIDER OF DARK MOUNTAIN

CHAPTER ONE

The wind had shifted an hour before the dawn, and the faint pattering of rain had stopped striking the taut tarp a foot above Cade Willcox's head. With the shifting of the wind had come a damp, penetrating cold. He hunched deeper in his hot roll, and his right foot found the one hole in the worn canvas cover. Cursing softly as his socked foot landed in a puddle just beyond the dripping edge of the tarp, he hastily drew in the wet foot and drew himself up until he could find his makings. He rolled a quirley and lighted it, surveying the wet, chilly world beyond the little square of the sheltering tarp with cold gray eyes. He felt as surly as a bee-stung bear.

Wasn't any use in stalling. He had figured to be in Bravo Creek Valley the night before, but the rain and mist had slowed him down on the mountain trail, and he had lost his way. He'd have to wait until he could get a sight of Dark Mountain so as to find Bravo Pass.

Cade cursed again as he pulled on his stiffened boots. His head struck the tarp, and water dripped on his left sleeve. By the time he bellied out from beneath the tarp, he was about as wet as if he had been walking in the rain instead of soaking up sleep in his hot roll. He scouted up enough dry squaw wood to start a fire in the shelter of a riven rock, and when he had a fair blaze going, he shoved the pot of Arbuckle's into the embers at the edge. Cade looked up through the soft woolly mist, hoping to get a glimpse of the dark, frowning head of Dark Mountain, but it was no use.

He had his simple camp struck and the sorrel saddled, pommel, and cantle rolls lashed in place when the coffee began to make the world a little more friendly with its cheerful bubbling and rich odor. He filled a tin cup and rolled another cigarette. The sorrel whinnied sharply.

Cade looked back over his shoulder. The mist-covered woods further down the slope were as quiet as the grave. He narrowed his eyes. This had once been Apache country, but the Indians had been on the reservation for some years. Not to say they were all tagged bucks waiting for government handouts while they tried to learn farming, for there were still a few rimrock 'Paches skulking about. A teamster down at Sulphur Creek had been killed for his rifle not more than three months past by some of the rimrock boys.

Cade sipped at his coffee, squatting on his heels, a cigarette dangling from the corner of his mouth. The sorrel was uneasy. Maybe a cougar was prowling through the drifting mist, thinking the horse was alone. When he got the man smell, he'd take off as silently as he had come.

Far up the slope, a rock clicked against another. Cade glanced up the slope, past the gaunt, fire-blasted trees. Nothing to see up there either. Possibly a rock had slid in the wet soil. Yet, there seemed to be something out in that mist.

Maybe, Cade thought, he was on the side of the Dark Mountain itself. If he was, there wouldn't be Apache around, for an Apache would go miles out of his way to avoid huge, lowering masses of rock and earth like Dark Mountain. Come to think of it; there weren't many white men who'd stay on the mountain after dark.

The sorrel shied and blowed. Cade quickly turned his head. The man was standing just beyond the riven rock, Winchester resting in the crook of his left arm, right hand gripping the small of the stock, and trigger finger lightly touching the trigger. His hat was pulled low over his shaggy brows, and his dark eyes moved slowly back and forth, studying the area of the camp.

Cade stood up. "You could get hurt indianing up on a man like that," he said quietly.

The sorrel whinnied sharply. Cade turned his head to see another man working his way slowly down the slick slope above the camp. "He's alone, Pierce," he said. He dropped lightly to the ground and rested the butt of his Winchester on the ground. "Nice hoss," he added.

Boots thudded on the ground beyond the shattered, blackened trees. Another man, limping slightly, led up three mud-plastered horses. It had been them the sorrel had scented. "No one down that away, Pierce," the man said. He tilted his head to one side and studied Cade. "Any coffee left?"

"Help yourself," said Cade. His Winchester was in its saddle scabbard, and the sorrel was twenty feet away.

The limping man took three cups from a saddlebag and came to the fire, kneeling down beside Cade. He looked up at Cade with a grinning face. "By God," he said, "mebbe we should'a waited until yuh had the bacon sizzlin'."

"I would have baked a cake if I had known you were coming," said Cade dryly.

The man named Pierce grounded his rifle. "If you had knowed we was comin'," he said coldly, "you'da been clear off Dark Mountain by now. Which way was you headin'?"

"West," said Cade. "Why?"

"From east of here, eh?"

"New Mexico," said Cade.

"From Quemado way? Or Buckhorn?"

"Neither," said Cade. "I crossed the San Francisco three days ago'."

"Hear, hear," said the man behind Cade.

"Shut up, Farley," said Pierce, looking at Cade from beneath dark brows. "You know where you are?"

"Somewhere east of Bravo Creek Valley."

"Yeh, but I mean right where you are?"

"Dark Mountain?"

Pierce nodded. "You ain't no local man. Any of you boys ever see him before?"

"Not me," said the man behind Cade.

"Muley?" said Pierce.

The little man glanced up at Cade. He sipped his coffee. "Can't say as I do. Looks familiar, though. You got kin around here, mister?"

Cade looked from one to the other of them. "What *is* this?" he asked quietly.

"Never you mind," said Pierce.

Cade placed his cup on a rock. "I *do* mind," he said.

A quick, darting smile raced across Pierce's dark face. "Don't get your tail in a crack," he said. "I'd hate to have to get fractious with you."

"I'll bet you would," said Muley. He grinned again.

"Muley asked you if you had kin around here," said Pierce.

"You'll get nothing out of me until I know what this is all about," said Cade.

"Hear, hear," said Farley.

Pierce sighed. He leaned his rifle against the riven rock and walked easily toward Cade. There was power in his sloped shoulders and meaty torso. "You just keep your hands off that cutter," he said. "Farley can part your hair with that Winchester." Muley hastily got out of the way, slopping coffee over Cade's boots.

Cade faced Pierce. The man smiled, but there was no mirth in his eyes. "I'm goin' to ask you three questions," he said. "You answer them pronto. If you don't, I'll beat the answers out of you. First, how come you came over the roughest damned mountains in this part of the country instead of the usual ways? Second, where you goin', and what's your business? Third, what's your name and what kin you got around here if any?"

Cade felt a slow fuse light up deep within his belly. "Maybe you'd better answer some questions first. Who are you? What's your game? What right do you have to ask me any questions at all?"

Pierce opened a solid right hand and spat into it. "Ready?" he asked.

The left fist smashed into Pierce's belly like the kick of a mule. His mouth opened and closed just in time to have a rock hard right fist meet the point of his jaw. He staggered backward. Cade whirled, kicking out at Muley. Muley's breath went out of him as the hooked heel drove into the pit of his stomach. Farley cursed and charged. Cade leaped to one side, gripped the rifle barrel, and dragged hard on it, pulling Farley across his outstretched left leg, smashing at the nape of the man's neck with the hard edge of his right palm. Farley cursed once as his face drove into the flinty ground, and then he lay still.

Pierce rushed Cade. Cade waited for the bear-like blows of the heavy man, danced back, stabbed a cutting left against Pierce's left eye, caught him twice with right hooks, and then as Pierce tried to close, Cade lined him up against Farley's prostrate body and hit him with a left and right to the jaw. Pierce fell heavily, struck his head, and lay still.

Muley, gasping and choking, looked up into the cold dark ring of a six-gun muzzle. He hadn't even seen the Colt rise from the leather. This tall, mean-looking stranger was stiff-legged with his hackles up, and Muley Smeed wanted no part of him.

Cade walked to the fire and picked up the tin cup. He filled it with coffee and drank some, the Colt hanging in his right hand. "Listen, mister," he said quietly to Muley. "My name is Cade Willcox. The younger brother of Dan Willcox of the Lazy W on Bravo Creek. I came over the mountains from San Francisco because I like those mountains and *preferred* coming that way. I'm going to the Lazy W to help out my brother's widow, now that Dan is dead. Those are the answers to your questions. Now, you tell me what your business is and why you jumped me."

Muley got slowly to his feet. "We work for Gus Cargill, owner of the Box C. We been losin' too many cows up this away. We seen you yesterday afternoon headin' in this way. We lost you and then smelled your fire and coffee this morning. Gus don't like strangers around here."

"This his land?"

Muley nodded. "All the area on this side of Dark Mountain is. Your brother's place is on the other side." Muley wet his lips. "You heard from his wife lately?"

"No."

Muley shrugged. "Won't be able to help her much," he said. "Ain't got but a handful of cows left. Been cleaned out, but then the sticky loopers was doin' just that when Dan was alive."

Farley groaned. He sat up and passed a shaking hand across his lacerated face. "Jesus God," he said. "Damned near skinned to the bone."

"Wait'll Gus hears about this," said Muley. He grinned. "Pierce Gatchell gettin' whupped in a fist fight. Hellsfire! He never even got in a lick at Willcox here. Farley Mosston gettin' flattened without never gettin' a shot off from his Winchester! Hawww!"

"You didn't do so well from the looks of you," growled Farley.

Muley shrugged. "Me, I ain't a real fightin' man like you two hombres. Hawww!"

Cade holstered his Colt. "Which way to Bravo Pass?" he asked.

Muley jerked a thumb over his shoulder. "Follow that little crick to the fork. The right fork goes through the pass. Yuh can't miss it."

Cade filled the three cups of the Box C men, carried the pot to his horse, tied the pot to the saddle, then swung up on the sorrel. "Follow the little crick to the fork. Take the right fork through the pass," he said as he rolled a cigarette.

"Keno," said Muley.

Cade lighted his cigarette. "Much obliged," he said politely.

"My pleasure," said Muley. He watched Cade ride down the slope and vanish into the dripping woods. "Well, I'll be double-damned," he said.

Farley picked up his rifle and walked stiff-legged to his horse. His face was white beneath the streaked blood of it.

"Wait," said Muley.

Farley thrust his left foot into the stirrup.

Muley stood up and drew his Colt. He cocked it. "Farley Mosston," he said quietly, "you got no call to gun that man. We walked into a bobcat with bristles on his belly. You mess with him, and you'll get another craw full. Lay off, kid."

Farley spat blood. "Keep your nose out'a this," he said.

"He's right, Farley," said Pierce Gatchell. He rubbed his swollen jaw and then gingerly felt the back of his skull. "Sonofabitch surprised me," he added.

"Sure as hell did," said Muley. "Hawww!"

Pierce stood up and eyed the little man. "One of these days," he said thinly, "I'm goin' to ram a fist down that gullet of yours when you bray like a jackass."

Muley's face went sober. He picked up his cup and sipped at the coffee. "Coffee's still hot," he said.

Pierce kicked out at his cup, scattering the liquid against the riven rock. "Let's go," he said.

Farley turned. He levered a round into his Winchester and fired, all in one fluid motion. The heavy slug smashed the remaining tin cup and drove it tinkling down the slope. The echo of the gun report slammed back and forth between the high rock walls until it died away. The acrid gun smoke drifted into the thinning mist. Farley's face looked like a death mask above the smoking rifle.

Pierce Gatchell walked to his horse. "Don't say nothin' about this to Gus," he said. He looked directly at Muley.

Muley drained his cup. "Cross my heart and hope to die," he said soberly.

"You talk, and you might just die," said Pierce.

Muley did not dare look at Farley Mosston. They all mounted and rode slowly down toward the creek.

Cade Willcox had heard the rifle shot far behind him. He sat for a moment in the saddle, big hand resting on the cantle pack. "One of these days, Hardtack," he said to the sorrel, "I'm going to learn how to keep a rein on this temper of mine. That was a damned close thing back there." Cade grinned. "Nothing like making friends as soon as you get into a new country."

He rode along the brawling creek until he reached the fork. The mist was clearing as the wind drove up the canyons and the pass. He looked up at the towering bulk of Dark Mountain. The sun was striking the other peaks beyond it, but a cloud hung over Dark Mountain. A chill-looking, dismal sort of cloud. Cade eyed the shattered lower slopes of the mountain, a tangled jungle of riven rock, talus slopes, fire-blackened, and lightning blasted timber. None of the other peaks seemed to have been the target for the primeval forces of nature as Dark Mountain had been. No wonder the Apache shunned it. Not even an early rising hawk or eagle hung on motionless wings above those blasted slopes. Cade shivered a little in the chilly wind.

He rode through the towering pass, eyeing the thin,

white rivulets of water that ran freely from high ledges and splits in the weathered rock to dissipate into sun-struck, shimmering veils of water that dropped on the shattered slopes far below to form again into rivulets that found their way to brawling Bravo Creek.

When the sun was fully up, he reached the narrow mouth of the pass and looked far below to where the creek flowed in sinuous curves and loops through a lush mountain meadowland. A thin wraith of smoke arose from some hidden source. As far as the eye could see was the Valley of the Bravo, and it looked good to Cade Will-cox. He had never been in that country, although Dan, in letters of years ago, had extolled the virtues of the Valley of the Bravo in an effort to get Cade to settle down with him on the Lazy W. That had been before Sarah, his first wife, had died on the slopes of Dark Mountain one rainy night when she had driven her buckboard over the side of the road. After that, there had been a long silence from Dan. The next letter, several years later, had been to announce Dan's wedding to Lucy Arnold. A later letter had said that Lucy was proving to be a good mother to their young son Grant. The next letter had spanned the gap of two years to let Cade know his brother was dead, found shot to death on the slopes of Dark Mountain, not far from where Sarah Willcox had died.

Cade rode down the slope toward the valley trail. It had taken a little time to get a leave of absence from the Arizona Rangers. Cade had wanted to resign, but Burton Mossman, head ranger, had told him to take a leave of absence for a year and then decide what he wanted to do. Therefore Cade still had his badge and credentials. The credentials were sewn into his waistbelt lining, and the badge was pinned inside his shirt, for Arizona Rangers rode undercover at all times, except when making an arrest.

Cade's last job for the Rangers had been to deliver a prisoner to the sheriff of Catron County, New Mexico

Territory. From there, he had ridden toward San Francisco to cross back into Arizona, with nothing but deer and bears and sky high and lonely hawks for distant company. He had liked it.

He looked back up the pass. There was a smell of death in this country, an odor of death and violence, and of deep and dark thoughts. He could have easily been killed back there. He had heard of Big Gus Cargill and the Box C. He ranked as high in the Dark Mountain country as John Slaughter ranked in Cochise County down along the Border. Cade would have to walk a little more quietly in this country.

The sun was fully up when he reached the Valley Road. He looked back at the sun-topped peaks, bright in the golden light, a shining backdrop to a beautiful and wild country, once beloved of the Apache. There was one distracting feature. Dark Mountain seemed not to absorb any of that lovely golden light. It seemed to force it back from the eternal gloominess and secretiveness of the massive pile it formed in the range. It seemed to be eternally waiting, waiting, waiting...

CHAPTER TWO

The Lazy W was well sited. Trust Dan Willcox to have an eye for such matters. In the timber beyond the ranch buildings, the sunlight shafted down between the trees and glinted from the rushing waters of the North Fork of the Bravo, and the subdued sighing of the swaying pines mingled with the steady murmuring of the creek. The log buildings were well constructed and well situated, but as Cade Willcox drew rein and began to fashion a smoke, his eye caught faint evidence of neglect here and there. There were, as yet, no signs of decay, but a hard winter or two would take care of that. The fences needed mending. Some of the windows of the outbuildings had either been boarded up or stuffed with paper. A door hung loose on its hinges. Weeds had sprouted alongside some of the buildings. The windmill had a rusty creaking sound to it as it swung to face the wind and began to turn. One of the vanes trembled spasmodically, just about ready to fall off.

The place seemed deserted except for a faint thread of smoke rising from the great chimney of the house. A mule bawled from a corral, and a dog barked somewhere beyond the timber. A door banged at the rear of the house, and Cade saw a woman walk to the end of the porch and pour a pan of water into a flower patch. The sun made her hair a golden helmet, and he could see that she was young and attractive. She saw him on the rutted road and placed a hand over her eyes to look at him.

Cade rode to the gate and opened it, leading the horse through. The woman walked to the front of the house. "Who are you?" she called out in a clear, pleasing voice.

Cade took off his hat as he led the sorrel toward her. "Cade Willcox, ma'am," he said with a smile. "I'm looking for Mrs. Willcox. Mrs. *Lucy* Willcox that is. Is she home?"

She lowered her hand and wiped her hands on her apron. "I'm Lucy Willcox," she said quietly. "You look a lot like your brother, Cade."

Cade narrowed his eyes. He almost whistled softly. Dan would have been thirty-five, no, thirty-seven, if he were still alive, with a fifteen or sixteen-year-old son. Sarah Willcox had been a year or two younger than Dan. Cade himself was ten years younger than Dan. There had been a sister between them, but she had died when young. This woman facing him could hardly be more than twenty-four or twenty-five at the very most.

She smiled. "Don't look so surprised," she said.

Cade grinned. "I had no idea Dan had found himself such a young, pretty wife," he said. "But Dan was a good-looking man himself."

"Like you," she said.

He shook his head. "Dan was the looker," he said.

By Godfrey, she was a looker herself! Clear skin, with a faint, almost imperceptible dusting of freckles. Clear blue eyes, almost with a violet shade, and a mouth that would make any man hungry to try. Even in her house dress, with the apron atop it, he could see she had a figure.

"You might have let us know you were coming," she said.

"I didn't know if I could make it," said Cade.

She smiled. "It doesn't make any difference. Grant will love to see you. He's off in the woods, as usual, but he'll be back in a few hours to do his chores. Come in! Come in!"

"I'll take care of my horse first," he said.

"I've baked a few pies, and the coffee will only take a minute. We had a good ham yesterday. How does ham, fried potatoes, and fresh-baked pie sound?"

He placed a hand over his heart. "You touch me deeply, Lucy."

She walked back into the house with an easy-swinging stride as Cade led the sorrel to the big barn. As he took care of Hardtack, he looked about the place. The barn needed chinking. There was an acrid, moldy smell about the place. Rays of sunlight peered through holes in the roof, and dust motes swirled in the light. A rear door was loose on one hinge.

Before he walked back to the house, he looked about the other buildings. The same general air of neglect had affected all of them. There were three horses, a mule, and a burro in the big corral. A pair of pigs grunted in a pen, and a few chickens wandered aimlessly about, pecking at the ground.

He looked at the area about the buildings. There was nothing wrong with the site. Plenty of timber and water.

Winter range shelter would be good, and the ranch was well shielded from the winter winds. If Lucy had a mind to sell, she'd get a good price for the spread. She'd do better if she ranched it, though. What was it Muley had said? "Won't be able to help her much. Ain't got but a handful of cows left. Been cleaned out, but then the sticky loopers was doin' just that when Dan was alive."

He walked to the house and scraped his boot soles, then rapped on the rear door, hearing her call out. He walked into the bright and cheery kitchen with its tantalizing odors of frying ham and potatoes, fresh coffee, and fresh-baked berry pies.

Lucy moved about the big kitchen like an expert, deft and sure of herself. After she had added the finishing touches to everything, she brushed back a stray strand of golden hair and sat down opposite him, pouring herself a cup of coffee.

"You're not eating?" he asked.

She shook her head. "Twice a day. Ruins the figure, Cade, and there isn't enough outside work to overcome all the eating I'd like to do."

He grinned. "Wish I could say the same."

"How long will you stay?"

He looked up at her. "Until you get back on your feet if you like."

"You've looked around then?"

He nodded. "Couldn't hardly miss. How many hands do you have?"

"Just two, not counting Grant. Grant is as good as both of them."

"How many head of cows?"

She shrugged. "Grant said there was about a hundred last tally."

He whistled softly. "Dan ran a lot more than that, didn't he?"

"We had a thousand head, not more than a year or two ago."

"Rustlers?" '

She nodded. "Bad, too. Everyone has been hurt. Even Gus Cargill."

"You mean to tell me you lost nine hundred head since a year or two ago?"

"Oh no! We had about two hundred head left after I sold off most of the herd. I couldn't see sitting here losing cattle month after month when I could get a fair price for them. At least we'd have the money in the bank."

"And a fine ranch like this supporting only a hundred head? It doesn't make sense."

She sipped at her coffee. "I've had a few good offers for the place," she said.

He looked at her. "What would you do if you sold out?"

"I can get work in town. Maybe move to Tucson or Phoenix. Maybe even California."

"What about the boy?"

She flushed. "He won't like it. He's a rancher, like his father. Every time I bring up the subject, he goes silent on me, like Dan used to do when you hit a sore spot with him. Remember?"

He nodded. "I remember," he said dryly.

"So you see, Cade, if I sell, there wouldn't be any use of you taking up your time to help out here."

"I've got the time, Lucy. I made it a point to have the time. I'd like you to reconsider selling, though. We can make a go of it, I'm sure."

She studied him. "There is a great deal of Dan in you," she said. "Thanks, Cade. Everyone who was friendly with Dan has advised me against selling. The others? Well, they see a fine bargain in the Lazy W, and they'd be the last to advise me against selling. Gus Cargill has always wanted the Lazy W, like he wants everything else in this country."

"The big noise, eh?"

"You know him?"

Cade shook his head. "Only by reputation. How did he and Dan get along?"

"Not very well. Gus tried to bluff Dan into selling out some years ago. He got pretty rough. He and Dan nearly fought it out in Pine Tree, but Gus was backed by some of his boys, and Dick Thornhill had all he could do to keep Dan from drawing. It was a good thing Dick was there, and he had some of his boys with him, or Dan might have been killed."

"Dan never would back down, odds against him and all," mused Cade.

She nodded. "Dan had his friends, but he also had his enemies. You know how his temper was."

Cade smiled. "I have some of it myself." He thought back on meeting the three Box C men that very morning up on Dark Mountain. He had taken his life in his hands up there, and only by the grace of God, and a little timing, had he won out against those three hardcases.

She refilled his coffee cup and then her own. "Then there was the trouble he had with Dude Carter, the gambler. Some years ago, Dan was gambling a great deal. He and Dude didn't get along. After Dan was killed, Dude claimed he had been playing poker with Dan the night before, and Dan had signed a note against a quarter share of the ranch, which Dude had won. Dude later said that Dan had absolutely refused to pay off, claiming that he had cheated. The two of them had been playing in Dude's room at the hotel, and there weren't any witnesses. Some people say the note isn't legal, and others say it is."

"Has Dude made a claim against you?"

"Several times. He has the matter up now to be brought into court."

"And Dan was killed the same night?"

"Either then or the next day sometime. Most people think it was the next day. He was a long way from Pine Tree when he was killed."

"Unless he was killed somewhere else, and his body was dumped there where it was found."

She narrowed her eyes. "What made you say that, Cade?"

"I was just thinking out loud."

She sipped at her coffee. "I don't think they'll ever find out who killed Dan. Dan had good friends and deadly enemies. He was like that. He had had trouble with the local Apache as well. He claimed they should be kept on their reservation and not allowed to wander about when and if they felt like it. He drove them off our place several times, although they claimed they had always hunted here and that Maje Simmons, the man who used to own this place, had always allowed them that privilege. Some people think Dan might have been killed by the Apache."

"On Dark Mountain?"

She looked at him. "You know about that then?"

"Only that the Apache give the place a wide berth. Seems as though a lot of white men do, too."

"I sometimes think that there is a curse on this whole area around the base of Dark Mountain. Perhaps the Apache know something we don't. I'm glad you've come to help us, Cade, but please forget about trying to solve Dan's murder. It won't do any good."

"You're wrong there," he said quietly. "It will do me a lot of good to find out who did it."

She stood up and began to gather the plates and cutlery from the table. "Let the dead bury the dead," she said softly. "We should be thinking of the living. Of Grant. His father's death struck him very hard. I've had a time with him, I tell you. He says he'll never rest until he finds and kills the man who killed his father. It's like an obsession with him, Cade. I wish you'd talk with him. Work with him." She placed the dishes and cutlery in the dish pan and turned to look at him. "You didn't tell me where you had come from and what work you had been doing. Were you ranching somewhere?"

"No. Ranching was Dan's business. I left the old home place years ago to see the elephant. I've traveled a lot and seen a lot, but I have yet to see the elephant."

"But how did you manage to live?"

He stood up and held out the makings. "All right to smoke, Lucy?"

"Of course."

He fashioned a smoke and lighted it, blowing a reflective puff of smoke. "I've had a good life," he said at last. "A little cowpunching. Some gambling. Worked for the railroad for a time. Did some mining and made enough to have a nest egg to fall back upon."

"You just can't drift about like that forever, Cade."

He smiled. "Why not?"

"You should have a wife, a home, a family. Have you ever thought of that?" she said over her shoulder as she filled the dishpan with hot water.

He eyed her golden hair, the shapely neck, shoulders, and back of her, the suggestion of hidden loveliness beneath the gingham dress and neat apron.

She turned and looked at him. "Well?" For a moment, she eyed him, then flushed prettily as she turned again to her dishes. "You'll likely find Grant beyond the timber, near the foothills. You'll hear the shooting most likely."

"Hunting?"

She shook her head. "You'll see," she said quietly. "Take a fresh horse. Supper is at six. Grant has his chores to do first, of course."

He left the house and saddled a blocky claybank in the barn. He rode toward the timber-lined creek. As he dismounted to open a Texas gate, he looked back at the house. She was emptying the dishwater in the flower patch, as she had been doing when he had first seen her. As he mounted, he saw her place her hand above her eyes to look toward him. She was young, pretty, and likely damned lonely. Maybe he reminded her of Dan. They had looked a lot alike. In some ways, they had been a lot alike. They both had the Willcox temper and stubbornness. The main difference had been Dan's desire to marry and settle down, to ranch and raise a family. There had been a yard of difference between the two of them in that respect. He looked back at the house and saw the fluttering of a skirt as she went back into the house. Maybe Dan had been right at that...

CHAPTER THREE

He heard the shooting when he left the second stand of timber. To the east, short of the mountains, was a low range of cut-up hills, thickly crowned with timber. To the left, he could see the dotted forms of grazing cattle. The sun reflected from a thin loop of the creek far to the north. A thread of smoke hung against the bright, cloud-dotted sky.

A dog barked, and the echo fled along the hills to die away, and a moment later, a gun cracked three times, and those echoes died away, too. Cade's sharp eyes caught a faint trace of bluish smoke drifting up from a wide-mouthed gully set deeply into the gap between two hills.

He rode slowly toward the gap and dismounted when he was fifty yards from the mouth of it. He walked quietly forward, cigarette dangling from a corner of his mouth. He saw a young man standing in the center of the gully, hands hanging loosely at his sides, body bent slightly forward. Beyond him, fifty feet away, a row of bottles stood on a flat rock. For a moment, the boy was as motionless as a statue, and then his hands swept down, both six guns cleared leather and rapped into life, filling the gully with noise and smoke. Two bottles were shattered, a third had the neck shot off, and a fourth was just skinned by a slug, whirling sideways to crash on the flinty ground.

The kid stood there, smoking Colts in each hand, looking at the havoc he had created. A dog loped out of the brush, saw Cade, and began to bark excitedly. The kid turned quickly, smoking guns still in his hands. "Who're you?" he demanded harshly.

Cade grinned. He held up his hands. "Black Bart," he said. "Hello, Grant."

The kid's lower jaw dropped. "Uncle Cade!" he cried. He stuffed the guns into their sheaths and ran forward. He gripped Cade about the waist and hugged him, driving the breath out of him. The kid was as strong as whang leather and wagon iron.

"Lay off!" said Cade. He gripped the kid about the shoulders. "By Godfrey! You're near as tall as me, kid."

There was a suspicious brightness in the kid's gray eyes. He looked away. "You might'a let us know you were coming," he said. "You see Lucy yet?"

"Had lunch with her."

Grant nodded. "She's a good one. I guess I've been giving her a hard time."

Cade looked at the shattered bottles. The ground around the rock was littered with shattered glass, punctured tin cans, and bullet-holed pieces of wood. Bright patches of lead scored the rock. Cade knew now what Lucy had meant about Grant's desire to avenge his father's murder.

Grant walked into the gully and picked up a box of cartridges. He opened the loading gate of a Colt and began to stuff cartridges into the cylinder. "I remember when I was little, when we had the old place down near Sulphur Springs, and you came to visit us one Christmas. You and Pa had a little too much to drink and had a shooting match out behind the barn. Ma was real mad about it. I hid in the barn and watched you." The kid turned, and his sober gray eyes studied Cade. "Pa was good with a cutter, but you made him look pretty sick. I didn't like you for that then, but I sure admire it now. I remember, too, when Pa said more than once that you were the best man with a six-gun he had ever seen. He said more than once, too, that he sure could have used you around here. It's too late now, isn't it, Uncle Cade?"

Cade rolled a fresh smoke and lighted it. "You should be spending more time with your books and working the ranch instead of burning up expensive ammunition, kid."

"You sound like Lucy now!"

"Ever occur to you she might just be right?"

Grant holstered the loaded gun and drew out the other. He began to load it, looking up at Cade now and then. "A man has to be able to take care of himself and his kin, don't he?"

"I'll buy that, kid."

"So?"

Cade looked down at the two holsters, the wide buscadero belt, the tied down tips of the sheaths. "A man has to be a bad shot with one gun to have to carry two," he said quietly.

"All the good gunslingers do!"

Cade blew a ring of smoke. "Carrying two guns, low and tied down, is an open invitation to every warped mind that fancies itself the best with a six-gun. Kid, there's *always* a better man than you are. Sometime... Someplace..."

Grant jammed the second Colt down into its sheath. "You sound like you're getting old," he said coldly.

Cade flushed. "Let's see how good you really are," he said quietly. He set up a bottle or two, then two half bottles, and the thick round bases of several others. He walked back behind the kid. "Shoot when you're ready."

Grant smiled. Biting his lower lip, he spread out his feet, bent his knees a little, crouched, and then drew. He was fast. The twin guns rapped noise and spewed flame and smoke. Every bottle and piece of the bottle was

smashed or driven from the rock. The echoes fled down
the canyon and died away. Smoke wreathed up from the
gully. Grant turned slowly. "Well?" he asked with a confident grin.

Cade flipped away his cigarette. "You telegraphed
yourself, kid," he said. "Spreading out your feet, bending
your knees, crouching and the like."

Grant flushed. "So?" He looked back over his shoulder. "I hit every one of them, didn't I?"

Cade nodded. He blew a smoke ring and punched a
nicotine-stained finger through it. "And not a damned
one of them was shooting back at you."

There was pure hell in the kid's eyes for a moment.
Cade had the uncomfortable feeling he was looking at his
brother Dan when Dan was angry. He could almost smell
the blood and guts. Cade flipped away the cigarette butt.
"Get your hoss," he said. "Show me over the place. Looks
like a better spread than the old place down at Sulphur
Springs. Your stepmother said you weren't running many
head. Sold some and had the rest rustled. You seem to be
able to run a lot more than you're keeping here." He
walked toward his horse.

"You afraid to match me, Uncle Cade?" said the kid
softly.

Cade stopped in his stride.

"Maybe you are getting old," said the kid.

Cade turned slowly. An uncomfortable feeling came
over him when he faced his own nephew. He remembered then a shabby cantina down near Nogales, the
night a two-gun punk had challenged Cade for dancing
with a slim Mex girl. She was nothing but a *puta,* a whore,
but the kid had thought he was in love with her. Cade
had walked away from the trouble and was mounting his
horse when the kid had come after him. Cade had put
three soft-nosed slugs into the kid's guts and had taken a
slug through the muscles of his right thigh. The *puta* had

laughed in delight because two foolish gringos had seen fit to fight over her.

"Well?" said the kid.

Cade fought with his ready temper. He remembered, too, what Lucy had said. If this kid faced men like Pierce Gatchell, Farley Mosston or Big Gus Cargill, or any other of the hardcase men in that country, he'd die before he'd plant a slug in any one of them. He was fast and accurate, but he wasn't dirty enough, *just not dirty enough*.

Was he to stand there and shoot a match with a punk who had big ideas? Was he to impress him with shooting with killing skill? The very thing Lucy did not want him to do. And yet the kid needed a lesson before he tried a real leather slapper in the moment of truth.

Grant grinned softly, almost evilly. "Well, maybe I'd better show you around," he said, "as long as the shooting is over for the day." He whistled to the dog and walked around the side of the gully, and a few minutes later, he came back leading a bayo coyote mare. He mounted and looked down at Cade. "What part do you want to see first, Uncle Cade?" he said politely, almost too politely.

Cade shoved back his hat. He dipped two fingers into a vest pocket and withdrew a Mex 'dobe dollar. He placed it on the back of his right hand, stretching out the hand so that his arm was parallel to the ground. For a moment, he stood there, and then he flipped up his hand, sailing the 'dobe dollar high into the sky, and as he did so, he drew with effort-less, liquid ease. The dollar stopped in its upward flight for a fraction of time before it dropped. The .44/40 cracked. The dollar spun upward again, and as it dropped, a second slug smashed it into shapelessness. Cade holstered the smoking gun. The instant the dollar hit the ground, the Colt was out, rapping four times, driving the shining silver along the ground with each shot. Cade slowly reloaded the Colt, slid it into its sheath, mounted the claybank, and looked at Grant. "Any part is all right with me, kid," he said quietly.

Grant spurred his mare and rode down the slope toward the far distant creek, not looking back. Cade grinned. He wondered how many expensive boxes of cartridges and how many mutilated 'dobe dollars that trick had cost him in the past ten years. It was a crowd pleaser, nothing else. Any man can learn to be a fast and accurate shot. It takes a top gun, a man of the gun-hard breed, to face another gunslinger shooting at you at the same time you are shooting at him.

In the hours that followed, Cade learned a great deal about the Lazy W, not so much from the conversation of his now rather reticent nephew, but by his own observations. No wonder Gus Cargill wanted the place. No wonder Dude Carter was pressing his suit for the quarter share he claimed Dan Willcox owed him. No wonder the Apache wanted to hunt on it, as they had hunted on it during the time of Maje Simmons and as their forefathers had hunted for generations past. Dan had picked an almost ideal place for his spread; almost ideal, for Dark Mountain had had its way with Dan Willcox. Maybe a curse was on that country.

It was getting along toward five o'clock when Grant led the way back toward the ranch buildings. He stopped a quarter of a mile from the house and ground-reined his mare. Up a slope, on a level knoll overlooking the wide meadows that flanked the rushing creek, was a fenced-in area. Five white headboards shone in the late afternoon sun. Grant opened the gate and walked toward the graves. He looked back at Cade. "My father and mother," he said. "My little sister Jennie. The other two graves are hands that worked here. Mack Rose, he was Pa's ramrod. Shot down by rustlers. The other grave is that of Lake West. He used to work for Grandfather Willcox, and you knew him. When he was old and sick, he came here to stay with us. He was like one of the family."

Cade nodded. "I knew him well," he said. "A fine old

man. Taught me how to chew tobacco, come to think of it."

Grant passed a hand across his eyes. "If it wasn't for Lucy, I'da never 'stayed 'here, but she says Pa and Ma would have wanted me to stay. Trouble is, Uncle Cade, I can't run this place the way it should be run. Not yet anyways."

"I'm here, kid," said Cade.

Grant turned. Gone was the hardness of the Willcox fighting man, and instead, Cade could almost see the gentle soul of the boy's mother looking at him through Grant's eyes. "Thanks, Uncle Cade. I'm sorry about what happened back there."

"Gunsmoke has a way of getting into a man's brain," said Cade. "Usually not to his own good. It's too easy to start killing, kid, and it isn't easy to stop or to stop someone else from thinking of killing you."

"That's what Ma used to say. Pa would always laugh. He was always so confident in himself. Leastways, until Ma died. After that, he wasn't quite the same. Lucy made the difference up some, though, I tell you. He was almost like his old self."

"She's a fine woman," said Cade.

"Prettiest gal in the Bravo Valley, Pa used to say. He was right, too."

Cade placed a wildflower on Sarah's grave. They mounted and rode toward the ford. "Do you know Pierce Gatchell, Farley Mosston, and a man named Muley? They ride for the Box C."

Grant looked quickly at him. "You run into them?"

"Casually. They told me how to get into the valley from the east."

"Were you on Box C land? A stranger?"

"Yup."

Grant whistled softly. "Muley Smeed isn't much of a hand, except that he's about the best tracker in these parts, outside of an Apache. Pierce Gatchell is one of

Gus Cargill's hired guns. He don't work much on the ranch, if at all. Mostly he patrols the Box C borders looking for rustlers, trespassers, and trouble. Mostly trouble. Got a big reputation, he has, and that's what Gus wants, I guess. Gus don't lose many cows to rustlers with those three riding fence for him. Farley Mosston is the best rifle shot in these parts, maybe the best in the Territory. Always takes first place in the Fourth of July shooting matches down to Pine Tree. One time the Army sent down a team from Fort Apache to take the cup they give out for the first place, and Farley made them look sick." Grant looked sideways at Cade. "You have any trouble with them, Uncle Cade?"

Cade rolled a smoke. "Not so's you'd notice," he said casually. He lighted the cigarette. "Who works for your mother?"

"Harry Nadeau used to work for Pa. He's all right. Lazy, but he gets by as long as we're running the place the way we are." The kid laughed. "No one else around here will hire Harry. Pa could make him work, though."

"And now?"

Grant shrugged. "He does his job. No more, no less. We have to get by with what we can get. Gus Cargill has most of the best men. Dick Thornhill has most of the rest. The hands we used to have mostly went to work for Dick because most of them can't stand Gus Cargill and his hardcases."

"And the other hand?"

"Joe Mahan? He's all right. Got a game left hand, but he does his job. Don't pay to get rough with Joe. He can get pretty mean at times. I guess his hand bothers him."

Cade looked about the place as they rode through the timber. It was a fine spread, run by a pretty young woman, a kid who was more interested in gunslinging and in revenging his father's death, a lazy good-for-nothing for one hand, and a mean-tempered cripple for the other. "Hard times come again no more," he said.

"What was that Uncle Cade?" said the kid. Cade looked at him. "I was thinking out loud," he said. "Your stepmother really wants to sell out, doesn't she?" He nodded.

"What about you?"

Grant looked away. "I like it here," he said. "I guess I'm a rancher like Pa was. How long can you stay, Uncle Cade?"

"As long as you need me."

They cleared the timber and rode toward the ranch buildings. The sun made the western windows look like they were on fire. Smoke wreathed up into the still air.

"There might be trouble," said the kid at last.

"So?"

"Someone wants us out of here. It's more than just rustling. Our fences are cut. Someone poisoned the springs at Apache Rock. Two of our line shacks were burned down. Never saw anyone doing it. Now and then, someone takes a shot at the hands when they're out riding fence or something. You know. Little things, but they add up. I'm afraid for Lucy, not for myself."

"You don't know who it is?" asked Cade.

Grant looked at him. "Gus Cargill is too smart to let himself get mixed up in such things. He wants this place so bad he can taste it. One time he offered an even trade with us for a place he owns south of here, near the Sulphur Springs country, but Lucy wouldn't have any of that. She says if Gus Cargill wants this place, he can darned well pay our price for it."

"You'd be foolish to sell or trade, kid. You wouldn't do anywhere near as well in the Sulphur Springs country."

"Some folks think it's the Apache who are hurrahing us. They still say they got a right to hunt over this land. Personally, I don't care, but folks look at you funny when you get too friendly with 'Paches. That's what Pa always said. What do you think?"

Cade shrugged. "I've known 'Paches that were blacker

in the soul than white men, and I've met white men that were blacker in the soul than any 'Pache I ever met. It's not the color of the skin so much, kid, as it is the color of the soul."

"Sometimes you talk like a walkin' preacher, Uncle Cade." Cade grinned. "Maybe I am, kid, maybe I am." Grant turned in his saddle. "You see that smoke low against the hills? Near that notch?"

"Yes."

"That's Ed Chilton's place. He's not a rancher. He traps, hunts, and suchlike. Knows these hills and mountains almost as good as the 'Paches." Grant shoved back his hat. "His wife was either whole or part Apache. Ed got that land through her. Some kind of deal from the government. Well, it's good land. Not for ranching, but because of the water. Ed wanted to dam up the South Fork to run a mill, and Pa went to the mat with him about it because part of the South Fork runs through our spread. There was hell to pay and no pitch hot until Dick Thornhill patched up the deal and let Pa use water from his place."

"Seems like you've got all the water you'd need."

Grant flushed. "Well, that's what Chilton said, but Pa ain't never had no use for 'Paches. One time he caught some of them hunting on our land and was whupping them when Ed showed up. Ed interfered, and him and Pa went to it. It was a dandy, and Pa was cut up quite a bit, but Ed Chilton was a mess. Pa walked on eggs for a long time after that. Them 'Paches move like shadows across the ground. They can sit within ten feet of you, and you won't see or hear 'em."

"I know," said Cade quietly.

"You've fought against them?"

Cade nodded. "And with them. Al Sieber was head of Apache Scouts under General Crook, later with General Miles. I served with Al and the Scouts. One time I spent five weeks alone with the Scouts along the Border, the only white man in the bunch, trailing bronco Apache. Caught 'em, too."

"And the Scouts let you bring them in?"

Cade looked at the kid. "They were as loyal as any soldier. They saw their duty and did it."

"Still swear you like 'Paches!"

Cade smiled. "Not all of them, kid. Not all of them."

"Well, like I said, the 'Paches had no love for Pa. Maybe it was them that cut the fences, poisoned the springs and suchlike. I don't know. Now you know why I'm learning gunslinging."

"Just don't let it take place over everything else, kid. There are far more important things."

The sun was low in the west when they reached the ranch. Cade put up the horses while the kid did his chores. The odor of cooking drifted from the house, and now and then, Cade could see Lucy passing back and forth in front of the windows as she bustled about the kitchen. Grant had told him the two hands were out riding fence and wouldn't be back until the next day.

The sun was gone, and a cold wind was sweeping up the Valley of the Bravo when Cade walked toward the house. Somewhere, deep in the dark hills, a wolf howled.

The huge, looming bulk of Dark Mountain seemed to move in closer at night, as though it was watching and listening to what was going on down in the valley. An evil coldness seemed to flow from its gaunt, rugged flanks and seep down into the lower ground about its base.

Cade shivered a little in the searching wind. A roaring fire and a well-cooked meal would drive the cold and the loneliness from his bones. That, and the smiling, lovely face of Lucy Willcox, his sister-in-law.

CHAPTER FOUR

The Three of them sat in the wide, pleasant living room of the big log house, looking into the crackling fire on the huge stone hearth. The place looked more than just familiar to Cade, for Dan had brought much of the furniture from the place down at Sulphur Springs, which in turn had come from the old Willcox place in the Pinon Creek country.

Lucy looked up from her sewing. "So you think we had best keep the place, Cade?" she said.

Cade slowly fashioned a cigarette, looking "into the fire. "Keep it until you get your price if you must sell. Meanwhile, there's work to be done around here. That barn needs repairing before the fall rains and the winter snows catch you. The fences are all in bad shape. How are you fixed for supplies?"

"Not too well," she said. "I haven't laid much in, thinking we might sell."

He looked at her. "How are you fixed for ready cash?"

"I'd rather not talk about it," she said quietly.

Grant looked up from where he was polishing one of his six guns. "That's Uncle Cade, Lucy," he said.

She flushed. "Well, we are short of cash. Dick Thornhill owes us for some stock he bought. Troy Burkitt owes us for some stock he bought three months ago, and Troy usually holds out as long as he can."

"Rancher?"

"Cattle dealer. He has an office in town. I think he's stalling to see what we do. He offered to pick up the rest of the stock for low prices and said he'd pay off the whole bill when we agreed to let him have the remainder of the stock. He and Dick Thornhill had words about that."

"And Thornhill owes you money, too?"

Grant looked up again. "Dick Thornhill is as good as gold for anything," he said. "His word is his bond. His wife has been sickly, and Dick has had a lot of doctor bills."

Cade lighted his cigarette. "I'll go into town tomorrow and buy supplies," he said. "Lucy, you make out a list tonight, will you?"

She nodded. "It's good to have a man around to make the decisions. It hasn't been easy since we lost Dan. Grant does his best, but he has a lot to learn. Thank God you came, Cade." She stood up. "I'll make out the list now."

The waggle-tail clock on the wall struck nine. Lucy walked toward the kitchen door. The window on the south side of the big room suddenly shattered, scattering shards of glass across the rug. The distant report of a rifle sounded. A second slug smashed the Argand lamp on the table, scattering flaming oil on the rug.

Cade pushed Lucy into the kitchen. "Lie down!" he barked. He crawled back into the living room. "Stay low, kid! Those slugs can't get through those logs!" He picked up a throw rug and doused the flames. The stink of burning oil hung in the big room. A breeze came through the shattered window. The fire danced and leaped, throwing bright light throughout the room.

"Belly into the kitchen, kid," said Cade. He crawled toward the north wall to where he had seen several rifles and shotguns racked against the wall. "These rifles loaded?"

"The rifles are," said the kid. "Let me go with you, Uncle Cade."

"Stay with your mother!"

Cade took a rifle, slid up a window, and dropped lightly to the ground outside. He bellied along the damp ground to the end of the front porch and looked across it toward the road.

A bright orange-red flash showed in the motte across the road, and another slug whined into the living room. The north window went out in a cascade of shattered glass.

Cade wet his lips. He studied the dark motte. There was no moon. Cade worked his way across the sloping ground to the fence line and levered a round into the Winchester. He rested the heavy barrel on the middle rail of the fence and sighted it on the motte. The bright flash came again, and Cade fired right at it, then pumped three more rounds into the motte. The echoes died away against the dark hills, but by the time they died away, Cade was thirty feet from where he had fired, rifle resting on a rock, sighted on those dark trees.

Minutes ticked past. The curtains were blowing from the shattered windows, and now and then, the firelight flickered up, giving a ghostly light to the broken windows.

Cade raised his head. A horse had whinnied beyond the motte. He fired three times at it. When the echoes died away, he placed his ear against the ground. The thudding of hoofs came to him through the ground, and then they were gone.

Cade walked back to the house and in through the kitchen door. "Don't light a light," he warned.

"Did you see them, Uncle Cade?" asked Grant.

"No."

"Why don't we chase them?"

"You'd never get near them. Then, too, they could wait for you and get you in the saddle."

Lucy came to Cade. "Did they mean to kill?" she said.

"I doubt it. A good rifleman could have hit either you or me the first shot out of the magazine if he had wanted to."

"Like Farley Mosston," said Grant from the living room.

Lucy rested her head on Cade's shoulder, and the sweet smell of her flesh and her hair did things to him. "You see now why I want to sell," she whispered.

Cade patted her cheek. "Don't let a hurrahing scare you out," he said.

She looked up at his face in the darkness. "It isn't that I'm scared for myself," she said. "It's Grant."

"I know," he said. "I don't think they meant to kill. How long has it been since something like this happened?"

"Some months ago. But they never shot at the house before, Cade. They killed my riding mare and shot at the hands a few times, but never at the house or the other buildings."

"There's likely a good reason they did tonight," he said grimly.

"You?"

"Yes."

"Who knows you are around here?"

"I had a little trouble with some of Cargill's hired guns up on Dark Mountain the morning I came here. Pierce Gatchell, Farley Mosston, and Muley Smeed stopped me to question me. I didn't like their attitude. There was a bit of a scuffle, and they came off second best."

"Three of them, Cade?"

He nodded.

"Oh, my God! Why don't you leave! Tonight! Now! I don't want you to be killed as Dan was."

"They haven't killed me yet. Besides, we don't know that it was them who fired into the house."

"What difference does that make?" she said fiercely. "You're as stubborn as Dan was! I had a feeling it was only a matter of time before they killed him. They did. Maybe this was just a warning for you, Cade. The next time they'll shoot to kill! It could happen anywhere! Please go! I'll sell out and move away. It's the best course, Cade."

He gently seated her. "I'll help Grant close off those windows," he said. "I can pick up some glass in town tomorrow when I go for those supplies."

"You're hopeless," she murmured.

Cade walked into the living room. "Stay away from the windows until the fire dies down," he said.

Grant was fondling a Winchester. "By Godfrey!" he exploded, "they might have hit Lucy! You think you hit one of them, Uncle Cade?"

"We'll take a look-see in the morning, kid."

Later that night, as Cade lay in his bed, looking up at the dark ceiling, hands interlaced behind his head, he thought of many things. He had walked into a seething hornet's nest of trouble in the short time he had been in the Bravo Valley country. Had it been Farley Mosston who had fired into the house? Grant had said Farley was the best rifleman in that part of the country, perhaps the whole Territory of Arizona. It had likely just been a warning. If Farley was as good as Grant had claimed he was, he could have easily killed Cade where he sat. The rifleman had seen Lucy move out of the way, leaving a clear shot at Cade. How long had he been waiting out there in the darkness? It had been some time since the place had been hurrahed, but then it likely hadn't been necessary, for Lucy had said more than once she was thinking of selling. They might have scared her off, but whoever it was now knew there was a man at the Lazy W, brother to Dan

Willcox, and the devil himself couldn't have scared Dan from his spread.

A man could go plumb loco trying to figure who had fired those shots. As lovely and bountiful as this country was, it had an aura of lurking fear and terror, of evil-doing and law-breaking under the clear skies.

Cade felt for the makings and rolled a cigarette. He snapped a lucifer on his thumbnail and lighted the cigarette. A thought struck him like a Comanche lance. "By God!" he said aloud, staring into the darkness. He winced in sudden pain as the match flame seared his fingers. He blew it out and lay there, staring up at the ceiling, his lean face alternately lighted by the glowing of the cigarette and its dying away. "I wonder if old Burt Mossman let me have a leave of absence to come up here not so much because Lucy and Grant needed me, but because there was a mess of rustler trouble in this country? I wouldn't put it past that old vinegarroon to do such a thing!"

Cade blew a smoke ring into the darkness. A year past, Clancy Barklew, one of the best men in the Rangers, had been found shot to death not far from the Bravo Valley. Someone had been sent to replace Barklew, but Cade had no idea who it was. His line of duty had kept him along the Border most of the time, and he had had little contact with the Rangers who worked the northern division.

Cade snubbed out the cigarette. He grinned into the darkness. Old Burt Mossman had been a jump and a holler ahead of him. The commanding officer of the Arizona Rangers was as sharp as a Barlow knife. He had to be to keep ahead of the hardcases he had enlisted in his select group of undercover officers. The Bravo country and the surrounding country had always been a hell's kitchen of sticky loopers, the heritage of the tough Texans who rode for the Hashknife outfit until they had rustled enough cattle on the side to start their own spreads, and even as "honest" ranchers, most of them were not averse to picking up a stray cow or two. He lay awake for a long time, and when he finally drifted off to sleep, it seemed to him that the faint fragrance of Lucy's flesh and hair had somehow drifted into his room to keep him uneasy company.

———

CADE WILLCOX PADDED through the motte, watching carefully for sign. The kid sat on the fence watching him. Cade knelt and beckoned to him. "Here," he said.

Grant came toward him. Cade pointed to a small rock. "See? The dark and heavy side is uppermost. Means someone disturbed it. A natural resting rock would have the lighter colored, lightest side uppermost. See these depressions in the ground? Elbows pressed down here, knees and boot toes down here. Rested the rifle on that rock. You can see where the lichens were rubbed off. Nice clear shot from here, not more than one hundred and twenty-five yards. Must have picked up the empty brass."

Grant rubbed his jaw, then looked at his uncle. "You talk like a lawman, Uncle Cade," he said quietly.

Cade stood up and brushed the knees of his levis. "Told you I served with the Apache Scouts. Old Al Sieber taught me a lot, and so did those bucks."

Grant nodded. "You never did tell me what kind of work you were doing in New Mexico."

"A little bit of everything, kid."

"Like being a lawman?"

Cade shook his head.

"Deputy-sheriff, maybe?"

"No."

"Marshal?"

"No."

Grant tilted his head to one side. "I wonder," he said.

"Dammit! Keep on wondering! I've got to get to town for those supplies."

"I still don't see why I can't go."

"Stay here with your stepmother. No pistol shooting today. Another thing: Get rid of that buscadero belt if you must wear a six-gun. Keno?"

"Keno, Uncle Cade."

They walked back to the road, and Cade climbed up into the buckboard. "Where do you trade in Pine Tree?"

"Charley Bidwell's General Emporium."

Cade nodded. He slapped the reins on the rumps of the horses and drove toward the distant Valley Road. The kid sat on the fence for a long time until Cade was out of sight. He looked back into the shadowed motte. "He's like a durned Apache," he said. "I would have walked through that motte a hundred times and never seen a thing."

———

IT WAS a beautiful day as Cade drove north along the Valley Road. Puffs of white clouds drifted across the clear sky, letting their swiftly moving shadows race downhill and across the valley, in a race that would never be lost and never be won. A crisp breeze swayed the trees, and carried the warm, pungent odor of the sun-bathed pines to Cade. The creek raced along the right hand side of the road for a time, then plunged into the thick shadows of the timber to vanish in a wide-sweeping loop, only to show up again, roaring in puckish delight as it passed beneath a bridge then disappeared into the woods on the lefthand side of the road.

The distant mountains stood out against the sharp, clear sky, like a magnificent panorama, with here and there small patches of snow still caught in pockets. Beyond the timber-line, the gaunt rock shoulders were tinted salmon, pink, yellow, brown, and red in pleasing contrast to the dark, velvety green of the swaying trees below the talus slopes.

Dan Willcox had not been wrong in picking out the Valley of the Bravo for his home, but perhaps he had been wrong in making enemies. Cade could not let Lucy and Grant Willcox lose the Lazy W. It would take time to build it up again so that Cade might return to his own work. He slapped the reins on the dusty rumps in front of him and felt for the makings, rolling a quirley with one hand, lighting it, and all the while drinking in the fresh beauty of this high meadows country. He would stay until they were on their feet. He owed that much to Dan, at least.

He blew a puff of smoke. "Dan," he said quietly.

The hoofs rattled on a creaking bridge, and the buckboard bounced a little over the rough planking.

"Lucy," said Cade Willcox. He shook his head. The memory of his brother would be too strong within her, and what's more, it would be too strong within Cade himself.

CHAPTER FIVE

Pine Tree surprised Cade Willcox as he drove across the bridge that spanned the Bravo and the main street of the town. It was larger than he had expected and had a bustling air about it. Lumber wagons ground through the streets, and the smell of freshly cut timber was in the air, mingled with the smoke of wood-fires, the pungent aura of freshly dropped manure and threading through it all, the winey mountain air. The main street was lined with buck-boards, a surrey or two, ranch wagons, a few freight wagons, and many horses standing hipshot at the racks. A two-storied hotel domi-nated the center of town, freshly painted white, with dark green trim and plenty of ornate gingerbread along the eaves. A neatly lettered sign proclaimed it to be *The Excelsior House*.

It wasn't difficult to find Charley Bidwell's General Emporium, for the establishment covered an area about the width of four average stores, with a wide boardwalk in front shielded by a roof. Behind the establishment was a big corral and wagon yard, lined with freshly painted, new wagons. At the end of the wagon yard was a black-smith's shop from whence came the steady, rhythmical beat of metal upon metal. Cade drove into the wagon yard and tethered the team to the rack behind the big store. There was a loading dock there, and several men were loading a big freight wagon marked *Gus Cargill Enterprises.*

Cade walked in through the back door down a narrow hallway that opened into several offices and storerooms. A pert-looking girl, in a high white collar, trim shirtwaist snug over fine breasts, looked up at him as he passed, and she quickly looked away as she saw his glance. Charley Bidwell evidently had the best of everything. Cade was beginning to like the Bravo Valley and Pine Tree better than ever.

The store was busy, and Cade suddenly realized it was Saturday. Three clerks were behind the long counter, and a white-haired man, a good inch taller than Cade, was checking the receipts. Cade placed the list in front of a clerk. "How soon can I have this?" he asked.

The clerk pulled a pencil from behind his ear. "Who is it for?" he asked.

"Mrs. Lucy Willcox, the Lazy W."

The clerk's pencil paused in mid-air. "Cash?" he asked.

"Yes."

The clerk grinned a little. "Time's changing out there, mister?"

"It's no concern of yours," said Cade.

"Say!" said the clerk angrily. "I got a right…"

"A right to what?" said a deep voice.

Cade turned. The white-haired man came toward them. "I've told you before, Caleb, I don't want any disrespect to my customers," he said.

"Sorry, Mr. Bidwell. I'll have this ready in an hour, sir," said the clerk. "Your name, please?"

"Willcox," said Cade. "Cade Willcox."

The clerk flushed. "Kin to Dan?"

"Brother," said Cade.

The clerk scurried off.

Charley Bidwell thrust out a big hand. "Pleased," he said. "Sorry about the clerk. Takes time to teach them, Mr. Willcox."

"Forget it," said Cade. "I was a little short myself."

"I didn't know Lucy was having you out there. Just get here?"

"Yesterday."

"Plan to stay?"

Cade shrugged. "I've been hoping Lucy would stay on the place. She seems to want to sell. The boy wants to stay."

Bidwell nodded. He reached under the counter and held out a box of long nines. Cade selected a cigar and bit off the end, accepting a light from the store owner.

"That's one of the best spreads in this part of the country," said Bidwell. "Dan had a future there when things cleared up. The timber alone would have made the place a success, but Dan was a rancher."

Cade nodded. "I suppose you'd be willing to make an offer for the place?"

Bidwell smiled. "Any time. Only you're leading me on, Mr. Willcox. As far as you are concerned, you don't want that place sold either."

"There's nothing in it for me," said Cade.

"I wonder," said Bidwell.

Cade took the cigar from his mouth. "What do you mean by that?"

"If you've got Willcox blood, you'll see the value of that place and fight to keep it."

"It isn't mine."

Bidwell nodded. "Does it make that much difference to you, Mr. Willcox?"

The penetrating blue eyes seemed to probe deeply into Cade. "You're a fighter by breeding and blood. I might warn you that Gus Cargill was doing some talking last night in The Excelsior House Bar. Something about you trespassing on his range. A little trouble with some of his boys. A bad start, Mr. Willcox, a bad start in this part of the country."

"I'll ride it out," said Cade shortly.

"You know, somehow you remind me of your brother."

Their eyes held each other, and Cade had a feeling he had found a friend. "I'm going to try to get Lucy to agree to restocking the place," said Cade.

"If you need credit, I can arrange it."

"Not right now. Where can I find Troy Burkitt?"

Bidwell smiled a little. "Troy usually keeps office hours in a booth over to The Excelsior House. Says it saves office rent, and besides, every rancher in the country, unless he's a Temperance man, usually passes through The Excelsior House Bar at least once a month."

"Thanks."

Bidwell watched Cade leave the store, shook his head, and then walked to the front of the store in time to see him cross the street and enter The Excelsior House Bar.

"What'd he have to get ringy for?" growled Caleb.

Bidwell turned slowly. "You act like a whiskey fool sometimes, Caleb. You walk and talk quietly around a man like that. That's Dan Willcox's brother. You remember Dan."

Caleb nodded. "I also know what happened to him. What happened to him can happen to his brother, tough as he is."

"You never did have enough sense to keep a checkrein on your tongue. You listen to me: Keep your mouth shut around him. He isn't just here to help his brother's widow. He's here about Dan's killing, and *don't you ever forget it.*"

The Excelsior House Bar was classy, as good as some of the best Tombstone bars. The light glistened from polished mahogany, brass, and glassware. By Godfrey, there was even a rug on the floor! The long bar was lined, well served by two bar critters in white jackets and well-waxed mustaches. Several men looked curiously at Cade as he passed, and one of them spoke out of the side of his mouth to another. The second man left the barroom as Cade reached the end of the bar. "Troy Burkitt?" asked Cade of the bartender.

"End booth, mister."

Cade walked to the end booth. A man sat there, poring over some papers, a wine glass at his elbow and a partially full bottle of wine in front of him. The smoke from a good cigar drifted up and wreathed over the booth. "Mr. Burkitt?" said Cade.

The man didn't look up right away, and when he did, it was as though he was just taking off enough time to be courteous. "I'm Troy Burkitt. Cattle dealer. Anything I can do for you?"

"It's a matter of a cattle deal."

"Sit down then." Burkitt smiled thinly. His eyes were a pale, washed-out gray, and his thin blonde mustache looked as though it was pasted to his upper lip. "That's my business. Glass of wine?"

"Beer," said Cade.

Burkitt beckoned to a waiter. The beer was served. Cade sipped it. Burkitt swirled the wine in his glass. "I didn't get the name," he said.

"Willcox, Mr. Burkitt. Cade Willcox."

Burkitt's face tightened.

Cade smiled. "Brother to Dan Willcox. I've come here to help my sister-in-law and nephew."

"You want to sell the rest of their cattle?"

"No. I want to buy."

Burkitt narrowed his eyes. "I offered a fair price for the remainder of their stock."

"And didn't pay them for the stock you already bought."

Burkitt flushed. "Well, it was good business."

"Rotten business, you mean."

"See here! I don't have to listen to that kind of talk!"

Cade leaned forward. "Don't get virtuous with me, Burkitt," he said coldly. "The Lazy W needs the money you owe it. We need stock. You've had three months to pay off."

"Well, there was some question about that stock. There's been a lot of trouble with rustlers, you know...." His voice trailed off as he saw the look in Cade's eyes. "I've got friends here in this bar," he added quickly.

"You haven't a friend in the world, Burkitt," said Cade softly, "unless you're buying him a drink at the moment. You're lying in your teeth if you're suggesting Lazy W cattle didn't have a clean bill of sale."

It was suddenly very quiet in the big barroom. Men were watching the two men in the booth.

"Well," said Burkitt in a nervous tone, "you haven't got the right to take payment for those cattle unless you've got a power of attorney."

"Pay off," said Cade quietly. "Now! In cash!"

There was a long silence. Burkitt risked a look away from those cold gray eyes opposite him. There were no friendly expressions on any faces lining the long bar or on the faces of the men in other booths or at the tables. Cade Willcox had called the shot. Troy slid a hand inside his coat for his bulging wallet. Slowly he withdrew it, not wanting to spring the trigger on that hard-faced man sitting across from him. He knew if he went for his derringer, he'd be dead before he cleared the pocket, and besides, he had never had the guts to draw on any man.

The bills rustled as Burkitt placed them one by one in front of Cade. Cade picked them up. "I hope, for your sake, Burkitt," he said with a thin smile, "that this is correct."

Burkitt's mouth was too dry to make a sound. He nodded.

Cade drained the beer glass and stood up. "A pleasure to do business with you, Mr. Burkitt," he said cheerfully. He walked toward the bar. A tall man leaned at the end of the bar, all dressed in gray, of the finest broadcloth, the linen of his shirt as white as snow, his gray fore and aft hat carefully brushed and spotless. His light gray eyes held Cade's. He hadn't been there when Cade had come in.

"Mr. Willcox, I believe," the man in gray said.

"Yes," said Cade.

"My name is Carter. Carl Carter. My friends call me Dude!"

Cade stopped short. A cold feeling came over him. This man was no Troy Burkitt.

Carter smiled. "I'd like to talk with you about a little matter that concerned your brother."

"The gambling debt? So-called?"

"Why so-called?"

The barroom was still very quiet. Troy Burkitt smiled thinly. There wasn't a man in Pine Tree who'd bully Dude Carter, and that included Gus Cargill and his gunslicks.

"I asked you a question, Mr. Willcox," said Carter.

"I heard you," said Cade. "My sister-in-law said there was some question about the legality of that claim of yours. I am only voicing her opinion."

Carter bent his head a little. "The opinion of a lady is not usually questioned, Mr. Willcox, but you also seem to question the legality of the note."

Cade felt his temper rise a little. "I understand you have brought the matter up before the court. I suggest you let it stand at that, Mr. Carter."

Carter studied Cade. "As you will," he said coldly. "I assure you, the matter is distasteful to me, as a gentleman."

Cade bent his head a little. "As a gentleman, Mr. Carter, this is hardly the place to bring up a matter of business."

Carter's face tightened. A muscle worked at the corner of his mouth, and fine lines etched themselves at the corners of his cold eyes. "I see," he said quietly. "You have a sharp tongue, sir."

Cade looked along the bar. "Are you through with me, Mr. Carter?"

"For the present."

"Good day then." Cade turned his back on the gambler and walked toward the door, and every man in the place expected Dude Carter to call out sharply, with the ring of steel in his voice, to stop this tall outlander and bring him to account.

Dude turned slowly to the bar. "Bourbon," he said quietly. He looked at Cade until the door closed behind him, and there was hell beneath the ice of his eyes.

Cade looked at the clock on the wooden tower of city hall and stepped into the street.

"Willcox," said a man behind him.

Cade turned. A broad-shouldered man stood on the boardwalk, an unlighted cigar in the corner of his mouth, dark eyes studying Cade.

"Yes?" said Cade.

"My name is Cargill. Gus Cargill."

"Owner of the Box C, headman of Gus Cargill Enterprises," said Cade.

Cargill smiled. He worked the cigar to the other side of his mouth. It was then that Cade noticed three men he had seen the day before, up on the wet flank of Dark Mountain. Pierce Gatchell, Farley Mosston, and grinning little Muley Smeed. One of Gatchell's eyes had a mouse under it, and Farley Mosston's face was a bruised and lacerated mess, but his cold eyes never left Cade's face.

Cade looked up and down the street. There were plenty of other people to the left and right of where Cargill and his three men stood facing Cade, but the immediate vicinity was quite clear.

"My boys here tell me you were on my land up on Dark Mountain," said Cargill.

"Just passing through, Mr. Cargill. Fact is, I got lost

and wasn't quite sure where I was. I had no intention of trespassing. I didn't know you Bravo Valley ranchers were so particular about lone riders crossing your spreads."

Cargill worked the cigar back to the other side. "We never used to be until a helluva lot of stock vanished right under our noses. A man has a right to protect his property. My boys were only doing their job."

"They sure were," said Cade.

Cargill glanced back at his three men. "What actually happened up there, Mr. Willcox? I don't see any marks on you."

Cade smiled. "Maybe the boys fell up a tree, Mr. Cargill."

Cargill smiled. "Yeh. You aim to stay around a spell?"

"That's the general idea."

"Run the Lazy WP"

"You're getting warm, Mr. Cargill."

Cargill nodded. "Nice place. I could use it. Mrs. Willcox is a little stubborn. Offered her a better place down in the Sulphur Springs country. No, go."

"If it was a better place, why offer it for the Lazy W?" asked Cade.

Cargill moved his cigar over to the other side of his mouth. "I happen to want that land," he said. "Meets with my plans. That place is losing money. Not enough cows on it to manure the weeds. Had a chance maybe when your brother Dan, God rest his soul, was running it, but that young lady ain't quite the type, and the boy is too interested in learning how to slap leather so's he can get killed in a hurry, to try to learn. You a rancher, Mr. Willcox?"

"I was born and raised on a ranch."

"Does that make you a rancher?"

"It does when I want it to."

Cargill shrugged. The cigar moved back the other way. "I wouldn't take you for a rancher."

"No?"

Cargill shook his head. "You're a fighting man, Willcox. I don't know what happened up on Dark Mountain yesterday morning, but I'd give a chunk to have seen it."

Cade looked at the three men behind Cargill. Only Muley was grinning, like a happy frog, but Cade didn't trust him any farther than the other two.

"I always have use for a good man on the Box C," said Cargill. "You ever ramrod, Willcox?"

"You just finished questioning my ability as a rancher. Why ask me about ramrodding?"

"I wasn't thinking of ramrodding cowhands, Willcox."

Cade smiled. "You mean ramrodding your hired guns?"

"You're getting the picture. A man has a right to protect his property, and I have a helluva lot of it. Damned near a quarter of this valley."

While they were talking, a man had walked slowly toward them. He stopped in front of the entrance to the Excelsior Bar. Pierce Gatchell glanced at him and then away. He said something out of the corner of his mouth to Farley Mosston.

Cargill glanced toward the newcomer. He nodded. He looked back at Cade. "You tell Mrs. Willcox to reconsider my offer. She won't do any better." He smiled. "I'll tell the boys you can ride over Box C land any time you have a mind to."

Cade looked at Cargill's three boys. "I'm not at all sure I'd think about it," he said.

Cargill nodded. "Come on, boys," he said. "The drinks are on me." He led his three men into The Excelsior House Bar.

"Willcox!" said the newcomer.

Cade turned. "Yes?" What was wrong now? He had been in nothing but hot water since he had walked into the barroom, and here evidently was more of it.

The newcomer was a handsome man, clear of complexion, bright of eye, with thick auburn hair and mustache. "My name is Thornhill," he said. "Dick Thornhill. Neighbor to the Willcox's."

Cade smiled and thrust out his hand. "They've told me about you," he said.

Thornhill looked over his shoulder. "My God," he said quietly, "I could almost smell the blood and guts."

Cade shoved back his hat and wiped the cold sweat from his forehead. "Maybe you helped me without realizing it."

Thornhill shrugged. "Maybe and maybe not. Gus Cargill doesn't look for trouble in public. I stopped by the Lazy W on my way into town and heard you had come to help out. Thank God for that! They need help there. Times are rough here in the valley, Cade. I'll do all I can to help you."

"I'm glad to hear that," said Cade. "You can start by returning the stock you bought. Lucy said you hadn't paid for it as yet."

Thornhill smiled. "Of course. Frankly, I was short of cash at the time and really didn't need any more stock, but I couldn't see Lucy handing over her stock to Troy Burkitt and not getting paid for it. She knows I'm good for it."

"I'm sure you are, Dick. By the way, I just made Burkitt pay off."

"Where?"

"In The Excelsior House Bar."

Thornhill stared incredulously at Cade. "You're joshing!"

Cade shook his head. He withdrew the wad of bills and showed them to the rancher.

Thornhill slapped his thighs. "That's the best yet! Cade, you send your boys over for the stock I got from Lucy. Haven't even changed brands as yet. Cut them out and drive 'em back to your place. I'll tell my foreman about it. Have to be careful. Helluva lot of sticky looping going on around here."

Cade nodded. "Who killed my brother, Dick?" he asked.

Thornhill's face sobered. "I'd give a lot to know," he said. He looked up and down the street. "He was at odds with Dude Carter, Ed Chilton, Gus Cargill, and half a dozen other hardcases around here, not to mention the Apache."

"If he was killed on Dark Mountain, that would eliminate the Apache, wouldn't it?"

"Possibly. Between you and me, Cade, I'd forget about the whole thing. It's dangerous to probe into these matters."

"He was my brother, Dick."

Dick placed a hand on Cade's shoulder. "I know this country," he said. "I know these people. You'll get into nothing but trouble trying to solve Dan's murder."

"Maybe you're right. My first consideration is getting the Lazy W on a paying basis."

"Now you're talking," said Dick heartily. "How about a quick drink? I'm due back at the ranch. My wife is feeling poorly, and I don't like to be away from her too long."

"Thanks, but I've got some business to take care of. I'd like to get back to the ranch in time for supper."

"Some other time then. Adios, Cade."

Cade watched the rancher walk toward his horse. He had the same feeling about Thornhill as he had about Charley Bidwell. He had a few friends in the Valley of the Bravo.

CHAPTER SIX

The valley road was dark, overshadowed by the swaying trees. The Bravo rushed along in its course, unseen by Cade Willcox, as he tooled the buckboard team along. The buckboard was heavy with supplies. He had spent more time in Pine Tree than he had anticipated, but he had taken care of enough business so that he wouldn't have to enter that hive of trouble again for some time. He had had a bellyful that day. He had managed to anger Troy Burkitt, Dude Carter, and Gus Cargill, and he had already angered Pierce Gatchell, Farley Mosston, and Muley Smeed.

He looked back along the dark road. He hadn't seen a human being since he had crossed the bridge at the edge of Pine Tree. He felt for a cigar and lighted it, drawing in the good smoke and blowing out a cloud of it. Things were looking up. He had collected from Burkitt, and Thornhill would return the stock he had not paid for, so as soon as Cade could round up a few more hands, the Lazy W would be in business again. Burt Mossman had given him a year's leave of absence, but Cade wasn't at all sure he'd need all that time.

He turned the team off on the side road that led to the Lazy W road. Faint moonlight was beginning to show over the dim, crested mountains to the east. A cold breeze swept leisurely through the valley. He drove up a slope where the trees had thinned out and then turned the team to enter the Lazy W road.

The gun flash blossomed in the trees beyond the road and across the rushing stream. The off horse went down as though pole-axed. His mate reared and plunged. Cade dived from the seat. A second slug smashed into the buckboard. Cade clawed for his Colt as he bellied under the wagon. The horse panicked, fighting the harness, frantic at the smell of blood.

A bullet smashed a wheel spoke, inches from Cade's head, and he winced in pain as a splinter gouged his left cheek, bringing tears to his left eye. He cocked the Colt and lay still, peering through the wheel, trying to spot the hidden rifleman. The echo of the last shot had died away.

The horse was whinnying in sheer panic, trying to drag itself free from the tangled harness.

Cade wormed his way from underneath the wagon into the ditch, cursing as the water worked its way through his clothing. The moon was shedding more light into the Valley of the Bravo, but he couldn't see any sign of life in the darkness of the woods.

Cade wormed his way out of the ditch and into the scrub brush by the side of the road. A rifle shot cracked, and the slug smashed into the load on the back of the buckboard. Inch by inch, Cade worked his way into the shelter of the trees as now, and then a bullet slapped into the buckboard or its load.

Cade bellied behind a mossy log just as a slug killed the second horse. Then it was very quiet except for the rushing of the stream, as the new moon rose higher and higher, shedding pale, washed-out light across the Valley of the Bravo.

He lay there for a long time, peering into the moving shadows, not daring to risk a shot until he saw something to shoot at for fear of getting too quick a return shot. The sweet smell of sorghum molasses drifted to him. The gallon jug he had bought must have been smashed.

The moonlight filtered through the trees, making silvery patches here and there. There was no sign of life. Cade stood up and then dived for cover again as a shot rapped out and a slug slapped into the mossy log. Cade lost his temper. He shook out three rounds in crashing crescendo and then dived for a hollow as the rifle gave him shot for shot. Something whisked through the crown of his hat.

The echoes died away down the valley.

Cade crawled from the hollow and behind a stump, from there to a tangle of broken branches and from there into another hollow. He raised his head in time to see a man run lightly through the woods. Cade fired until the Colt ran dry. The acrid smoke swirled about him, blinding him for a moment, and when it cleared, the man was gone like a phantom into the night. A few minutes later, he heard the thudding of hoofs up the road, and then they, too, died away.

Cade reloaded the hot Colt and walked into the moonlit woods. Boot marks showed on the soft ground, and empty brass hulls were scattered here and there. He picked one of them up. It was still warm. It was a .44/40, a cartridge interchangeable between Colt and Winchester, and most of the men in that country carried .44/40's.

He walked to the road and looked up it. It was empty of life. The drygulcher was gone, at least for that night. Cade walked to the buckboard, looking ruefully at the dead team. The load was shot up, but outside of the smashed sorghum jug and some holes in a flour sack, the supplies hadn't suffered too much.

Cade sheathed his Colt and walked toward the ranch. "Little man, you've had a busy day," he said dryly. He wiped the blood from his face. He wouldn't be able to conceal this affair from Lucy. By Godfrey, she had enough troubles as it was.

The ranch house showed cheerful light as he walked toward it. The smell of good food drifted to him, and he suddenly realized how hungry he was.

Two men were washing up outside the bunkhouse when Cade rounded the side of the house. One of them whirled and stabbed a hand down toward his Colt. "Take it easy," said Cade. "I'm Cade Willcox."

The taller of the two men peered at him. "'Oughta, watch how you walk up on a man," he said testily.

"Little nervous, aren't you?" asked Cade.

"Well, dammit, we heard some shooting down the valley," the tall man said angrily.

"Who are you?"

"Harry Nadeau. This is my partner Joe Mahan."

"Pleased," said Cade. "Get a team and go back to the road junction. Both of my horses were killed by a drygulcher.

Unharness them and pull them into the woods. We'll have to take care of them later. Bring the buckboard back."

"Now?" said Nadeau.

"Why not?" said Cade. He wiped the blood from his face.

"We ain't et yet," said Mahan.

"Lucy!" called out Cade.

The kitchen door opened. Lucy came out on the back porch. "Cade! You're so late! What happened?"

"A little shooting down the road," he said. "Both horses killed. The load was shot up a little."

"Are you all right? What's that on your face?"

"Splinter wound. I'm all right. How soon do we eat?"

"It'll be late. I was waiting for you. In an hour or so."

Cade turned. "Get the team," he said.

"Can't it wait until later on?" said Nadeau.

"I said: Get the team," said Cade quietly.

The two men eyed him.

"Are you working here?" asked Cade.

"We take our orders from Mis' Willcox," said the smaller man. His voice had a sour ring to it. He looked at Lucy.

"My brother-in-law is in charge now, boys," she said.

Nadeau looked at Cade. He walked toward the bunkhouse. "Come on, Joe," he said over his shoulder. "We can get the buckboard after supper."

"Now," said Cade.

Harry kept on walking.

"You can draw your time," said Cade.

"You got no right to say that," said Mahan.

"Will you go and get the buckboard?"

"If Harry goes, I'll go."

"Then you can draw your time, too."

"Hands ain't that easy to get around here, Willcox."

Cade's temper had been fanned all day but hadn't reached a hot enough pitch for action, but it was getting dangerously close now.

Nadeau turned. "What's for supper, Mis' Willcox?" he said insolently.

Cade walked slowly forward. He reached Mahan. He looked at Nadeau. "Get off the place," he said. "You'll either take orders or leave."

"Damn you to hell!" snapped Mahan. He dropped his good hand to his Colt.

Cade backhanded him, driving him back against the wall of the bunkhouse, washbasins clattering to the ground. Mahan cursed.

Nadeau whirled and ran toward Cade.

"Watch him, Cade!" cried Lucy. "He used to be in the ring!"

Cade glanced at Joe Mahan. Mahan wiped the blood from his mouth and grinned. "You're safe from me," he said. "Harry can take care of you, mister."

Nadeau raised his hands. "Keep your hand off that

cutter," he warned. He danced about throwing punches, bobbing, and weaving.

Cade smiled coldly. "If you want to fight, Mr. Nadeau," he said, "stand still for a minute."

The left tapped Cade's bleeding cheek, then dropped and tapped his jaw. The right came so quickly that Cade wasn't ready for it. It staggered him. A left and a right drove him back still further. Nadeau measured him and threw a Sunday punch that landed Cade flat on his back. Nadeau blew professionally through his nose, hunched, lowered his shoulders, and smiled thinly. "Enough, Mr. Willcox?" he asked.

Grant Willcox came from the corral and stood beside the bunkhouse, staring in disbelief. Joe Mahan was laughing silently.

Cade stood up and wiped the blood from his left cheek. Nadeau moved in swiftly, throwing fast and accurate punches that stung Cade like whip strokes. He had indeed been in the ring. Cade backed away, gauging the fast-moving man, taking punch after punch, arid, then he noticed Nadeau was breathing just a little too hard for a professional. Grant had said the man was lazy, and it was likely he was too lazy to keep himself in top condition.

"Enough?" questioned Nadeau.

The left jab caught him low in the belly. His head came down, and a right cross shook him. He danced back, stabbing viciously at Cade's damaged cheek. A left smashed into his gut. He split Cade's lower lip wide open and ripped at the torn cheek. A left and right thudded into his guts, and he whitened beneath the tan. "Time!" he gasped.

"Time?" said Cade coldly. "You're not in the squared circle, Mr. Nadeau. You're in a stinking barnyard."

Nadeau made his play. He rushed Cade, throwing desperate punches, and the rock of a man facing him took every one of them while he smashed steadily at ribs and belly like a man chopping wood until Nadeau dropped his arms and a right caught him on the side of the jaw, nearly snapping his neck, and he went down into the mud and manure with blood flowing from his mouth and nose.

"Keep your hands away from that six-gun, Joe," said a cold voice.

Cade turned, dropping his hand to his Colt. Grant Willcox stood behind Joe Mahan, six-gun in hand. Mahan slowly raised his hands to shoulder level. "I'll fix you for this, kid," he said fiercely.

Cade took Joe's pistol from its holster and sailed it into the darkness of the corral. "Get your partner out of here, Mahan," he said.

When Nadeau came to, Mahan helped him to the bunkhouse while the two Willcox men waited outside. In a little while, the two hands came out with their gear. When they were gone, Cade looked at Grant. "Thanks, kid," he said.

"You can't trust Joe Mahan, Uncle Cade. You've made a bad enemy with him. Harry hasn't got the guts to give you trouble unless Joe prods him into it, and he will. You mark my words."

Cade washed up, wincing as the water stung his cuts. "Get the team," he said over his shoulder.

"You're not taking him with you?" said Lucy.

Cade turned slowly. "I don't aim to leave those supplies out there all night," he said.

"There might be more shooting."

"I'll have a rifle this time," said Cade.

"It was Grant I was thinking about."

Cade wiped his face. "I'll go alone then," he said.

"No, you won't, Uncle Cade," said the kid.

Lucy turned on a heel and walked to the house. "It might have been better if you had stayed away, Cade," she said.

Grant came to his uncle. "Don't pay her no mind," he said.

"She's your mother," said Cade.

"Stepmother," corrected Grant. "My real mom would let me go with you."

Cade looked at him. "That would be because your father was there, kid. Maybe Lucy is right. There's been nothing but trouble since I got here."

"Someone is trying to drive you away," said the kid. "Don't you let 'em, Uncle Cade!"

Cade put on his hat after examining the bullet hole in it. "Damn!" he said. "Twenty dollar Stetson ruined."

The kid grinned. "Could'a been your head that was ruined."

Cade slapped him on the back. "Let's go," he said.

The moon was fully up by the time they finished the job. The kid's face was set with anger as he saw the team pull the last of the dead horses from the road. "Don't make any sense," he said. "Killin' horses like that."

"It could have been me," said Cade.

Grant turned to look at him. "You think they really were after you, or just throwing the fear of God into you?"

"Who knows? It was just a little too dark for a clear shot, and from the angle of the first shot, the one that killed the first horse, the drygulcher, was either a lousy shot or wasn't aiming at me. No, I don't think they meant to kill me yet."

"You have any idea who it was?"

Cade shook his head. As they rode back to the ranch, he told the boy of what had happened in town. "So, you see, it might have been any of them, but then again, there was shooting before I went to Pine Tree."

"But it's been pretty quiet around here for some time. Until you got here, Uncle Cade."

"Maybe I'd better leave then kid."

Grant slapped the reins on the rumps of the team. "No," he said quietly. "I ain't about to leave this place. It was my pa's place. Him and my ma are buried here. He picked out the place and always told me I'd really have something here someday. I ain't leaving, Uncle Cade. The two of us can hold this place until hell freezes over."

"You've got Lucy to think of," said Cade.

"We can always send her away until things clear up."

"You know she won't go," said Cade.

The kid nodded. "Yeh. She's the true grit, all right."

Later that night, after the delayed supper, they sat in the living room behind the boarded windows. Lucy sat with the wad of money from Troy Burkitt in her lap, but she wasn't much interested in the money. There was a worried look on her lovely face. "I don't think it's a good idea to get that stock back from Dick Thornhill," she said. "He's good for the money. We can sell off the remaining stock and put the place up for sale."

"No," said Grant.

She looked at him. "Do you want to die here like your father did? Do you want to see your uncle die as your father did?"

Cade slowly rolled a cigarette. "I won't run from a fight," he said quietly, "and I don't think the kid will either. It doesn't sound like you either, Lucy."

She sighed. "We've just been lucky so far." *

"We can leave the stock over at Dick's until we have enough hands to take care of them," said Cade. "Tomorrow, Grant and I will try to round up as much of the remaining stock as we can and herd them close to the ranch here. We'll have to get help. Maybe Dick can loan us a few hands for a time, at least enough of them to keep guard over the herd."

Grant nodded. "Sounds good," he said.

His stepmother stood up and placed the money on the table. "It seems like the decisions are out of my hands," she said. She looked at Cade. "I can see a great deal of Dan in you. Isn't it possible to avoid trouble instead of looking for it?"

Cade stood up. "No one is looking for trouble, Lucy," he said. "This is a man's way. I don't know of any other."

She shrugged and left the room.

Grant held out his hands, palms upward. "Man, she's riled," he said. "Another week or so, and we would have been out of here. I know she doesn't want to leave the place, but she's afraid for me."

"With good reason," said Cade. "We'll pull out of here an hour before dawn. I'd like to get part of that herd moving this way. Maybe better take along our hot rolls and some grub. Might have to stay out a night or two. You think Lucy will be all right?"

The kid nodded. "No man in his right mind is going to bother a woman in this country," he said. "Even Gus Cargill wouldn't stand for that."

Later, as Cade lay in his bed, staring up at the ceiling again, he thought back on Lucy's words. Cade's arrival had brought trouble. Maybe he should have stayed away, but it wasn't in his breed to run away from trouble. Still, he knew he had only been warned. The next shooting might not be a warning.

CHAPTER SEVEN

"Fifty head," said Cade in disgust. He reined in the sorrel and felt for the makings. "Kid, are you sure there isn't some other place around here the rest of them might be hidden?"

Grant shoved back his hat and reached for his canteen. It had been hot work under the sun rounding up the last few head and starting them toward the ranch. "We covered every possible place, Uncle Cade," he said.

"When was the last time a check was made?"

"Harry and Joe made one about a week ago."

"How many head?"

"A little over a hundred. Hundred and ten, I think."

Cade lighted the cigarette. "Did you believe them?"

"No reason not to."

"Maybe you should have done it yourself instead of playing Billy the Kid."

Grant flushed. "Well, I wasn't thinking," he said.

"Damned right you weren't!"

Cade looked up at the nearby flank of Dark Mountain. The North Fork of the Bravo curled around the base of the huge pile and vanished into a narrow canyon. The mouths of somber-looking canyons yawned down on Cade and the kid.

"You won't find anything in there," said Grant.

"You ever look?"

"Pa did a couple of times. The last time he never came out. Tracked some stolen head one time plumb into Lost Canyon, then lost the trail. Gus Cargill took a bunch of his waddies in there one time, right after Pa was killed, and they didn't find a thing either. Muley Smeed even lost the trail, and Muley can track durned near as good as any old 'Pache."

"Can you handle these critters alone?"

"The dog can help. I'll take it in easy stages."

"Bueno! I'm going to take a look-see over toward the mountain."

"Maybe Gus Cargill won't like that."

Cade grinned. "I got a safe passage from him the other day."

"You believe him?"

Cade nodded. "He wants me to work for him. As long as I don't give him a definite answer, he'll take real good care of me."

"You're a gambler at heart, Uncle Cade."

"I may camp out a night or two. Tell Lucy everything will be all right. You go over to Thornhill's and see if Dick can let you have some help."

"Lucy said she was going over to see Mrs. Thornhill. She's been feeling poorly. I'll let her ask Dick. Maybe I ought to stay around the place and keep an eye on these cows."

"Keno," said Cade. He touched spurs to the sorrel and rode toward the distant creek. He looked back now and then to see the kid slowly driving the few head toward the distant ranch with the dog working the side of the herd to keep it from drifting toward the bottoms. Cade grinned. "Might make a rancher out of him yet," he said.

The Bravo flowed through a green bottomland, sparsely timbered, and then flowed into a thicker tangle of timber filled with deadfall, the trees hung with weathered squaw wood. No one could drive cattle through such a barrier. Cade rode around the timber until the mouth of the canyon loomed before him, a flow of cool air sweeping from it, rustling the branches, and swaying the trees. Here the talus slopes of shattered detritus covered both banks of the creek right to the water's edge, and some of it had even flowed into the stream, shallowing it, until it was only a few inches deep, running clear and cold over the rock.

High to the right were the rough, flanking hills of Dark Mountain, sun swept and empty of life. A man could wander into those hills and canyons and spend days in there, never retracing his steps. Yet, this was likely the only place stolen cattle could be driven without being seen by other ranchers. The Box C was to the north of the Lazy W, then curled around in a vast sweep of the broken country to end on the northern flank of Dark Mountain. Somewhere to the south of the Box C, east of the mountain was Ed Chilton's place. Dick Thornhill's Dark Mountain Ranch, with a Circle Dot brand, was west of the mountain, running on both sides of the Bravo Valley Road, and adjoining the southern border of the Lazy W. To the east, beyond the Box C and Chilton's place, was rough mountain country, once the haunt of the bronco Apache, which extended clear to the New Mexico border, without a ranch, house, village, or town to despoil the natural beauty of a virgin wilderness.

Cade worked his way up the canyon, and half a mile from the mouth of it, he found some fairly fresh droppings. He poked at them with a stick. About twenty-four hours old, hardly more than that. They could have come from a stray. If a stray went into that country, he'd fall prey to a mountain lion most likely or stay lost until he died.

He ground-reined the sorrel and waded across the stream to work the far bank, but it was a barren expanse of spray-washed rock, with the sheer wall of the canyon rising above it, stained by weather, cracked by heat and frost, and entirely unscalable by man or beast.

The sun was slanting to the west when he came out into a more open area. Here the creek was joined by another fork that foamed and raced from a slit of a canyon. Cade looked dubiously up it. The fork almost filled the canyon from wall to wall. He rode up the first canyon, looking for signs, cutting back and forth, and all he was rewarded with was the picked bones of a calf, lying stark and white under the late afternoon sun, with weeds sprouting up between the ribs. To the right was a savage tangle of wood, brush, and shattered rock that had been brought down through many years by the Bravo when in flood. No one could ride through that mess, much less drive fifty head through it.

Cade hooked a leg around his pommel and rolled a quirley, his gray eyes studying the lonely canyon. Maybe he had been misled. If Cargill was behind all the rustling, he'd likely have the steers driven over onto Box C land and across it, to hide it in some of the many box canyons to the east, under the rimrock mountains, until such time as he could change brands, or get rid of the cattle. It would be easy enough to do, inasmuch as he kept his range well patrolled by hardcases like Gatchell, Mosston, and Smeed.

Cade lighted the cigarette. This man Chilton had tangled horns with Dan because of the Apache who had insisted on hunting over Lazy W land. A hunter and a trapper, not a cattleman, and yet that wouldn't stop him from snapping up a few head when and if he got the chance. The Apache would help him, and yet they wouldn't go near Dark Mountain, which likely ruled out their participation in cattle stealing if the cattle had been run off through the Dark Mountain country.

"Beats the hell out of me," said Cade loudly.

"Beats the hell out of me... Beats the hell out of me... Beats the hell out of me..." echoed the narrow canyon.

Cade grinned. He looked back at the sun. It was getting late. Too late to work his way back out to the ranch. He rode back to the narrow-mouthed canyon and looked up it again. He had enough light to poke up there a piece and still time enough to find his way back to this canyon for his night's camp. He didn't know whose land he was on if he was on anyone's land at all. The area seemed deserted, but one never knew.

He rode the sorrel up the fork, eyeing the sheer dark walls, noting the loose rock that was scaling off here and there in slow decay. One of those slabs could smash a man and his horse into jelly. A mess of cattle being driven up this narrow slot would surely cause enough tremors to loosen some of that rock.

The canyon twisted and turned, almost doubling back on itself at times, and much of the time, the fork nearly filled the canyon from wall to wall. High on the sheer walls, he could see dark water stains, and here and there shaggy tufts of dried brush, and now and then a broken branch or two indicated plainly enough that a flash flood would fill that canyon from wall to wall. It was no place to travel and certainly no place to camp.

He kept on, knowing that darkness would trap him in there but also knowing that there would be a good moon that night if he ever got out of the canyon.

The darkness came suddenly, like a black mantle hung by the hand of an unseen magician over the mountains and canyons. The noise of the stream drowned out the clatter of Hardtack's hoofs on the naked rock. Cade dismounted and led the sorrel on, feeling his way slowly and cursing his stupidity for letting himself be caught in there. He felt as though he were probing into the hidden guts of Dark Mountain itself. Coupled with the rushing of the stream came the cold moaning of the wind down the canyon, seeking the lower ground far to the west.

He felt rather than saw when the canyon widened. High above him was the dark, looming bulk of the mountain. He tethered the sorrel and dropped his cantle pack on the ground. The ground sloped upward toward the canyon wall to the north, high enough so that the stream would have to be at full flood to sweep over the rock-studded ground where he planned to make his camp. He found enough driftwood to start a cheery blaze, although the flickering light seemed to have little effect on the shadows of Dark Mountain looming beyond the rim of the canyon. He was east of the mass of the mountain, likely somewhere on either Box C land or possibly Chilton's land. Thornhill's Circle Dot was too far to the south for Cade to be on it.

When the fire died down, he placed the battered spider over the glowing coals and filled it full of bacon, placing the coffee pot in the embers at the edge. He unsaddled the sorrel and picketed it where there was some scant grazing. After he ate, he sat for a long time, with his back against a tilted rock, smoking, sipping his coffee, and watching the soft, almost imperceptible light of the rising moon touch the eastern sky. It was a pleasant enough place. The wind moaned softly down the canyon, and the rushing of the stream made gentle music, but still, there was an uneasiness in the night, a feeling the firelight and the rising of the moon could not dispel, and time and time again he found himself looking at the strange, eerie-looking mountain. Sometime in ages past, a great chunk of the eastern side had subsided, leaving a deep notch effect, like a crescent, in the harsh flank of the mountain. There was likely a chaotic tangle of broken rock, dead timber, and thorny brush filling the gap beneath the crest, a no-man's-land if there ever was one.

When the moon arose and filled the canyon with light, he walked along the bank of the stream, looking for signs, and sure enough, on an area of decomposed rock and silt washed up by the stream during higher water, he found tracks. He knelt beside the area, studying them. He lighted a cigar and held the flickering light of the lucifer over the nearest tracks. They were fresh. Maybe not more than twenty-four hours old as the droppings he had found earlier had been. He circled the trodden area and worked his way through a tangle of catclaw and wait-a-bit brush, and in a clear area in the middle, he saw the plain print of a horse's hoof and an empty bag of Bull Durham caught on a thorn.

Two hundred yards up the canyon was a great wide place, where the canyon walls had collapsed, leaving a jumble of shattered rock on each side that flowed almost to meet together, stopped by the rushing stream. There were no more tracks, no droppings, not a sign that cattle and horsemen had passed that way. Beyond this area was a place where the canyon narrowed and where the light of the moon did not penetrate very deeply, and the mingled sound of the stream and the wind poured from it.

It was too dark in there for Cade to find signs, so he walked slowly back to his simple camp. In daylight, he could penetrate still further. He might just as well keep on. Those cattle had to be driven through an outlet somewhere to the east or the south-east, there was no other way they could go unless they were spirited out of the canyons along a threadlike trail clinging to sheer cliffs, and that was out of the question.

He let the fire die out and lay atop his hot roll for a long time, watching the moon and listening to the night sounds. Before the chill of the night drove him into the hot roll, he levered a round into his Winchester and placed it beside him, piling rocks on either side of his bed. Hardtack was as good as any watchdog.

He slept fitfully. Twice during the night, he opened his eyes to see the dying moon, and once, as the wind shifted, he heard faint sounds, almost as though cattle were bawling in the darkness to the southeast.

He was up before the dawn, breakfasted, saddled the 'sorrel, and broke his camp in the space of an hour. The first light of the dawn was tinging the eastern sky when he rode Hardtack up the dark canyon, shivering in the clammy wind that swept around the flank of the great mountain.

By midmorning, he was at a dead end as far as signs were concerned. The canyon had broken up into a mess of branches, and each one of them had to be investigated, and each one of them was a box canyon, forcing him back to the main canyon where the Bravo, constricted, frothing, and leaping, roared out of the tangled country to the east.

It was slow going. By noon he had reached a wider place in the canyon, the right bank of the stream thick with shattered, sun-silvered deadwood, while the left bank was hardly more than a narrow ledge seemingly tacked to the sheer wall that rose high above it. Here the Bravo was deep, swirling about hidden boulders in its constricted bed, frothing against the far wall. He sat the sorrel, fashioning a cigarette, idly watching a big piece of driftwood whirl about a bend and race toward him, leaping and plunging in the liquid grip of the current. He lighted the cigarette, and when he raised his head, the driftwood had vanished. He looked downstream. It was nowhere in sight. Likely the current had a fierce undertow. He sat there a long time until another piece of wood shot into view. He kept his eyes on it until it passed him and vanished far downstream.

The next piece of wood swirled about as it rounded the bend, then suddenly shot from sight. It did not reappear. Cade rubbed his bristly jaws. The stream couldn't be that deep. He studied the far bank, noting that there was a deep curve in the canyon wall and that a mass of driftwood hung against it in a deep eddy, pinned to the far wall by the force of the current.

Cade dismounted and pulled off his boots. He stripped off his gun belt and selected a stout staff from the driftwood on his side. He waded in, feeling the strong current grip on his calves, then his thighs, then his waist as he reached midstream. He probed with the staff. The water was about five feet deep beyond him. A chunk of wood shot around the bend and headed toward him, and he began to work his way back, not being anxious to get clobbered with the heavy piece of wood. When he looked for it again, it was gone. He shook his head in bewilderment. It hadn't passed him, and it wasn't likely it had dived to the bottom. He waded out of the cold water and began to wring out his levis. It was then he saw the piece of driftwood pinned against the far wall, caught by the eddy. He reached for his left boot, and as he did so, he saw the piece of wood vanish before his very eyes. Cade pulled on his boots and stood up, eyeing that mass of driftwood, noting the set of the current. Maybe there was a deep undercutting on the far side, drawing in wood and debris or holding it against the side of the canyon. Cade turned toward the sorrel. The rifle shot cracked from the canyon rim. A mallet seemed to slap Cade alongside the head, just above his left ear. He fell backward into the stream, and the Bravo, roaring in delight, gripped his motionless body and swirled it out into the middle of the stream and raced to the west with it.

CHAPTER EIGHT

His aching skull was gripped in a red-hot vise while an unseen demon pounded out a devil's tattoo on it, and yet his lower body seemed to be in the grip of ice. For a moment, he seemed doomed to whirl off again into the black pit from which he had slowly emerged. He opened his eyes to see wet stones inches from them. He slowly moved his hands and felt about himself. He was laying on wet stones, and from his waist down, he felt cold water, inches deep. He raised his head a little. Faint moonlight was tinting the sky, but the canyon in which he lay was thick with murmuring darkness. Slowly he raised his left hand and felt alongside his aching skull. The skin had been furrowed and was sticky with coagulated blood and hair.

"Creased, by God," he said.

He closed his eyes again. There was little feeling in his lower body, and for one god-awful moment, he thought his nerve system might have been damaged by the bullet, paralyzing his lower body. He tried to wiggle his toes within his soaked boots, and they wiggled, but just about. Slowly, inch by inch, digging in his clawed hands, he drew himself from the chilling waters of the Bravo until he lay belly flat on the harsh, flinty ground beyond the water's edge, his fingers bleeding and his heart pounding.

The moon rose slowly, sending down streamers of soft light into the canyon of the Bravo, while the soft night wind murmured through the scant brush and whispered about the eroded rock, and nocturnal animals scuttled furtively about on the night's business of hunting and being hunted. From somewhere up on the rimrock came the howling of a coyote, greeting the moonrise.

Cade slowly drew himself up into a sitting position and looked up at the canyon rim, and as he did so, he saw a man move swiftly back out of sight. An icy chill shot through Cade's body. The man had had a thick mane of hair, bound about the temples with a dingy cloth and no hat. There was only one race of people who did not wear hats in that country. *Apache!* Cade slid his hand down to his gun and touched the wet leather of his empty holster. The Bravo had disarmed him while it had played with his helpless body.

He looked up the canyon. Hardtack was likely still up there somewhere with Cade's Winchester scabbarded on the saddle. The Apache were supposed to be reservation bucks, but plenty of them had drifted off to become broncos again, not being farmers at heart, and they likely never would be. This was lonely, almost deserted country, and if a white man vanished, it might be a long time before anyone came looking for him, and by that time, the Apache would have thoroughly covered their tracks.

The moon rose higher, revealing the sharp line of the canyon rim, the scant brush standing out like silhouetted drawings or as though they had been cut from black paper. There was no sign of life. Yet he knew there was someone up there. Perhaps the very rifleman who had creased him, waiting for Cade to make his next move. He lay belly flat behind a rock and eyed that mysterious rim. In a little while, the canyon would be filled with clear moonlight, and not even a lizard could cross it without being seen by those sharp eyes up there.

Waves of sickness flowed through his bruised body, and his head ached intolerably. He knew he'd never have the strength to work his way out of the canyon on foot. The best thing to do was hide, but if they really wanted him, he'd never be able to hide from them. They knew it as well as he did. Maybe they were playing with him. Maybe they thought he was still armed. They'd find out soon enough.

The wind shifted a little, and he heard a faint but unmistakable sound, the striking of a shod hoof against the stone. It came from up on the rim. A few moments later, he heard the sound again, and this time it was closer. It was then that he saw a person on a horse, leading another horse. The rider and his horses vanished, but Cade could hear the hoofs clattering on loose rock. He turned his head. He could see the rider slowly coming down a narrow, precipitous trail that slanted to the canyon floor fifty yards from where he lay. Despite his fear of the unknown, Cade couldn't help but admire the iron nerve and skilled horsemanship of the rider. Stones fell from the trail and clattered on the canyon floor.

Cade looked up at the rim, and his heart skipped a beat. There were two thick-maned heads now where he had seen but one before. His skin crawled. He had no chance to escape. He picked up a fist-sized rock and felt in his pants pocket for his clasp knife. He opened the blade with his teeth and then waited.

The horseman stopped and slid from the saddle, looking toward Cade. He could not see the man's face, for he was in shadows, just beyond the clearly defined moonlight. For a few minutes, the man was still, and then he walked slowly forward, and Cade could see the rifle in his left hand. He stopped again and peered toward Cade as though he could not see Cade.

Cade raised his head a little. "Stay where you are!" he warned. "I've got a bead on you!"

The head turned a little to look directly at Cade.

"Leave one of those horses here," said Cade. "Then get the hell out of here!"

The man came slowly forward, hardly making a sound on the loose rock. Cade got slowly to his feet, rock ready in his left hand, knife in the other, ready to attack, on the chance he could get this one, grab a horse and hightail it out of there before the others had a chance to get him.

The man stepped into the moonlight just as Cade was about to hurl the rock and then attack. His breath caught in his throat. It was a woman, a young woman. Her dark, lustrous hair was braided and hung in front of her shoulders, flowing out on the high breasts beneath the man's shirt she wore. Her face was oval, creamy skinned, with a pair of the loveliest dark eyes he had ever seen.

The rock hit the ground, and the knife dropped from Cade's hand. He narrowed his eyes. It was like a dream.

"You've been badly hurt," she said in a soft voice, speaking excellent English. "I've come to help you."

Cade passed a hand across his eyes. "Who are you?"

"Alma Chilton."

He looked up at the rim. They were still there, looking down at Cade and the young woman. "And them?"

"My cousins," she said.

"You are Apache? Chilton's wife?"

She shook her head. "His daughter. My mother passed away."

"Nice cousins," said Cade. He gingerly touched his wound.

"They did not shoot at you."

"No?"

She shook her head. "They would not come down into this canyon. Where was the man who shot you?"

He pointed to the south wall of the canyon.

"Then it was not them who fired at you. No Apache would go beyond the north rim of this canyon." She looked at Dark Mountain. "This country is taboo for them."

"And you?"

She laughed. "Not for me, although I must admit I don't care to go beyond this canyon, nor even come into it."

"But you came for me?"

"Yes. My cousins saw you down here. They came for my father, but he's away hunting and won't be back until tomorrow. I knew I'd never convince my cousins to come down here, so I came myself. Let me look at your wound."

He sat down on a rock, and she came to him, and he caught the faint, almost perceptible perfume of her, and a breast brushed his shoulder as she bent to look at his wound. Her hands were exquisitely cool on his fevered head. He looked up into her dark eyes as she stepped back.

"A fraction more, and we would have buried you here," she said quietly. "You have a hard skull, Mister..."

"Willcox," he said. "Cade Willcox."

She drew in her breath.

He grinned crookedly. "Yeh. I know. Your Dad had a feud with my brother. It doesn't concern me."

"You do look familiar," she said. She looked up the canyon. "Strange," she added.

"What do you mean?"

"My cousins said your horse is still up the canyon. His reins evidently caught in the brush when he tried to run."

"So?"

She looked at him with a strange look on her lovely face. "They say it is the same place where the body of your brother was found."

An indescribably eerie feeling flowed through Cade. "Are you sure?"

"They do not make mistakes in such things," she said. She looked up the canyon again. "There was another man killed in here last year. No one ever found out who did it. He was trailing strays. He worked for your brother. His name was Mack Rose. My father brought him out. Your brother was ready to kill my father, saying he had killed Mack Rose, but there was proof my father had been in Pine Tree at the time."

Mack Rose… Cade remembered the simple head-board in the Willcox graveyard on the Lazy W. Likely shot down by rustlers, Grant Willcox had said.

"Do you want me to get your horse?" she asked.

"I'll get him," he said.

She looked up at him. "Supposing they are still there?" she asked.

Cade walked to the spare horse. He looked back at her. "Why do you say 'they,' Alma?" he asked quietly. "Only one man shot at me. I never even saw him."

She shrugged as she mounted. "I don't really know. Pa always speaks of them as being 'they,' Cade."

"Rustlers?"

She nodded.

"You think it was rustlers then?"

She touched her horse with her heels. "Do you have other enemies, Cade?"

He opened and then closed his mouth. By God, yes I do, he thought. He saw in his mind's eye the hard, rough-hewn face of Pierce Gatchell, the lean, cold features of Farley Mosston, and the grinning face of Muley Smeed. He remembered the coyote-like face of Troy Burkitt and the handsome, though cold, face of Dude Carter. Then there was Gus Cargill, cocky Harry Nadeau, and venge-ful-looking Joe Mahan. Cade hadn't wasted any time in racking up an imposing array of men who'd cut out his heart for sheer bloody pleasure.

"You don't have to answer," she said. "I can see the answer on your face. Can you ride all right?"

He touched the horse with his spurs and clattered along the banks of the rushing stream. He looked at the cold, frothing waters and shuddered a little. It had been so close; it had been too damned close.

"My father says the Bravo never gives up its dead," she said.

"I wasn't killed," he said.

"Not this time."

He looked back at her but did not answer.

The sorrel was patiently waiting for Cade. Cade swung down from the horse he had been riding and staggered a little in his stride. A rocket seemed to burst inside his aching skull. He walked to the sorrel, freed the reins, then rested his head against the saddle.

"Are you all right?" she asked.

"I'll live," he said.

"There speaks the brave heart," she said.

He mounted the sorrel, feeling better because of the sheathed Winchester beneath his leg. He followed her to the trail and then up it. When they reached the top of the canyon, the place was deserted. "They've pulled out," he said.

She smiled. "No. They just don't want to have anything more to do with you, Cade."

He looked about. There wasn't a sign of any of them, and yet he knew she was right. A cold finger seemed to trace the length of his spine. "Can I leave you here?" he asked. "Will you be all right?"

"Safe as though I was in church," she said. "I can't say the same for you. Frankly, Cade, you look awful. My home is only five miles from here. In Lost Canyon. You'd better come home with me."

For a moment, he looked at her stubbornly, and then he nodded. It was easy to nod. She was a lovely thing and evidently well educated, and Cade couldn't find it in his heart to ride away from her. Not yet, at any rate.

He saw no sign of the bucks while they rode to the

Chilton place, and yet he knew they did not leave until Alma and Cade dismounted in front of the sprawling, well-built log house on a branch of the Bravo, with the moonlight streaming down almost as bright as the day. A dog barked from the barn, and another came growling toward them until the girl sent him packing. She took the horses, letting Cade wait for her on the wide porch. Despite his pounding head, he had to admire the view across the canyon, with the timber mantling the slopes of the distant mountains and the curious rock formations beyond the stream. Dark Mountain was to the south-west, dark despite the clear light of the moon, somber and brooding as always. Somewhere rode the man who had nearly killed him.

She came back to him, and in a little while, she had hot food on the table. She watched him eat after she had bathed his wound and bandaged it. He found the touch of her hands and the nearness of her more pleasant than he cared to admit to himself.

"Prime," he said as he pushed back his plate and refilled his coffee cup.

She arose and got the makings for him, and he watched the graceful, swaying motion of her hips as she walked back to the fireplace and poked the burning wood. She looked back at him, and he knew as sure as hellfire she knew he had been eyeing her lush body. Cade flushed as he quickly rolled a cigarette.

The young woman was as fine a mixture of white and Apache blood as he had ever seen. He remembered a girl, hardly more than seventeen, he had known in Bisbee, whose mother had been a pure Tarahumara, while her father had been born of a Mexican mother and an American father. She, too, had been lovely and dangerous, for when Cade had left her, breed that she was, she had given him a parting memento of a knife cut on the left shoulder and deep teeth marks in his left hand. But Alma was different, inheriting the best features of both races.

Her complexion was clear and creamy, almost ivory in color, while the eyes and hair were pure quill. Her face was a little too angular for an Apache but perfect for a white. She was young, perhaps nineteen, possibly twenty.

He lighted the cigarette and walked to the big armchair beside the fire. She sat on a hassock and picked up some darning. He watched her deft hands as she worked, the glowing of the firelight on her soft cheek and on the lustrous sheen of her hair.

"Do you plan to work the Lazy W?" she asked.

"My sister-in-law wants to sell out," he said. "The boy wants to stay. It's a good ranch."

She nodded. "Lucy Arnold is not the ranch type," she said.

"What makes you say that?"

"I went to school with her in Pine Tree," she said.

"She married Dan," he said.

"Yes. He was a good man."

"That sounds odd, coming from you."

"It's my father's opinion as well."

He blew a smoke ring. "Perhaps it's foolish," he said. "There are only fifty head left on the place. We have more stock coming in and no one to handle it. I've made a few enemies in the few days I have been here."

She looked at him. "You won't quit," she said. "You're much like your brother. He wouldn't quit either, and things were going badly for him. He wouldn't quit, but they made sure of him."

He looked into the fire. She had used 'they' again. "What is in the Dark Mountain country?" he asked.

"Ghosts," she said.

He grinned. "There speaks your mother's people."

She shrugged. "Tangled canyons. Twisted stream courses. Mountain lions. Wolves and bears. Places where a man can get lost and wander until he dies without ever getting out of that country again."

He rolled another cigarette. "And stray cattle?"

She looked quickly at him. "Why do you say that?"

"I could have sworn I heard cattle bawling up there one night."

"I have, too, when the wind is right. My mother's people say they are ghosts, that no cattle can live in there for long. That no man can live in there for long either."

"Apache?"

She looked into the fire. "No one knows why they shun Dark Mountain, but they have for generations. They don't know why they should shun it, but they know they should. It is enough for them." She picked up her darning. "My father will tell you all he knows about the place."

"Has he been in there?"

"He has never said so. He avoids it. His Apache relatives' and friends have asked him to stay away from the place. He will not go against their wishes. It is for his own safety, they say."

It was more than just plain pleasant sitting there with her. He learned that she had gone to school in Pine Tree until pressure from people who didn't want their children going to school with a breed' had forced Ed Chilton to take her to a private school elsewhere. She had lasted there a year, and the same thing had happened. After that, she had returned home. Her father was an educated man. He had brought crates of books back with him from a trip to EI Paso and had taken her education on himself. Later, as Cade lay on his bed, staring up at the dark ceiling, he thought about her. Some white man would marry her and consider her below his level, or she might end up as a squaw. Neither course was right for one so lovely and human.

The pain lanced through his head, and he shrieked aloud during the long night. He sat bolt upright, staring at the wall, unseeing, but still, terror marked his sweat-dewed face.

She came to him quickly; a wrapper was drawn about

her body, soothing him with soft words and softer hands. He lay still, looking up at her dim face, feeling the pressure of her breasts against his chest as she adjusted the bandage. He slid an arm about her slim waist, and she did not resist. He drew her close, and despite this throbbing skull and the weakness of him, he wanted her. God, how he wanted her!

She looked down at his sweating face. "No, Cade," she said softly. "Not this way."

She was only a breed and likely soul starved for love and affection. They were alone in the house. She was his for the taking, and he knew she'd never use a knife or teeth on him.

"Cade," she pleaded.

For a long moment, he hesitated, and then he withdrew his arm. "I'm sorry," he said.

"It was my fault," she whispered. "Coming to you like this."

She pressed her soft lips on his burning forehead. "Sleep now," she said as she stood up. She walked to the door and turned. "You have a hard head, Cade Willcox. Another thing: You recover fast. Too fast! Good night!"

He grinned at the ceiling, in relief for letting her go, and at her words. She'd be safe with him. She had completely disarmed him. He dropped off to sleep, and as he did so, he could have sworn that the night wind, creeping up from the southwest, murmuring through the trees, brought the faint, ever so faint, bawling of cattle with it.

CHAPTER NINE

"He'll live, Alma," the dry voice said.

Cade opened his eyes. A broad-shouldered, gray-haired man stood beside the bed, looking down at him. The cool gray eyes studied Cade. A dented scar showed on the man's bronzed face, on the left cheekbone, tracing a course to the tip of the ear.

"You're Ed Chilton," said Cade.

"The same. One of the boys came to tell me they had found you in the canyon of the Bravo. You took a helluva chance poking in there. You won't ever find strays in there."

"I wasn't looking for strays. I was looking for about fifty head."

Either way, you took a chance. Thank God the boys saw you. It's a good thing Alma was here to come and get you. She's part Apache, but Dark Mountain doesn't bother her."

"Not as much as the others," she said.

"Can't say that I care much for it myself," said Ed. "Get some coffee, Alma." He looked after her. "That damned place bothers her more than she'll ever admit." He looked again at Cade. "I heard another Willcox had shown up in the Bravo Valley. A man tough as a cob with a low boiling point. All you Willcox's alike?"

"I'm afraid so."

The hunter touched the deep scar on his cheek. "I ought to know," he said dryly. "Your brother gave me this. I'm not complaining. It was a fair fight. I used to think before he was killed that either him or me had to go."

Cade slowly sat up, feeling his head throb. "You did?"

"It wasn't me that killed him, Cade. Maybe Dan was getting close to something, as Mack Rose had done, and as you did."

"What makes you think so?"

Chilton shrugged. He took the coffee cups from Alma as she came into the room and handed one to Cade. "This is my home here in this canyon, Cade. I'm no rancher. The mountains feed me and let me take care of Alma here. The Apache are my relatives by marriage, and above that, they are my good friends. It's a good life. Lonely, but I don't mind. I feel differently about Alma. Sometimes I think I'm part Apache. Not by blood but by inclination, for, by the Bible, I won't go into the Dark Mountain country. But there's something in there, Cade. Something someone is guarding."

"Like the Lost Dutchman's Mine?"

"Something like that." Chilton sipped his coffee. "You know the Apache?"

"I served with the Apache Scouts along with Tom Horn and Al Sieber, under both Crook and Miles."

"Chiricahuas. These are White Mountain Apache around here. My wife was of their blood. A fine woman. A man couldn't find a better. Gus Cargill tried half a dozen ways to get this land of mine, but my wife had it through a government grant, and even Big Gus Cargill couldn't break that! I put this land in Alma's name, so her blood would hold it. Cargill might have beaten me out of it. Best timberland in this part of the country. Once I planned to lumber it, but someone stood in the way."

"My brother?"

Chilton nodded. "It's just as well. I couldn't stand to see the woods stripped from this country."

Cade sipped his coffee. He couldn't help but like the man. "If rustlers ran cattle up this way, where could they get them through the mountains?"

"They couldn't. There's absolutely no place they could get through. Farther south, they might, but certainly not around here."

"It just doesn't make sense."

"Sometimes, when the wind is right, we hear cattle bawling."

"Near where I was shot?"

"Somewhere beyond that, I think. The wind has to be just right. I used to think the sound came from the Lazy W or Dick Thornhill's Circle Dot, but that's hardly possible. The Apache say they are ghost cattle, and sometimes I think they are right. This is a strange country, Cade. There is a great deal we do not know about it."

"They are real cattle," said Alma.

"You believe that?" said Cade.

"My mother's people would see any cattle driven through here. No cattle could be driven east of the Box C, the Lazy W, or the Circle Dot without my mother's people knowing about it. Nothing can pass through this country without them knowing about it."

"Like me?" said Cade.

"They will not go near that canyon. They would have no reason to follow you or *shoot* at you."

"My brother refused to let them hunt Lazy W land as they had been accustomed to doing," said Cade.

Ed Chilton fingered his scar. "Their feud was with him, not with you," he said. "I convinced them they should stay away from the Lazy W. We want no trouble with the white people."

Cade looked at him. It was almost as though Chilton

considered himself one of them. Squawman thought Cade.

Chilton emptied his cup. "You can stay here as long as you like," he said.

"I'll have to get back," said Cade.

"Today?"

Cade nodded. He looked at Alma. She flushed a little and left the room. Chilton looked after her. "Fine girl," he said absent-mindedly. "Damned shame she has to live like this."

"You like it."

He nodded. "It's my life. White men don't like mixed blood. Breeds are fine for bedding but not for marrying. Apache bucks are chary of white blood."

"She's lovely," said Cade. "Damned lovely."

"Would you marry a breed?" said Chilton bitterly.

Cade did not answer. He emptied his coffee cup and thrust his legs out from beneath the covers. He felt weak, but he had to go. His clothing had been dried and several rips had been mended, and as he reached for his shirt, he suddenly remembered he had been wearing his Arizona Ranger badge inside the shirt. He felt the weight of the badge as he picked up the shirt. He glanced at Chilton. The hunter was standing at the window looking out across the sunlit canyon. Did he know? Alma certainly did. Had she told him?

He swung his gun belt about his lean waist and buckled it.

"Alma said you lost your six-shooter," said Chilton. "I've an extra one you can borrow. Might as well keep it, come to think of it, for I never wear one of the things. A rifle is good enough for me."

Cade nodded. "They are a damned nuisance," he said.

"I've heard you were mighty good with one of them."

Cade did not answer. He picked up the makings and rolled a cigarette, then followed Chilton out to breakfast. There was no expression on the girl's face as she served them. If Chilton was mixed up in the rustling, and he had learned who Cade really was, Cade knew he'd never get back to the Lazy W alive. The girl certainly never would cover up Cade if she knew her father was in danger.

"I'll guide you back," said Chilton as he finished eating. "I'll go get the horses." He left the room.

Cade refilled his coffee cup. He looked at Alma. "Do you know who I am?" he asked.

"Cade Willcox," she said.

"Don't play foxy with me, Alma," he said.

She closed the outer door and came to the table. "You mean about the badge?"

"Yes."

"Your secret, if it is a secret, is safe with me," she said.

"I am not in the Bravo Valley on Ranger business," he said.

She smiled. "They could use you. It doesn't really make any difference to me, Cade."

"What about your father?"

She studied him. "He is not a rustler or a killer of men," she said. "He has never killed a man. Can you say the same?"

Cade drained his coffee cup and stood up. "No," he said quietly. "But I have killed only in the line of duty."

"A reasonable excuse," she said.

Cade suddenly hated her. He hated her for her hold over him. He hated her for her loveliness. He hated her for her mixed blood.

She walked to a cabinet and withdrew a Colt six-shooter from it. She placed it on the table in front of Cade. "My father said you could have this. There are fresh cartridges in that drawer there." She walked to the sink and began to do the dishes.

Cade loaded the Colt and put a dozen fresh rounds in the loops of his gun belt. "Someone has to do the job," he said suddenly.

"That is true."

"But not me, is that it?"

She turned slowly and looked at him. "It doesn't make any difference to me what you do, Mr. Willcox," she said.

He walked to the door. "Thank you for coming after me," he said.

"You would have lived," she said.

"Are you sure about that?"

Her great dark eyes studied him. "Men like you are not easy to kill," she said. "Some men are born to be killed, and others are born to be killers."

"And I am one of the latter?"

"I didn't say that. There are other men than killers and those who will be killed." She turned away. "Do not harm my father. He is not one of those for whom you are looking. If any harm comes to my father, through you, or any of those others in the valley..." Her voice trailed off.

Her meaning was plain enough. She still had close bonds with her mother's people. "I apologize for last night," he said.

She looked at him again. "I am used to it," she said. A bitter sort of a smile fled across her face. "Goodbye, Cade."

He closed the door behind him. He mounted Hardtack and rode beside Chilton. Neither of them spoke as they followed the trail beside the stream and then up the side of the canyon to the rim. Here Chilton drew rein and began to stuff his pipe. Cade rolled a cigarette, looking at the vast spread of country before them. Even Dark Mountain looked good with the morning sunlight flooding it with golden light. Already puffs of clouds had formed, and the east wind was driving them toward the mountain and the Valley of the Bravo.

Ed lighted his pipe. "I have often thought that this rustling is engineered by a man who can out-think any rancher or lawman in this country," he said.

"Such as?"

Chilton shrugged. "Gus Cargill has the brains and the

guts. Stoney Underhill, on the far side of the valley, spent five years at Yuma for rustling, some years ago."

"Maybe he's at it again."

Ed shrugged. "Maybe, but from what Stoney has told me, five years in Yuma ought to be taken off your time in hell. Besides, Stoney is a sick man. His boys are good men. Upright."

"Maybe it's them."

Chilton grinned. "Not likely. One of them is deputy marshal up at Holbrook, and the other is a Mormon bishop in the Little Colorado country."

"Maybe it's being done by outsiders."

"Maybe. It wouldn't be easy. My Apache relatives and friends know when a stranger comes around. I knew you were here the first night you set foot on Dark Mountain." He looked at Cade. "It was the next morning when you tangled with Gatchell, Mosston, and Smeed."

"You knew about that, too?"

"You walk a thin line, Mr. Willcox."

Cade blew a smoke ring. "What about Troy Burkitt, or Dude Carter, on this rustling business?" he asked.

"Troy hasn't got the guts, but he's sneaky enough. Might have some boys working for him. Carter? There's a horse of a different color. Cold, calculating, and deadly. Always well-heeled. You know he always claimed your brother had lost a part of the Lazy W to him. Maybe he's getting paid off his own way by running off your cattle."

"He's a townie, isn't he?"

Chilton shook his head. "Dude is as good a man in the open as any man in the valley. He can ride, rope, and shoot with the best of them. Don't let those clothes and that dandy look fool you. He wanted part of the Lazy W because he wants to own property in this valley. Maybe he figured he'd eventually get all of the Lazy W." He looked at Cade. "Maybe you didn't know it, but Dude was mighty soft on Lucy Arnold before your brother married her. They say Lucy would have married Dude if it hadn't been for his profession."

"Curiouser and curiouser," said Cade.

Chilton rode on, leaving a trail of powerful pipe smoke behind him. He did not speak again until Cade found himself coming out of a thick tangle of timber to see the Lazy W spread out before him, with the Bravo looping across the meadows like a silver cord on green velvet.

Chilton turned in his saddle. "I'd give you some advice if I knew you'd take it, Cade, but you won't. I'd say stay away from the Dark Mountain country and watch yourself on the Lazy W range, but you won't do it. I hope to God you win out. You'll keep on going. It's your type of breed. Good luck."

Cade took Chilton's proffered hand. "Tell Alma I thank her again," he said.

A fleeting change came over Chilton's bronzed face. "A fine girl," he said. "God help her." He spurred his horse and rode to the east, followed by Cade's curious eyes.

The hunter reined in within earshot. He turned in his saddle. "The secret is on Dark Mountain," he said cryptically, then he was gone in the thick timber.

Cade rode down the steep slope until he reached the timber, then passed through it until he could see the Bravo sparkling in the sun. There wasn't a sign of life anywhere on the Lazy W range. It was a damned shame cattle couldn't be run on that fine range. A cold, hard feeling came over Cade. He raised his hand and touched the bandage on his head, then traced the fresh scar on his cheek where the wood splinter had hit him the night he had been dry-gulched on his return from Pine Tree. His innate stubbornness welled up within him. He looked at Dark Mountain. He must have been too close to the secret when he had been creased. Ed Chilton had said the secret was on Dark Mountain. Likely he knew more than he'd ever admit. He evidently minded his own business and expected others to mind theirs. It was a good policy for a man who had been a squawman and who acknowledged Apache as friends and relatives.

He splashed across the ford and rode toward the ranch buildings, glancing sideways to see the sun reflecting from the white headboards in the little cemetery. Two good men lay there, killed by rustlers, and there might have been another one there if the rifleman who had fired at Cade had fired a mite more to the left or had allowed for windage. This time the unseen marksman had not been playing with Cade, warning him, but had meant to kill. The chips were down in this dark and deadly game.

The wind shifted as he passed through the timber, and he caught the odor of wood ashes. He narrowed his eyes. Helluva big fire in the house for that time of day. He cleared the timber and looked toward the ranch house. The ranch house and the big barn were gone, leaving nothing but huge rectangular patches of ashes on the ground. The wind stirred them fitfully, spiraling up thin, ghostlike streamers of ashes. There wasn't a sign of life about the place.

Cade slid from the saddle, swiftly withdrawing his Winchester, levering a round into the chamber. He slapped the sorrel on the rump and stepped behind a tree, scanning the terrain with narrowed eyes. The place was deserted, indescribably lonely, and a feeling of foreboding hung in the air along with the acrid smell of wood ashes.

Cade padded softly across the ground. The bunkhouse was empty. The shed doors gaped open. The windmill was turning slowly in the wind, pumping water into the overflowing tank. Cade shut it off. He walked to the corral. Another smell greeted him there. The stench of burned horseflesh. A mare lay there, seriously burned, stiffened legs outthrust, and a neat bullet hole in her head. Beyond her lay a dead mule, also with a bullet hole in the head. It, too, had been burned beyond hope.

Cade wet his dry lips. They had struck while he had been gone, whoever they were. Maybe it had been Harry Nadeau and Joe Mahan. Maybe not.

There was no use in staying around the Lazy W. Not a head of cattle was in view. They had either drifted off or had been runoff.

Cade walked back to the sorrel and mounted, keeping his rifle ready in his right hand as he rode toward the road. Lucy and Grant had likely gone to Dick Thornhill's place. There wasn't a thing for Cade to do on the Lazy W. No stock, no house, no barn. There was nothing left but the land itself. That and the graves in the little motte.

CHAPTER TEN

The Circle Dot was situated on a broad sloping area west of the broken country at the foot of Dark Mountain. Through the many mottes of trees on the open land, Cade could see grazing cattle. Smoke wreathed up from the many ranch buildings. Several riders were moving away from the ranch toward the broken country beyond the creek. The sun shone on the big frame house, white painted with dark green shutters. To one side of it was an aging log house, smaller than the one that had been burned on the Lazy W. There was a neat, well kept up look about the place. Dick Thornhill was evidently prosperous and lucky.

Cade tethered his sorrel to the fence and opened the gate. There was no one in sight, although he could hear metal ringing against metal from one of the many outbuildings. The big Eclipse windmill whirled steadily in the fresh breeze sweeping down from Dark Mountain.

Cade slapped the dust from his clothing with his battered hat. He was a sorry looking sight to go calling, and from the looks of the place, Mrs. Thornhill was a smart housekeeper. Cade rapped on the front door. He heard a feminine voice call out for him to come in. He opened the door. The living room was huge and well furnished. Near the wide window on the south side of the room, looking out across the rangeland to the purple-hued mountains in the distance, was a wide bed, and in it, a frail-looking woman was propped up with huge pillows, while her thin, transparent looking hands rested on the thick quilt.

"I'm looking for Mr. Thornhill, ma'am," said Cade.

She smiled wanly. "I'm Mrs. Thornhill. Abigail Thornhill. My friends call me Abby. You must be Cade Willcox. I think I'd know you anywhere. You look a great deal like Dan." She eyed the bandage on his head. "Have you been hurt?"

"A little," admitted Cade.

"Dick is around the place somewhere. Your sister-in-law and nephew have moved temporarily into the old place. It was a terrible thing, Mr. Willcox."

"The burning?"

She nodded. "Everything is gone, the boy said, the stock, the horses, the house, and the barn. He'll be all right, though."

"What happened to him?"

"He tried to get the horses out of the bam and was burned. Dr. Walsh, who is my doctor, too, said it would be quite some time before Grant can get about. His hands were badly burned, Mr. Willcox."

"And Lucy?"

She nodded her head. "She's fine. She didn't want to stay here, but Dick insisted on it. What will you do now, Mr. Willcox?" She tilted her head to one side. "You may smoke if you like."

"Thanks, ma'am." Cade rolled a cigarette. "We can stay in the bunkhouse until we get a house built. The barn will take time."

"You mean to stay there?"

He nodded as he lighted the cigarette.

She shook her head. "You're much like your brother," she said.

"Where can I find Lucy and Grant?"

"The boy is in our old house. Dick took Lucy to look over the stock. He said you had wanted the stock back Lucy had sold to him. Lucy said last night she couldn't see how you could take care of it, now that you have no hands, Grant is burned, and the house and barn are gone."

Cade picked up his hat. "I hope you're feeling better, Mrs. Thornhill," he said.

She waved a hand. She had once been a rather pretty woman, although now her face was thin and drawn, and her dull hair was shot with gray. "I'm of little use to anyone," she said.

"You shouldn't say that."

She looked out the window. "Dick is so full of life, so virile. I have been this way for over a year now. Dick needs a woman. More than most men. He works so hard and lives every minute of his life. I am of little use to him now."

"You shouldn't say that," said Cade.

"You must see your nephew. You will have dinner with us tonight, Mr. Willcox?"

"I'm not sure. I'd best be getting back to the Lazy W."

He closed the door behind him and walked over to the older house. He entered and found Grant sitting in a chair by the window, his hands and forearms heavily bandaged and a bandage about his face.

"What happened, kid?" asked Cade.

Grant shrugged. "We were asleep. Must have been about two o'clock in the morning when the barn started a fire. I was too late to stop the fire, and while I was trying to get the horses and the mule out, the house started up. There wasn't any wind, but maybe the updraft of the fire whirled embers over there. All I know is when I went to the house to get a gun to kill the two animals that were too badly burned to live, the fire was roaring all through the living room. Lucy got out all right. I sent her to the Circle Dot for help. I tried to put out the fire in the living room, but it wasn't any use. I got pretty badly burned. Lucy was a long time in coming back with Dick, and by the time they got here, there was nothing that could be done."

"What about the rest of the stock?"

The kid looked up at him. "Is that gone, too?"

Cade nodded. "We're cleaned out, kid, except for the stock Dick owes us."

"What happened to your head?"

Cade sat down and rolled a cigarette. "After I left you, I worked back into the edge of the Dark Mountain country. Someone 'creased' me. I'm lucky I'm here, kid." He looked at the boy. "It was Alma Chilton who came to help me."

"She's all right," said the boy.

Cade nodded. "I don't think our rustling problem is there, kid."

"I never believed Ed Chilton had anything to do with it."

"How does Lucy feel?"

The kid shook his head. "She says we've had our lesson. She insists we sell out."

"How do you feel?"

"I want to stick, Uncle Cade. I won't be of much help to you now, though."

Cade lighted his cigarette and looked through the smoke at the kid. "They can't hurt the Lazy W anymore," he said quietly. "No stock to run off. No buildings to burn. No hands to scare off. This leaves me free to find out where the stock vanished to."

"You were lucky up there, Uncle Cade. Maybe this time, they'll make sure of you."

"I won't go in there like a damned fool this time."

"Dick Thornhill will loan you some help."

Cade shook his head. "I'll go alone," he said.

Cade left the boy and went to his horse. He mounted it and rode out toward the open range. As he did so, he saw the sunlight glint from metal in a motte close to the edge of the stream. A cold feeling came over him. He remembered all too well the rifle shot that had almost killed him. He kneed the sorrel into the cover of some trees and looked toward the stream. The place looked deserted, but as he watched, he saw a movement. A few minutes later, two horsemen appeared on the far side of the timber, splashed across the stream, and rode up the broken slope beyond. One of them was tall in the saddle, and the other was a short man who held his reins in his right hand. Cade turned to get his field glasses from a saddlebag, but by the time he freed them, the two horsemen had vanished into the broken country.

The afternoon sun was slanting its rays down on the far range of the Circle Dot when Cade saw two riders approaching him. He had seen enough of the Circle Dot to know that Dick Thornhill had a gold mine in the place. Well-timbered and watered, good range, and fine stock. He had seen some of the Lazy W stock amidst the Circle Dot cattle. They'd have to make some arrangement with Dick for their care after the Lazy W stock was moved to their home range. It would be a good enough start, and with the money Cade had gotten from Troy Burkitt, they could get more stock. It would all take time.

He heard a woman laughing as he sat his sorrel in the thick timber. He looked more closely at the two riders and saw that one of them was Lucy Willcox, her hat hanging at the middle of her shapely shoulders and the sun glinting on the highlights of her golden hair.

Cade rode from the timber. Dick Thornhill drew rein and stared at him for a moment and then yelled in greeting. Cade spurred toward them. Lucy's face was sober when she saw him. Dick stared again at Cade. "By God," he said quickly, "you must have had a close one up there!"

Cade nodded. "Closer than I like to admit."

"Did you see who fired the rifle?"

"No. It happened so quickly I was hit about the time I heard the report of the rifle."

"How the devil did you get out of there?"

"Some of the Apache found me, but they wouldn't come down into the canyon of the Bravo. They went and got Alma Chilton, and she came for me."

"I'm surprised she went down into that canyon," said Lucy. "She's half Apache herself."

"She forgot about that in order to help me," said Cade.

Dick hooked a leg about his pommel and felt for the makings. "What do you aim to do, Cade?"

Cade grinned wryly. "There's nothing else to fight for on the Lazy W. They can't run off, shoot, or burn the land. That will always be there."

"You plan to stick then?"

Cade nodded.

Lucy shook her head. "It's no use, Cade. You saw Grant?"

"Yes."

"Only by the grace of God did he get out of that barn. Dr. Walsh said he might be disfigured for life."

"He'll live. You can't hurt a Willcox."

She flushed. "Don't say that! I've heard Dan say that too many times! Grant has been saying that as well! Look what happened to Dan! Look at you! Almost shot to death in that canyon! Look at Grant! Almost burned to death!"

Cade slowly rolled a cigarette. He lighted the quirley and looked at her through the wreathing smoke. "Neither of you have to go back to the Lazy W," he said.

"And you?" said Dick.

Cade nodded. "I'm sticking with this thing. Those cattle are somewhere on the Dark Mountain. I aim to find them."

"I'll get some of the boys to help you," said Dick.

Cade shook his head. "No need for them to risk their lives for Lazy W cattle."

"What about you?" demanded Lucy. "I won't let you go, Cade!"

"You've no hold on me," he said slowly. "I make it my choice to go."

Dick looked at her. "He's right," he said. "I'd do the same thing, Lucy."

They rode together toward the distant ranch, marked by a streamer of smoke spiraling toward the sky.

Cade glanced at Lucy. She wasn't smiling or laughing now, and there was almost a tense look on her lovely face. Did he affect her that much? Maybe he was a damned fool for going back into that hostile country by himself, and yet he could not expect anyone else to risk their lives along with him. Further, he liked to work alone. This wouldn't be much different than his Ranger work along the Border. He knew now why Burt Mossman had been so eager for him to take a leave of absence. The old coyote had figured Cade would get his long nose into this sticky looping business in the Bravo Valley country.

"You'll stay for dinner?" asked Dick.

Cade shook his head. "I already told your wife I didn't think I could stay."

"Abby? You were at the house then?"

Cade nodded. "You keep a nice place, Dick."

"It was Abby who did the house," said Lucy. "You can see her touch all over the place. That was before she became ill, of course."

"How long has she been ill?" asked Cade.

"Over six months," said Dick quietly. "It came on her slowly. Doc Walsh doesn't seem to know what it is. Frankly, Cade, we have little hope for Abby."

"She was such a pretty woman," said Lucy. "The change has come so quickly. She doesn't seem to care about life anymore."

Cade glanced at Dick. His face was tense. "You'll keep the Lazy W stock here until we can get it?" said Cade.

"Certainly, Cade. We're quite busy now, but when you're ready, I'll have some of the boys come over to help you." He began to roll a cigarette. "By the way, Cade. Harry Nadeau and Joe Mahan have been making threats against you. Some of my boys saw them in town. You've made a few enemies around here. Are you absolutely sure you want to go ahead on tracking down these rustlers?"

"Positive."

"You won't change his mind," said Lucy bitterly.

There was nothing for Cade to say to her. He looked at Dick. "Where are Nadeau and Mahan now?"

"My boys told me they had left for the Little Colorado country. By God! They had better not come around here!"

It was dusk when they reached the Circle Dot buildings, and once again, Cade refused dinner, although he did replenish his supplies from Dick's well-filled storehouse. He almost changed his mind when he smelled' the cooking. He looked in the kitchen of the big house. Lucy, pretty as a picture in gingham and a crisp apron, was officiating at the stove while Dick helped her, peeling potatoes at the table. Cade said his goodbyes and rode past the house. He looked in from the darkness, seeing Abby Thornhill in her great bed, like a frail doll, her thin hands on the covers and her large eyes looking out into the darkness beyond the window. She did not see the thoughtful look on the scarred face of the tall, lean man who rode past on his way to the deserted Lazy W.

The wind shifted as he rode down the valley. He carried his Winchester across his thighs, and his head never stopped turning as he rode. This time he hoped to get in the first shot. The time for avoiding trouble was past. It was getting to be the time for killing.

The moon was rising when he reached the Lazy W. It was deserted, or seemingly so. He rode toward the remaining buildings. He'd bunk that night in the bunkhouse or one of the sheds. The moon lighted the foothills to the east as he dismounted and looked about. Hardtack whinnied sharply. Cade peered into the shadows. The sorrel was smelling the dead animals.

He made his simple accommodations in the bunkhouse, cooking his beans and bacon atop the stove, boiling his coffee while he ate. He finished his meal and made up his bunk. He set his battered alarm clock for four a.m., Cade pulled off his boots and lighted a cigar he had cadged from Dick. He dropped on the bunk and looked up at the fly-specked ceiling, trying to organize his thoughts. He was tired, and the blow on his head hadn't helped him any. It would be a few days before he was up to par. He half-closed his eyes.

Hardtack whinnied sharply outside. Cade meant to get up and see what was bothering him, but he just couldn't quite make it.

"Very cozy," the dry voice said from the door.

Cade thrust himself upward and swung his legs toward the edge of the bunk, glancing at his gun belt hanging from a nail. He looked toward the door. Dude Carter stood there, immaculate in gray.

"I'm not quite ready to receive visitors," said Cade dryly. There wasn't a chance he could reach his Colt before Carter could draw and shoot if that was what he had come to do.

Carter looked back over his shoulder. "What happened here?" he asked.

"Burned out," said Cade. "I wasn't here."

Carter eyed the bandage on Cade's head. "You look like you had been. Where are Lucy and the boy?"

"At Dick Thornhill's place."

Carter nodded. "I thought they would be. Lucy anyway."

"What can I do for you?" asked Cade.

"I came for a settlement. I didn't know this had happened."

Cade picked up the makings from the table. "Smoke?" he said.

"Have a cigar," said the gambler. He tossed his cigar case to Cade. Cade selected a short six and lighted up. "Prime," he said. Carter had him puzzled. The first and last time he had seen the man, he had been quite sure Dude Carter would kill him if he had the chance, with provocation, of course. His type did not kill unless it was in "self-defense."

Carter lighted a cigar and looked at Cade through the smoke. "You've had a pretty thin time," he said.

"Don't make it any worse, Carter."

Carter waved out his match. "I don't intend to. After all, you didn't make the deal with me. It was your brother."

Cade blew a smoke ring. "You said you'd settle it by legal means. Go ahead and do so. I'm sure Lucy will settle with you if the court orders her to."

"I do not like to force a woman, a widow, into such a thing."

"It's the only way you'll get it, Carter."

"You won't take my word that Dan actually signed a note indebting himself to me before he died?"

Cade smiled thinly. "The word of a gambler?"

Carter's face tightened. "I'm a man of honor!"

Cade shrugged. "Take it to court. That's all I can say. Legally I can do nothing about that debt. I don't own this place."

"They say you're standing in the way of Lucy, who wants to sell it. If you were to stand out of her way, she'd sell. I could get my share of the ranch then."

Cade looked at the glowing tip of his cigar. "I was thinking more of the kid," he said. "It was his father's ranch. My brother and Grant's mother worked like Trojans to build up this place. It has a future, Carter, and you know it well; otherwise, you'd not be so damned anxious to get your hands on a piece of it."

Carter smiled coldly. "If I can convince you to sell, you could convince Lucy. Of that, I am sure. Besides, this is not a good place for the boy under the present circumstances."

Cade looked steadily at the gambler. "I don't know about Lucy," he said, "but the boy wants to stay, and I aim to stay with him."

"You'll die here then," said Carter.

Cade slowly took the cigar from his mouth, and as he did, so the sorrel whinnied sharply. Just beyond Dude Carter, who was squarely silhouetted in the lighted doorway, Cade had almost felt rather than saw a furtive movement. "Get out of the doorway, Carter!" he snapped.

Carter hesitated. Cade drove from the bunk hit Carter low as the startled gambler fumbled for his hideout gun. A gun cracked flatly in the darkness beyond the door, and a slug whipped through the air where Carter had been standing, shattering a mirror on the opposite wall. Cade doused the lamp as he heard booted feet thudding on the ground. Guns cracked outside.

"That wasn't Willcox!" someone yelled.

The glass shattered at a side window, just behind Cade. A rifle barrel poked through the window. Dude Carter fired from the floor an instant before the rifleman's finger tightened on the trigger. The rifle exploded, the bullet thudding into the ceiling. Smoke filled the bunkhouse. Cade ripped his Colt from its sheath. A bullet eerily sang as it hit the stove and ricocheted.

Another window shattered, and again Dude Carter fired. A man grunted in pain. Boots thudded on the ground. "Clear out!" yelled a man. "There are two of them in there!"

A moment or two later, hoofs sounded on the road and then faded away.

Dude moved slowly. "You see what I mean?" he said dryly.

"You saved my life," said Cade.

"I can say the same for you. Put on the lamp. I've been hit."

Cade lighted the lamp and then knelt beside Carter. His right upper arm was already soaked in blood. Carter dropped the short-barreled Colt from his left hand. "Good thing I learned how to use the Border Shift," he said quietly, "or he'd have got you in the back, Willcox."

Cade worked quickly, stripping off the gambler's coat, vest, and shirt. He examined the wound. "Clean through the meat," he said with satisfaction. He cleansed and swabbed the wound and then bandaged it, forming a sling from Carter's scarf. "That'll do until you get to a doctor," he said.

Carter jerked his head. "Take a look outside," he said. "You'll likely find a dead one out there."

"How do you know?"

The cold gray eyes had the ghost of a smile in them. "I rarely miss," he said with quiet pride.

Carter was right. A man lay on his belly outside the window through which Carter had fired. Cade rolled him over and looked into the set face of Joe Mahan. The man's bad left hand was curled like a claw about the forestock of his Winchester. Cade knew then whose voice it was that had called out of the night. "Harry Nadeau," he said.

"Harry and Joe were supposed to have gone to the Little Colorado country," said Carter from the window.

"They certainly hold a grudge," said Cade.

"It was likely more than that," said Carter. "There was someone else with them."

Cade nodded. Two men set to make a grudge killing likely wouldn't have taken others with them. Such things were private matters. An eye for an eye...

Carter coolly relighted his cigar with his one useful

hand. "Load that murderous bastard on my horse," he said.

"Why?"

Carter smiled evilly through the wreathing smoke. "I'll dump him in the Bravo," he said. "I fancy you don't want his corpse lying around here. I doubt if his friends will turn us over to the law."

Cade loaded the dead man across the pommel of Carter's saddle and then gave the gambler a hand in mounting. "Thanks," he said. "Once the smoke clears around here, Carter, I'll see that you get what is coming to you if the court says so."

"They will." Carter looked down at Cade. "You plan to keep on then?"

"Yes."

"Good luck. I wish I could ride with you, but it's out of the question now. Adios, Cade."

"So long, Dude."

He watched the gambler ride off into the darkness. That eliminated Carter. He turned and looked up at Dark Mountain. The secret *and* its answer was up there...

CHAPTER ELEVEN

He had left the bunkhouse several hours before dawn, leading the sorrel through the timber, waiting now and then to see if he was being followed, before he worked his way into the broken hills to the east of the Lazy W. It was dawn when he stopped to make a smokeless fire and brew his coffee. The sun was striking the western face of Dark Mountain when he finished his coffee and eliminated traces of his fire. He believed someone had been watching him or had information about his movements. The several ambushes he had been through testified to that. He'd have to act as though he was always being watched. Memories of his work with the Apache Scouts came back to him. No white man could move as silently and unseen as they could. Hardly any white men, that is, for when a white man was *really* good at the game, he could out-Indian most Indians.

While the sun rose and warmed his back, he lay belly flat in low brush, studying the mountain through his field glasses. The part that particularly interested him was that great depression, like a huge saucer, where the eastern flank of the mountain had subsided in ages past. What secret did that gigantic hollow hold? If there were cattle hidden in or about Dark Mountain, that would be the logical place to hide them, but how in blazes were they driven there? Even Ed Chilton didn't know, and no man knew the country better than he did, with the exception of the Apache, and they knew absolutely nothing about Dark Mountain because they would not cross the invisible boundary line drawn by their ancient taboo.

There was only one answer for Cade. He could not ride into that huge hollow, and the only way to get near it was to scale the crumbling southern canyon wall of the Bravo. He had prepared for that. He had taken long spikes from the shed at the Lazy W to use as *pitons,* and he had brought as much good rope as he could find about the place. But he knew those cattle had never scaled that canyon wall. There was no indication of an entrance into it from the outside, but a man might be able to find it from the inside.

Now and then, he scanned the surrounding country, making sure he shaded the lens of his glasses to keep them from reflecting. He sighted no one. A wraith of smoke arose from Ed Chilton's place in Lost Canyon. A thread of dust hung over the far distant Valley Road. A hawk hung against the clear sky, seemingly motionless. He saw no one, and yet he had not seen anyone until the ringing of a rifle shot had warned him, once too late, that he was being fired upon.

He moved several times, keeping to the lower ground, picketing the sorrel in a hidden place, while he wormed his way through the clinging brush and scrub trees to scan a different angle of the approaches to Dark Mountain. The results were always the same. Visually, there was no way to get into that gigantic hollow.

He cooked his noon meal and slept until the late afternoon shadows crept down the rugged flanks of Dark Mountain, and the wind began to shift. By the time it was dark, he had worked his way on foot to the very canyon where he had been creased, listening to the rushing of the stream and the murmuring of the evening wind as it flowed down the canyon toward the lower country to the northwest.

He pulled off his boots and replaced them with a pair of thigh-length, thick-soled, button-toed moccasins given to him by old "The Coyote Saw Him," in the days when Cade had ridden with the Scouts. The footgear had no peer in this kind of country. As he pulled them on, he thought of Pretty Hands, the old man's granddaughter, who had made them for Cade. He remembered her well, but there had been nothing between them, for Apache women are chaste, and adultery was punished horribly. An adulterous married woman would lose her nose along with her chastity.

He fashioned a sling for his rifle, thinking about Alma Chilton as he did so. He had first thought a great deal about Lucy Willcox, but gradually, as time passed on, he found himself thinking more and more of Alma.

In the thick darkness, laden with his ropes and *pitons,* he crept along the floor of the canyon beside the rushing stream, scanning the dim southern rim of the canyon until he could find a likely place to climb if there was such a place. The whole rim looked as though a mouse could crumble the edge if he scampered along it.

He had to start somewhere, so he found the place where he had been creased. Mack Rose had been murdered somewhere in that area, and Alma had told him Dan's body had been found there, right about where Cade had been wounded. The dark stream did not look too inviting. He cut a pole and probed about until he found a place where he could ford the stream. He was puzzled until he saw where a great slide had scaled tons of rock from the canyon wall to roar down into the stream. In time the stream had cut its way through and had washed away the lighter rocks, leaving a fine fording place beneath the dark waters. He was wet only to the waist when he reached the south side of the canyon to stand on a narrow, partially submerged ledge, looking up at that uninviting wall.

There was no choice. He had to be up on top of that rim before the full moon arose. Cade set about it carefully, wedging in his improvised *pitons* where he could not find foot or handholds. Several times he gained by casting a *reata* up to a projecting rock, then trusting his weight to the *reata* as he pulled himself upward, the cold sweat breaking from his body. Again and again, he had to rest, his fingers raw and bleeding, clinging to that naked rock face, listening to bits of the decomposing stone break loose beneath his weight to plummet down into the rushing Bravo. By God, he wanted a drink and smoke, but tobacco was in his shirt pocket, and the flask was in the light pack on his back, and a man needed both hands and feet to hang on, as well as thick-headed stubbornness and sheer faith in his Maker.

Another frightening thought crept into his brain. He was not progressing swiftly enough. Already the eastern sky showed the first faint suggestions of moonrise. If he was caught on that cliff face, he'd be like a fly in amber.

He forced himself upward and then reached a narrow ledge where he clung with aching muscles, not daring to look down because of the fear of falling and not daring to look up for fear that there would be no way to ascend. He could feel the cold sweat working down his body, setting up an intolerable itchiness and no way to scratch. He pressed his face against the rock and tried to think. He looked up and saw no way to gain footage. A piece of the ledge cracked off and fell to the stream. He could have sworn the whole ledge had moved as though getting ready to crack away from the cliff face. He drew in a sharp breath, and then he felt the ledge sink a little. If it fell, he'd be dangling there, hanging onto the *reata* and one lone *piton,* insecurely wedged in the rotting rock.

Minutes ticked past. The ledge sagged a little. Cade looked up desperately. He *had* to get off that ledge!

Already the moon was lighting the tips of the eastern mountains. A rifleman could hardly miss him this time. Slowly he eased a hand down to his belt and pulled loose a rope coil. He had already fashioned a running noose in it. He extended it by holding it in his teeth and working the loop wider with his free hand. He lowered the coil and cast it upward. It struck the cliff face and fell, catching Cade squarely across the face, half blinding him. He moved too quickly in his reaction and felt the ledge drop from beneath his feet. He clawed for the other rope and missed it. He scrabbled at the unyielding cliff face with bleeding fingers. For a moment, he clung there, and then he, too, fell, turning end over end to land with a splash in the cold waters of the Bravo, going under, feeling his rump strike the harsh bed of the stream, and the breath was driven out of his gaping mouth in a mass of bubbles. He felt the rifle sling break, and the weight of the rifle was gone. His feet tangled in a rope coil, and he struggled desperately with it to free himself while the powerful current rolled him over and over, grinding at him with sharp-edged stones.

He tried to get to the surface, and his head struck rock. He clawed at a mass of brush and driftwood. His head struck rock again, and he knew he was going to drown.

He opened his mouth to yell, and it filled with fresh air. He stared about him, but it was pitch dark, and yet he had surfaced. He should be able to see the sky, the dim canyon walls, and the faint luminescence of the rising moon. But it was pitch dark! He felt his way with his bleeding hands. His feet were on rock but beneath water. The water was up almost to his waist.

Cade looked behind himself and thought he saw a faint line of light against the dark waters. He carefully waded back, and his extended hands struck damp rock, but it ended a good two feet from the water level. He carefully worked his way under the rock facing and ran into a thick barrier of brush and driftwood, held against the side of the rock by the water pressure of the current, but he could see the sky and the far side of the canyon, now faintly bathed in moonlight.

He pushed at the brush. "Sonofabitch!" he barked. He had rammed his hand into a thorn caught in the brush. He sucked at the wound and felt his shirt caught against the thorn. As he worked it free, he thought it was the stiffest, sharpest thorn he had ever made unwilling acquaintance with. Then he felt it more carefully, then peered at it. "Barbed wire," he said. He felt his way upstream along the driftwood and brush until he reached a narrow ledge running along the creek edge. The floating mass was firmly bound with the barbed wire. The upstream end was anchored by thick strands of the wire fastened to heavy iron stakes driven into the rock.

Cade squatted on the ledge, trying to reason. Why had such a contrivance been fashioned in this out-of-the-way place? He looked back and saw where he had emerged from the darkness. It was a low, semicircular opening in the cliff face right at the water's edge, and yet it could not be seen from the far side of the canyon unless someone towed the free end of the wire-bound brush and driftwood against the current like opening a gate.

He looked across the canyon and figured out he had been standing over there the time he had been creased. He remembered something else as well. He had seen driftwood swirling down the Bravo, leaping, and plunging in the grip of the current, sometimes disappearing, but always bobbing up again, and yet had seen other pieces of driftwood plunge out of sight and not return to the surface. He remembered, too, that there was a wide and shallow curve in the canyon wall right about where he was squatting and that he had noted the mass of driftwood pinned against this wall the last time he had been in the canyon.

Cade worked his way back to the opening beneath the sheer face of the cliff. He was about to let himself down into the cold water again when some instinct made him look back over his shoulder. A horseman was riding slowly along the far side of the canyon. Cade slipped into the water, with only his upper body protruding but well hidden by the screen of brush and driftwood. The moonlight had not yet touched the north side of the canyon; although it gave light to most of the bottom of it, the south wall was still dark.

The horseman stopped and looked toward the south wall. His face was well shielded by his hat brim. His rifle was across his thighs, the metal shining dully in the moonlight. He sat there for some minutes, looking almost directly at Cade, giving Cade the uncanny feeling that he could be seen. He knew if he moved, a rifle bullet would come his way. The water was cold, and he felt his legs stiffen. He couldn't stand there much longer.

The horseman moved. He felt in his shirt pocket, drawing out the makings. He deftly rolled a quirley and then lighted it, illuminating his lean, bronzed face. It was Farley Mosston, the skilled rifleman, the line rider for the Box C. He sat his horse, still scanning the south wall, the glow of the cigarette tip coming and going, alternately lighting and darkening his expressionless face. Just as Cade was about to creep back under the opening, Mosston touched his horse with his spurs and rode slowly to the west, looking back over his shoulder now and then.

Cade cursed as he stiffly made his way under the overhanging lip of rock into the unknown darkness beneath the cliff. He kept his matches in a waterproof case made out of a big Sharps Big Fifty cartridge case. He stood in water just below his waistline and lighted a match with shaking hands. He was in a wide, low-roofed cave. Water lapped the right side of the cave; on the left, there was a rocky shoreline a few feet wide, littered with dry driftwood and brush. He waded out and squatted, teeth chattering, as he felt for his whiskey flask and took a stiff shot. He rolled and lighted a cigarette, looking about as he did so. The cave disappeared into darkness, floored with smooth dark water, ledged at the left. He tossed a bit of driftwood into the water. It drifted to his left, into the cave.

Cade patiently formed an improvised torch from driftwood. He took stock of what he had left with him after his dangerous fall. He still had his six-shooter and cartridges, field glasses, whiskey, tobacco, some food, matches, a coil of line, and his sheath knife. He carefully wiped the six-gun. The cartridges likely had not been immersed long enough to have spoiled. At least he hoped they hadn't.

He tossed in more driftwood. All of it drifted to the left. Even as he watched, a big piece of driftwood bobbed up out of the water as though it had come from the Bravo and drifted into the cave. Cade formed half a dozen torches. The sorrel would be all right for a few days. There was a little grazing where he had been hidden, as well as a shallow *tinaja* full of rainwater. When the water ran out, he'd pull his picket line loose and make his way to the Bravo and then to the lower country.

He lighted a second torch from the dying first torch, casting the burned-out torch into the water. It, too, drifted into the cave.

There was no choice. Cade Willcox was committed to the unknown darkness beyond the flickering pool of uncertain light cast by his torch.

He walked slowly along the narrow ledge. The cave roof got lower, leaving just about enough room for him to stoop and walk under, and then he found himself in a much larger, higher domed area of the cave. His feet grated on something, and he looked down at a burned-out torch, similar to those he had made. Here and there, on the walls of the cave, he saw sooty patches as though torches had been too close to the rock. Others had been in there before him, but how long ago had that been, and who had they been?

The roof got lower again, and he crept through on hands and knees to find himself on the edge of the ledge. Close to his hand was a rusted, shattered oil lantern. He eyed the dark flowing water with distaste. Slowly he pulled off his wet moccasins. He unbuckled his gun belt and placed it in the pack, hoisting the pack high on his shoulders. He felt his way into the cold water and was delighted to find that it was only waist deep. He waded on, holding his extra torches in his left hand and the flaming torch in the other, peering ahead into the darkness. The roof would get lower and then rise, but there was no ledge on either side of the underground channel. He knew now that it was not a cave or a manmade tunnel but a subterranean fork of the Bravo.

The water deepened and then shallowed so that he was knee-deep in it. Now and then, he looked behind him. If the light went out, it would be black as the inside of an inkwell, with not a ray of light, and little enough of hope, for him to find his way. He looked back again, and as he did so, he stepped off into deep water. Before he could recover, the torch hissed out. He splashed out, striking on, feeling the grip of the strong, cold current. His head struck the side of the cave. He swam just enough to keep himself afloat, feeling no bottom beneath his dangling feet, unable to see the cruel rock that now and then he struck head or hands against. A greater coldness crept through him, more than that of the water; it was the chilling grip of fear. Fear at being borne deeper and deeper into the guts of Dark Mountain. There was no way back now. He was committed to going on.

His head bumped the side of the channel, and he went under, rolling over and over in the current, and another fear came over him, a mad sort of fear; *he did not know which way was up.* All he knew was that the current was carrying him where it would, and there wasn't a damned thing he could do about it this side of hell.

His head broke water. He drew in a deep breath or two and then went under again. He began to fight the water in panic, striking his hands against the rock. His knees were gouged by the bottom of the stream, and he experienced a blackness, coldness, and despair he had never known in all his life.

It was the end. There was no question about it. His lungs seemed about to burst. The best thing to do was to draw in as much water as possible and drown quickly. The biggest game of all was over. Death was waiting for his chips.

The fighting spirit came back to him. He fought savagely. He went down deep and then braced his feet against the bottom, pushing hard. His head broke water, and he saw a moonlit sky, high above him through the lacy branches of trees bordering the stream. On each side of him was a wide shoreline of rocks and pebbles, washed by the now silvery-looking waters of the stream, reflecting the full moon.

Cade stood up, knee-deep in water, and waded stiffly ashore. His body ached as though he had been put through a stamping mill. He dropped on the dry stones of the shore and lay still, drawing in painful gulps of the cool night air. He closed his eyes and felt life slowly come back to him. A great lassitude swept over him, and he thought he was going to pass out. His senses wavered, then slipped toward the abyss of nothingness.

Cade's head jerked up, and his eyes opened. He turned his battered head.

Somewhere beyond the stream, cattle had bawled.

CHAPTER TWELVE

Cade sat in the shadows of the swaying trees. He had cleaned his six-gun for the second time. He desperately wanted to smoke but did not dare light up. He satisfied himself with a stiff jolt from the whiskey flask. His body still ached dully from the battering he had taken. He pulled on the moccasins and got to his feet, working his way through the trees that bordered the stream. It now rippled over the clean stones of its bed, hardly more than a foot deep.

He reached the edge of the woods and lay down flat behind a tip-tilted slab of rock to look into a huge bowl, stippled with mottes, with the stream looping itself across the ground like a huge snake. All about Cade were the towering walls of rock except to the west, where a huge, familiar bulk arose, dark despite the clear moonlight. Dark Mountain...

He was quite sure where he was. He had penetrated beneath the northern wall of this huge natural bowl. It must be the great subsidence he had noticed from the outside. As yet, he had seen no cattle. He took out his field glasses and wiped the lenses, focusing them on the far side of the bowl. The floor of the great bowl was littered with great slabs of rock, half-buried in the earth.

Slowly he began to pick out the dun shapes of cattle here and there throughout the bowl. He whistled softly between his teeth. He took a spot check, getting a count of the number of cattle in a given area, then multiplying that by the size of the bowl. He shook his head in disbelief. If his estimate was anywhere near right, there would be somewhere between five and seven hundred head in the bowl. It didn't seem possible there was enough grazing to keep them fed, and yet the bowl was good rangeland. Still, it didn't seem possible that many cattle could exist in there.

Cade cased his glasses and faded back into the timber. The moon was full, shedding clear light into the bowl so that one could read by it. Shadows of rocks and trees were sharply etched on the ground. Cade worked his way through the scattered timber, taking to his belly when he reached open areas, crawling behind rock slabs. In an hour's scouting, he had seen cattle aplenty, but not one sight of a human.

He knew now the cattle were driven up the canyon of the Bravo, ten to perhaps fifty head at a time, then driven into the stream. The brushwood and driftwood that cloaked the entrance to the underground channel would be pulled aside by a *reata* cinched to a saddle horn, and the cattle would be driven into the underground channel. They could not fight the current in the deeper places, and they would be driven, bellowing, through the torch and lantern-lit tunnel to the fair range deep-set into the looming flank of Dark Mountain, as safe as if they were in a peeled-pole corral. By Godfrey, maybe they didn't even need herders in the place. The cattle certainly wouldn't attempt to get back through the underground channel, and even if they tried, the current would likely force them back. It was a perfect setup. The cattle could be kept there indefinitely, hidden from prying eyes, with a perpetual water supply and good grazing.

Cade risked rolling a cigarette and lighting it as he

crouched in a hollow on the side of a huge monolith half-buried in the soft ground. He knew now how the cattle were brought into the hollow, but who had brought them there? Those cattle he had seen in his scout had mixed brands. There were a number of Box C cattle in there, as well as Lazy W and Circle Dot, and several brands with which he was not familiar.

He studied the towering walls of the great natural cup within which the cattle were penned. It was impossible to drive those cattle back through the channel or over the northern or eastern rims of the bowl, and they certainly couldn't be driven over Dark Mountain, which formed the western border of the bowl. That left the south rim. It was more broken than the others. The stream had to leave the bowl somewhere.

He snuffed out the cigarette butt and worked his way to the south. He was several hundred yards from the wall when he stopped and stared. There was a chunk missing from the side of the bowl, and within it, he saw the pale, whitish unmortared stones of a cliff dwelling. He focused his glasses on it, seeing the T-shaped doorways, the little, uneven windows, the protruding roof beams, and the great talus slope that slanted down to the greenery of the more level ground.

Cade nodded. It was a perfect place for a cliff dwelling, a hideout for the peaceful Hohokam farmers. The Southwest, New Mexico, and Arizona were full of them hidden away in remote places, many of them as yet unseen by white men. The nomadic Apache avoided these dwellings of the Old People. "By God," said Cade, "no wonder they shun Dark Mountain!"

The drought had driven the Old People from such places. A twenty-year falling water supply had at last driven them elsewhere. Cade moved the glasses, studying the sheer wall, and then he saw a notch at the end of the wall, close under the flank of the mountain. It indicated a box canyon perhaps or a hidden and tortuous pass to the more open ground to the south.

Cade was about to start toward the notch when something caught the corner of his eye. He turned to look at the cliff dwelling. Three windows in one of the end dwellings *showed faint yellow light.* An eerie feeling crept through Cade. There was no one there; there couldn't be anyone there. They had been gone from that place for hundreds of years.

He narrowed his eyes. The flickering light came again and then glowed steadily. Cade padded toward the great slope of detritus below the dwellings. He was within a hundred yards of it when a horse whinnied sharply. Before the whinnying stopped, Cade had hit the ground and was circling downwind of the unseen horse.

He saw the animal in a motte, not far from the edge of the stream, picketed and unsaddled. Cade looked about. There was no sign of life anywhere near him. Slowly he worked toward the animal, talking softly. The horse whinnied. His gray flank was in the moonlight, and Cade clearly saw a Box C brand.

Cade padded back into the shelter of the trees and looked up at the cliff dwelling. He caught the bittersweet scent of woodsmoke. He moved silently to the far end of the dwellings, then took a long chance, moving swiftly up the loose detritus slope taking advantage of the few scraps of cover he could find until he rolled over the low, crumbling wall at the end of the broad, uneven terrace that had been built in front of the dwellings. Here and there, the tops of crude ladders thrust themselves up out of squared openings in the terrace, leading down to the kivas once used by the men's societies.

Cade faded in between two of the crumbling buildings. At the rear of them was a triangular passageway formed by the rear of the buildings and the slanting wall of the huge opening in which the dwellings had been constructed ages past. He drew his Colt and checked it.

He hoped to God the cartridges were all right after being in the water.

He walked like a great lean cat until he reached the last of the dwellings. The mingled odors of bacon and wood smoke drifted to him. Cautiously he edged up to a small window and then peered quickly inside, withdrawing almost instantly. He had seen enough. Muley Smeed squatted over a firehole, stirring bacon in a battered spider over the flames. Several hot rolls lay against the front wall, and a Winchester leaned against the sidewall.

Cade wet his lips. Was the little man alone? He had seen Mosston out in the canyon, but that wasn't to say the rifleman hadn't come in after Cade had traversed the passage the hard way. There wasn't any doubt in Cade's mind that Gus Cargill was behind the mysterious rustling. Part of the Dark Mountain country was on his range. No wonder Cargill had so much money. His greed was stupendous. His sounding Cade out as to working for him now made sense. He could use men fast with a gun if Gatchell and Mosston were his examples.

Cade moved softly around the side of the dwelling. He looked down the moonlit slope. The only movement he saw was swaying brush. He heard a sound at the doorway of the dwelling, and he froze against the sidewall. Smeed stepped outside and looked down the slope. Cade had to make someone talk. It might as well be the little man. Cade stepped around the side of the dwelling and touched Smeed in the middle of his back with the muzzle of the six-gun. "All right, Muley," he said. "Back inside."

"Sounds like Willcox," said the little man without turning.

"Correct! Now move!" Cade plucked Muley's Colt from its holster and shoved him inside the room.

Smeed turned to face him, leaning against a rude ladder that led up to the next floor of the primitive

dwelling. "Beats the hell out'a me," he said conversation-
ally, "how you got into this hideout."

Cade nodded. "Where are the rest of them?" he said.

"Who?"

"Mosston, Gatchell, and Cargill."

Sneed's little eyes narrowed. "Don't you know?"

"I wouldn't be asking you if I knew."

Smeed reached down for the spider and placed it to
one side. "I'm alone," he said over his shoulder.

"You aim to eat all that bacon yourself?"

Smeed grinned. "I fancy bacon," he said.

Cade wet his lips. One horse and one man, but a
helluva mess of bacon in that spider. Smeed was likely
expecting someone. A cold feeling came over Cade.
*Muley wouldn't have put on the bacon if he hadn't expected
someone right soon.* Something warned Cade. He jumped to
one side. A gun exploded in the rear window. Cade risked
the ancient ladder. He was halfway up it, feeling the
rungs crack and give beneath his feet when Muley leaped
at him, dragging at his legs. In that instant, the gun
exploded again, and Muley Smeed took the heavy slug
between his shoulder blades. He pitched forward atop
the bacon-filled spider, scattering grease and bacon over
the floor as he died. Well, thought Cade as he stepped
out on the second floor, feeling the last rung snap
beneath his foot, he had fancied bacon.

The gun smoke swirled up through the floor opening.
Boots thudded on the hard ground. Cade saw there was
no ladder going up to the top floor of the dwelling. He
crouched and leaped, thrusting his hands through the
hole, and pulling himself up. Thank God the Hohokam
had been little men and had built low ceilings. He fell
across a pile of trash where the roof had partially
collapsed just as two slugs drove up through the opening
and ricocheted eerily from the sloping rock above the
dwellings.

Cade leaped to the next building. He dropped behind

the low wall of the roof and lay flat. It grew very quiet as
the gunshot echoes died away. He raised his head to
listen. A steer bawled down in the hollow. The acrid
stench of gun smoke mingled with the smell of bacon
drifted about the dwelling, soon joined by the odor of
burning cloth and leather and then the smell of burning
flesh. Muley had died lying partly across the embers of
the fire. The smoke drifted up and hung against the
smoke-stained rock over the dwellings.

Cade bellied across the roof and looked into the rear
passageway just in time to see a booted foot disappear up
the next lateral passageway. Cade softly walked across a
roof, feeling it give a little beneath his weight. He lay flat
behind the front wall and then peered over it. A broad-
shouldered man stood there in the moonlight, pistol in
hand, peering the other way. Cade dropped a pebble
behind Gatchell, whom he had recognized. Gatchell
whirled. Cade stood up. "Grab your ears, Gatchell," he
said. The roof collapsed, dropping Cade in a shower of
mud, stones, and broken rafters into the ground floor
room.

Gatchell's six-gun slammed three rounds into the dust
filling room. Cade rolled to his feet as the slugs smashed
against the hard-baked floor and bounced crazily from
the inner walls. Cade stood up, poked his Colt through a
window, and fired point blank at Gatchell. The big man
staggered along the terrace.

Cade leaped through the doorway and fired twice
from the hip, just as Gatchell fired once. The two slugs
smashed into Gatchell's guts, raising puffs of dust from
his shirt. He fell heavily, rolled over, and lay still, his
sightless eyes staring up at the rock ceiling high above
him, smoke drifting lazily from the muzzle of his hot
Colt.

Cade wiped the sweat from his forehead and walked
toward the man. A rifle cracked from the lower edge of
the slope, and the slug plucked at the slack in Cade's

shirt. He dropped flat as another round whined past his right ear. The echoes bounced from the rock wall behind and above the dwellings, then died away, and it was quiet again.

Cade reloaded. He wished desperately for a rifle. Smeed's Winchester was in the smoke-filled dwelling where the little man had been killed by his riding partner Gatchell. Cade lay flat, listening for the sound of boots against the loose rock of the slope. It had to be Mosston. Yet it might be Cargill or some of his other boys.

Minutes drifted past. Cade raised his head. A slug bounced from the wall, an inch from his head, driving stinging shards against his face. The echo died away.

Foot by foot, Cade bellied along the terrace until he reached the end of it. He lay on his back, picked up a large stone, and hurled it as far toward the other end as he could.

The instant the rifle spoke, Cade was over the wall and lying flat behind a bush. He cursed softly. There was hardly enough cover, and if he was caught on that moonlit slope, it would be all over.

Five minutes went past. It was very quiet; it was too quiet.

"Gatch!" called out a man from the far end of the slope. "Muley!"

There was no answer. The dead don't talk, thought Cade with a bitter smile.

He saw the rifleman move slowly up the slope and step over the wall. Cade bellied along the slope side of the wall. He stopped when he reached the midway point and lay still, fully bathed in moonlight. Boots grated on the terrace.

"By God," said the rifleman, a few feet from Cade. "He got them both!"

There was no mistaking the voice of Farley Mosston.

Cade felt the icy sweat run down his sides. The man

was deadly with his long gun. His nephew, Grant, had tabbed Mosston the best rifle shot around.

Boots scraped again. Cade looked up. Mosston was standing right at the wall, looking to the west, and all he had to do was turn his head and look down, and he'd see his quarry.

"Beats the hell out of me where he went," said Mosston.

"Mosston!" yelled Cade as he came to his feet like an uncoiling spring.

Six-gun and rifle spoke almost at the same instant, and Mosston died with his smoking rifle in his hands.

Cade stepped over the wall. It had been too close, much too close.

He picked up Mosston's smoking rifle and removed the fresh cartridges from Mosston's well-filled belt, replacing the rounds in his own six-gun and filling the magazine of the fine rifle. Once again, he had met Gus Cargill's three hard cases, and once again, he had defeated them singlehandedly, with a little unwilling help from Gatchell, of course.

He'd have to find his way out of the hideout and contact the law to come for the bodies as well as the stolen cattle. They would settle with Cargill as well. He had no desire to push his way back through that damned underground channel to the canyon of the Bravo. There must be another way out of the place; there had to be.

He hauled the two bodies into the room where Muley had set up camp, covered with their tarps from the hot rolls, helped himself to a huge bacon sandwich and whatever else he needed, then put out the fire and blocked off the doorway to keep the coyotes out.

Cade walked slowly down the slope, trailing the rifle.

The moon was waning, but there was still a great deal of light in the bowl. Enough for him to find his way through that notch.

CHAPTER THIRTEEN

I t didn't seem as though the notch would lead the way out to more open country. It zig-zagged back and forth, and at times Cade was in almost complete darkness, so narrow was the notch, but here and there, he noted signs of passage by man, horse, and steer. Midway down, he found a stout barricade of barbed wire with a solid gate to let a horseman through. He closed the gate behind him. The stolen cattle would be safe enough until they could be driven out unless Cargill or some of his men got there first. If Cargill didn't know his hideout had been exposed, it would be easy to apprehend him.

The passageway widened and then narrowed, and suddenly Cade was out of it, reining in his horse on a wide area of scattered rock and scrub trees, beyond which was badly broken country. Unless one was within several hundred yards of the notch, he'd hardly be able to see it.

The trail divided, one fork drifting down to the broken country, but still wide enough and good enough to drive a small herd of cattle along it. The right-hand fork was narrower, but cattle could be driven along that, too. Cade followed it. He rolled a smoke. This side of the mountain was new to him. The moon was dying when he rode down into a shallow canyon and up the other side. He drew rein quickly. A well-built line shack stood in a little motte. The windows shone dimly with yellow lamplight. Two saddled horses were tethered to trees behind the shack. A wisp of smoke rose from the chimney.

Cade slid from his horse. He hadn't expected any habitation in this country. He studied the shack as he stood there. He had no idea whose range he was on. It certainly wasn't Cargill's, for that was clear on the other side of the mountain.

His horse whinnied sharply. Cade slapped him on the rump. He trotted back into the timber and whinnied again. The light went out in the shack. Cade stepped behind a tree. He heard the shack door creak open, and a man stepped out into the shadows of the trees.

Cade cursed as the horse whinnied again.

"Who's out there?" demanded the man.

Cade grinned. He recognized the voice of Dick Thornhill. "It's me, Dick! Cade Willcox!"

Thornhill walked forward. "What in the devil's name are you doing up here?"

"This your land?"

"No. Gus Cargill owns this section, but he doesn't use it for ranching. Too far from his home place. Had an idea of mining here, but nothing came of it. He lets me use this shack when I'm up this way. I'm hunting strays. Seen any?"

Cade grinned as he walked toward the rancher. "You have no idea!" he said with delight. "I've found the rustler's hideout, Dick. It was Cargill, after all."

"What are you talking about?"

Cade leaned his rifle against a tree and felt for the makings. "I got into the Dark Mountain area, east side, by following an underground channel from the Bravo. There's a huge natural bowl in there, with plenty of water and grazing, and about five hundred head of steers in there. Some of them are yours, and some are from the Lazy W; funny thing, there are a lot of Box C cows in there, too."

"What are you going to do now?"

"The cows can't get out, and there's no one left to drive them off. I'm heading to Pine Tree for the sheriff."

Dick looked at him incredulously. "No one watching them?"

Cade rolled a cigarette. "There was," he said dryly. "Muley Smeed, Pierce Gatchell, and Farley Mosston. They won't ever throw a sticky loop again."

"You captured those three hard cases by yourself?"

Cade shook his head. "They're dead, Dick."

"You?"

Cade nodded as he lighted up.

"Jesus God! You might have a murder charge pinned on you! Maybe they didn't have anything to do with the rustling."

"They did. I was doing a job, Dick. In the line of duty. You might as well know I'm an Arizona Ranger. I didn't come here in the line of duty, but as long as I was here, I thought I'd better investigate this rustling."

"By God, I find this hard to believe."

Cade reached inside his shirt and unpinned the badge. He held it out in the palm of his hand. The moonlight glittered from the polished metal. "Who's with you?" he said. "We can send him down for the sheriff, and I'll take you back with me to see those cattle. You won't believe it."

Thornhill eyed the badge. He stepped back and drew swiftly, cocking the six-gun as he leveled it at Cade's belly. "I believe it," he said quietly.

Cade's eyes "narrowed. "What is this?" he said.

Thornhill glanced over his shoulder. There was someone else in the unlighted shack, standing just inside the doorway, fifteen feet from the two men.

"Well?" said Cade.

Thornhill studied Cade. "Don't try a draw, Willcox," he said. "I've killed before, and I can do it again."

The truth struck Cade like the blow of an Apache war club. "You!" he said.

Thornhill nodded. "No one ever suspected," he said. "Not even you, Ranger."

"But why? You've got everything you need. A fine ranch, a good wife, a future in this business."

"Granted," said Thornhill. "But there was something else I wanted. Something I couldn't get any other way but the way I did it. I had to ruin the Lazy W. I had to get rid of you."

"I don't follow you."

"It doesn't matter."

Cade knew then that Thornhill intended to kill him.

The waning moonlight shone on the handsome face of the rancher. "One bullet," he said coldly. "You won't feel a thing, Willcox. I nearly had you that afternoon in the Bravo Canyon. Half an inch, and you would have been killed."

"Like you killed Dan?"

"Yes."

"And Mack Rose?"

"Mosston did that."

"And all the troubles of the Lazy W came from you?"

"You guessed it."

"I still don't know why."

"Stop stalling for time, Willcox."

The person inside the shack moved a little. The floorboards creaked.

"Ready?" said Thornhill.

"As ready as I'll ever be."

Thornhill stepped forward. Cade jumped to one side as the Colt flashed. A sickening sledgehammer blow struck his left upper arm, and he knew it was broken. He staggered sideways as Thornhill fired again.

"No, Dick! No!" screamed a woman from the shack. It was the voice of Lucy Willcox.

The rancher turned his head. "Keep out of this, Lucy!" he snarled.

"No, Dick! No more killing! Please! For my sake!"

"You're in this as deep as I am," he said.

Cade was down on one knee. He fought against the waves of faintness and drew his Colt just as Thornhill turned. Cade fired. The rancher grunted as the big slug rapped into his gut. His Colt flashed, whipping Cade's hat from his head. Cade fell flat and fired from the ground, driving the rancher back with slug after slug until he sprawled backward against the side of the line shack and then fell heavily to the ground in front of Lucy.

The smoke wreathed about the beautiful young woman, "Dick!" she screamed.

Cade gripped his arm, feeling the hot blood flow down his forearm and begin to drip thickly from his fingers. An intolerable thirst gripped his throat harshly. Somehow he managed to drive off the waves of faintness.

She stepped over the sprawled body of her lover. "Cade!" she said. "You're hurt! Let me help you!"

He shook his head. He ripped away his shirtsleeve with his teeth.

"It was Dick who did it," she said. "Not me! Look! I was afraid of him, Cade! You didn't know him!"

Cade worked his scarf loose with his free hand and awkwardly worked it around his upper arm.

"Let me help you!" she said. She ran toward him.

He looked up at her as he tightened the improvised tourniquet. "Keep away from me," he said quietly. "Mourn for your dead. It will likely be more than you ever did for Dan."

She placed a shaking hand against her throat. "Take me with you," she said. "No one has to know about Dick and me."

"No one but me and you," said Cade. He got clumsily

to his feet and walked slowly past her into the line shack. There was enough moonlight streaming through a window for him to find the little medical kit on a shelf above the washstand. He undid the scarf and slowly worked a bandage about the wound. Things began to come back into his mind. Things about Lucy. How she had let Dick Thornhill take all those cattle without paying for them. Thornhill had been behind those mysterious shootings. Lucy had known that. Likely she was the one who had kept him informed about Cade's movements. At first, they had only tried to scare him away, and after that, it had been to the death. She had cast suspicion in Cade's mind against other men. He remembered, too, something Grant had said about the burning out at the Lazy W. The kid had been sleeping when the fire had started. It would have been easy for Lucy to have started it. When the kid was getting the burned animals out, the house had started a fire, but there had been no wind, and the flames had started inside the house. Something else clicked in Cade's mind. "Lucy was a long time in coming back with Dick..." he had said. No wonder. It was a good chance for Lucy and Dick to be together.

He tightened the bandage with his teeth. There was a bottle of rye on the same shelf as the medical kit. He drew out the cork with his teeth and took a stiff drink. He corked the bottle and slid it inside his shirt. He'd need it before the night was over.

What was it Abby Thornhill had said? "Dick is so full of life. So virile... I have been this way for over a year now. *Dick needs a woman. More than most men.* He works so hard and lives every minute of his life. I am of little use to him now." Lucy had been laughing with Dick when Cade had found them on the Circle Dot range. She had been laughing with him while preparing the evening meal at the Circle Dot. Waiting for Abby to die. He remembered, too, the haunting sadness on the face of Abby Thornhill. *She had known all along.*

Bit by bit, the last pieces of the puzzle fell into place. They had been clever, the two of them, in their dirty underhanded game. Meeting secretly in Cargill's line shack. Hunting strays... Cargill knew nothing of his three hardcases riding secretly for Thornhill. Cargill had no need of cattle; he had all he wanted.

Cade walked outside, stepping over the stiffening body of Dick Thornhill. Lucy had brought up his horse and her mare. She stood there in the moonlight, pretty as a cameo, with dying moonlight on her lovely face. The fragrance of her came to him on the shifting breeze. "Let me help you mount," she said.

Cade fashioned a cigarette with his free hand. He placed it between his lips as he looked steadily at her. She could not look at him. By God, she was lovely]

"Let me go back with you, Cade," she said in a faltering voice.

The moonlight glistened on Dick Thornhill's sightless eyes. Too many men had died because of this woman. Other men might die because of her. The curse would follow her. She'd never outrun it, and she'd have to live with her memories. It would be punishment enough.

"Cade?" she pleaded. "Forgive me! I'll make a good wife to you. Grant loves me. He believes in me!"

He took out his wallet and threw it at her feet. "Take all the money in it," he said.

She hesitated.

"Take it!" he snapped.

She emptied the wallet and handed it back to him.

Cade walked to his horse. "Write to me from wherever you end up," he said over his shoulder. "Don't put a return address on the envelope. I'll contact you about your willing the Lazy W fully to Grant. I'll take care of Carter's claim against the place. You'll get a check every month as long as you need it from the estate."

He swung clumsily up into the saddle and looked down at her.

She walked slowly to her horse and mounted it. Once more, she looked at him, but never at the body of the man who had been killed because of her. She sat her horse there as Cade turned and rode back the way he had come. "Cade!" she called out once more.

There was no answer. There never would be an answer.

He rode down into the shallow canyon. With the grace of God and half a quart of whiskey, he hoped to make Lost Canyon. There was a young woman there who could take care of a wounded man, as she had done before.

The moonlight slanted toward the dark western face of the mountain. The secret of Dark Mountain no longer existed. The curse was off the Bravo Valley range. Blood had been shed to keep the secret, and blood had been shed to solve the mystery.

Cade Willcox rode on into the darkness east of the mountain. There would be work to do on the Lazy W, for the kid would need help. After that? Well, a man might find a better place to settle than the Valley of the Bravo, but Cade Willcox was satisfied. He had come home at last.

Story action and reader satisfaction...

SHADOW OF A GUNMAN

CHAPTER ONE

The steady shooting that had been going on for most of the day began to die away an hour after sunset. Now and then, a posseman's Winchester cracked flatly from the shadows beyond the adobe, and a slug would hum through a window or thud against the bullet-pocked walls.

Thorp Barrett slowly reloaded his Colt while he sat below a window with his back to the wall. He was bone weary, but it wasn't weariness which took the steadiness from his hands; there wasn't a chance of getting out of that adobe alive, and to surrender was out of the question, at least as long as Travis Barrett was still alive.

Thorp looked up at his elder brother. Travis was flattened against a wall, cocked Colt upraised in his right hand, eyeing the outer darkness beyond the courtyard wall like a lean hunting cat. The hunter was always dominant in Travis Barrett.

Thorp looked away. It was the first time he had ever doubted his brother's invincibility, and it wasn't nice to think about. Somehow an idol was tottering on its feet of clay.

The Barrett Corrida would be wiped out like ants

when the posse closed in; a final, vengeful stamping out of the five-man core of the gang which at times had numbered as high as fifty men, gun-slingers all, who had either died with their boots on or had faded into the obscurity of the owlhoot trail.

Thorp closed the loading gate of his Colt and wondered if he had loaded it for the last time.

Clay Farrar sat against the far wall with his empty pistol in his hand. It seemed to Thorp that Clay was watching him, which was impossible because the tall man's handsome face was set and blue with death. Three slugs had chewed into his chest, and a man could cover the area with the palm of his hand.

Jim Finley lay outside, just beyond the scummed horse trough. It had taken him hours to die, and it seemed to Thorp that he could still hear the man's slobbering breath as his life had ebbed away by inches.

Porter Angus had been shot from his bay a mile from the adobe in the last hell-for-leather dash of the gang for cover. *"Go on!"* he had yelled. *"Go on, amigos! My tack is drove! Vaya con Dios!"*

Thorp wiped his mouth with the back of a dirty hand and wondered how long he and his brother had to live. Who would die first?

A slug grooved the sill of the window just above Thorp's head, showering him with adobe flakes.

Travis moved a little. "Take a siesta, Kid," he said, "while you still have a chance."

"I can't sleep, Travis."

Travis spat. "They always say Texas is fine for men and dogs but hell on women and horses. I'm beginning to think it's hell on outlaws, too."

The dusk was quiet now, so quiet they could hear the soft wind moaning between the vanes of the rusted windmill near the dry stock pond.

Travis moved about restlessly, and his spurs jingled musically. He was six feet tall, big-boned, and proportioned like a Greek athlete. Even though his lean face was covered with stubble and alkali dust, it was still as handsome as ever. He was twenty-three, six years older than Thorp, and in his short life, he had seen and created more excitement than a dozen men his age.

"Barrett!" the harsh voice broke the stillness like the snapping of a whip.

Travis edged toward the window.

"Barrett!"

"That's US Marshal Doug Scott," said Travis in a low voice. "I'd know that damned voice of his anywhere."

"Barrett!"

"Yeh?" called out Travis.

"I've got fifteen men out here. We know we got two of your *corrida*. You haven't the chance of a fiddler in hell. Throw out your guns and come out with your hands up."

"What happens then?"

"Jail and a trial... a fair trial."

Travis spat. "Tell you what, Scott. You divvy up those men out there and give me half of them. Then we meet at dawn, on the road, fair and square. You win I go to the *calabozo*; I win I cross the *rio* into Chihuahua. What do you say?"

There was a muttered curse in the darkness and the shuffling of boots on gravel. "You loco bastard!"

Travis laughed softly.

The wind crept in through the windows and did little to dissipate the miasma of powder smoke, adobe dust, sweat, and blood which hung in the room like a semisolid body. It was an old house, and more than one vagrant had eased himself in a corner with the innate filthiness of their kind.

It wasn't the way Thorp had figured on dying. None of the border songs told it this way. They always told of the heroic cowboy or vaquero, driven from his home by treachery, who fought for the poor against the rich and then was shot down in the street while beautiful girls wept unashamedly over the cold clay of a hero.

Travis squatted beside Thorp. "*Muy Malo,* eh, Kid?"

Thorp nodded. It was more than just very bad; it was pure hell and no pitch hot.

Travis slowly pinwheeled his Colt, letting the smooth ivory butt slap into his palm. Its mate hung in the carved leather holster at his left side. That pair of engraved Colts were known from Denver to El Paso Del Norte and from Dodge City as far west as Yuma. Nine men had died under the flaming muzzles of one or the other of those beautiful forty-fours.

"You game to make a break, Kid?"

A slug rapped into the warped door.

Thorp looked down at the littered, filthy floor. It had been great stuff riding with the Barrett Corrida since his mother had died the year before. It was true enough he hadn't been much help, but he had done the best he could, holding the horses, casing the towns, buying the supplies. All of the boys had said he had been all right.

It had been a thrill to ride through sleepy New Mexican *Placitas,* with his hat slanted low over his gray eyes, eyeing the girls, and staring down the insolent looks on the faces of the lounging men.

There wasn't much left to show for their forays. Horse stealing, rustling, robbing had shown little profit; the Barrett Corrida spent their money as fast as they stole it. A short life and a merry one, and to hell with the reckoning.

"Well, Kid?"

"What are the chances, Travis?"

Travis shrugged. "We can't stay here. There's not much of a moon due tonight. Beyond the corral is a deep arroyo, thick with brush. If we can make it, we can give them the slip and head for the *rio*. It's only fifteen miles to the border, Kid."

"On foot."

Travis looked away. He began to rub the muzzle of his Colt with the palm of his left hand.

"It's almost hopeless, isn't it?"

Travis stood up. "I told you never to talk like that!"

Thorp crawled away from the window and stood up. He was almost as tall as his brother. For the first time in his life, he began to see clearly what his brother really was.

"You hear me, Kid?"

Thorp nodded. He didn't want to argue. There was too much love in him for Travis, and in a matter of minutes, they might both be dead.

Travis gripped him by the shoulder. "We're on the western slope of the Sierra Viejas. The *rio* is due west. There isn't a hell of a lot on the Mex side of the *rio*. Maybe a few *ranchos,* but you can get food and water there. They don't ask questions."

"Aren't you coming?"

Travis grinned. "Sure, but we might get separated, see, Kid?"

He was lying like hell, thought Thorp.

A gun spoke in the darkness, and the slug smacked against the wall. Another Winchester cracked, and the bullet sang eerily through the air as it ricocheted.

"Go to the back door, Kid. Try to make it to the arroyo. It's dark as the inside of a boot back there. There hasn't been a shot fired from back there for an hour or more."

Thorp tightened his wide gun belt about his lean waist. "What about you?" he asked.

White, even teeth gleamed in the dimness. "I'll be along. If we get separated, head for Ciudad Juarez. There is a man there, a *campanero* of mine from the old days, named Bernardo Parillo. Find him and stay with him until I get there. If I make it first, I'll wait for you there."

"*Si.*"

"And, Kid, if I *don't* make it, tell Bernardo to give you

the box. He'll know what you want. You might need what's in it."

Thorp stared at his brother, and his voice seemed to come from a long way off. The spurs jingled a little. Travis crossed the room with his catlike stride and paused near a rear window. "I'll cover you," he said quietly.

CHAPTER TWO

Thorp eased the rear door back. It was pitchy black beyond the littered yard. That would be the arroyo. He stepped softly outside and flattened himself against the wall with his Colt in his hand and his heart in his dry mouth.

A coldness seemed to settle about him. In the day-long fight, he had traded slug for slug with the possemen without thinking too much about getting hit. But that had been in the heat of conflict. This was different and called for the chilled steel nerves Travis Barrett had in such abundance.

Thorp started across the hard-packed *caliche* of the yard. There was a ragged row of brush at the lip of the arroyo. He turned and backed towards it, peering back at the house.

There was a wall to the right and to the left of him, across the yard. He saw a vague movement as Travis left the house and started toward him.

Something scratched in the darkness beyond the wall, and there was a sudden faint flickering of light, which brightened as a torch sailed over the wall and struck the caliche, scattering flame and sparks. The fitful light revealed Travis, catfooting it toward the arroyo. He turned sideways and fired his left-hand Colt at the top of the wall.

Then it seemed as though the wall tops blossomed with fiery flowers which leaped and stabbed toward the lone man standing there in the changing light.

Travis leaned forward as though facing a strong wind. His body jerked, and dust puffed from his clothing.

Thorp fired two times, and the third time he pulled the trigger, the Colt misfired. He cursed and hurled it at one of the heads showing atop the wall to his right.

Travis was staggering forward with ridiculously short steps trying to regain his balance. "Light a shuck, Kid!" he yelled hoarsely. "I'll never make it!"

Travis fired toward the wall and then staggered against his brother. He shoved Thorp into the thick brush and then went down on one knee. He shook his head and got up, both sixguns at waist level, twinkling as he walked toward the nearest wall. A posseman grunted in pain.

The torch burned out as Travis Barrett went down.

Thorp ran toward his brother. A slug picked at his shirt. Thorp went down on one knee as another torch sailed over the wall and struck close to Travis. Travis got up on his feet and then fell heavily, but he thrust his Colt forward with a grimace of pain on his bloody face.

A tall man broke from the cover of the wall and started toward them with a Winchester in his hands. His hat fell off, revealing his graying hair.

"Get back, Scott, you bastard!" said Travis. He fired, and Scott sank down on one knee. He shook his head as blood darkened the left thigh of his trousers.

Thorp snatched up one of Travis' Colts and aimed it at the marshal, but the gun clicked dry.

Thorp darted for the brush and then turned to go back for his brother. Travis was grinning, as though at last he had met death face to face and knew it for what it was.

Scott fired from the hip, levering round after round into the repeater while the heavy slugs rapped into Travis Barrett and tore the life from him.

Thorp hurtled into the brush, yelling in pain as the thorns ripped through clothing and flesh like Apache knives.

"Scott got Travis!" yelled one of the men.

"Where's that sonofabitch of a Kid?"

"In the brush!"

"He won't get far!"

Thorp hit the bottom of the arroyo and got to his feet to cross a dry stream bed. He clattered across rounded stones and climbed driftwood piles as guns flashed along the arroyo lip.

There was a darker patch to his right, and he plunged toward it. It was a branch of the arroyo. He scaled the side as slugs hummed like bees through the brush, and then he tumbled out onto the open ground.

He was dead beat, thirsty, and scared, but he drove his legs on until he was across the field. He entered a motte of willows. A horse whinnied.

He stumbled as he looked back. Fire flickered near the house, and he could hear men calling out to each other as they beat through the brush after him.

The horse was Porter Angus' blocky bay. There was blood on the saddle. Thorp swung up on him and spurred him to the west. He reloaded his brother's Colt as he rode, and there was a cold hatred in him for Doug Scott. He could see the hard face of the marshal as he pumped lead into Travis with the precision of a machine, and there had been no mercy on his face.

There was a scabbard repeating rifle beneath his right thigh, and there was food in the saddlebags, a full canteen hanging from a strap, while a cantle roll had blankets and slicker.

The tumult and the shouting died away, and a warm

searching wind crept from the mountains and dried the sweat of exertion and fear from his face.

He reached the river just as the faint moon began to show. There was no hesitation in him as he spurred the bay into the dark waters and let the reins drop on its neck. The bay swam strongly, as though it, too, wanted no part of Texas.

The moon was up when Thorp Barrett swung down from the saddle and led the dripping bay up the slope into the willows and cottonwoods on the Chihuahua side of the Rio Grande.

The moon shone on his face, and if a man didn't know that Travis Barrett was lying dead in the filthy courtyard of an abandoned ranch in the Sierra Viejas, staring toward the moon with gray eyes that did not see, he would have sworn it was Travis himself who stood there on the west bank of the Rio Grande, looking toward Texas with a newly born hatred which boded no good for Marshal Doug Scott.

It was a long way to the city of Ciudad Juarez, north-west along the winding Rio Grande, that river of blood and violence.

He mounted the bay when they cleared the thick growths along the bank. Then he rode at a slow but steady pace. He had an appointment with Bernardo Parillo, who had in his keeping a box that now belonged to Thorp Barrett.

CHAPTER THREE

The sun had a curious yellow haze about it. The wind, which had been blowing half a gale all morning, had died away, and a curious sort of stillness hung over the land.

Thorp Barrett wiped the sweat from his face. His water was low, and he had avoided the few faint traces of road he had seen. Twice that morning, he had seen smoke against the sky.

The temperature was rising again, and there was an odd sort of feeling about the land as though something was going to happen, something which boded no good for the people who lived in the desolate land west of the Rio Grande.

The bay raised its head. It seemed to sense something. Then Thorp heard it. A faint, singsong moaning sound. The empty country to the north slowly changed as though a yellowish veil had been hung across it, and it wasn't until the hot wind struck Thorp and the bay that he knew it was the father and mother of all sand storms coming to open another suburb of hell for him to visit before he made Juarez.

The wind and sand had been driving him for over an

hour, and there seemed to be no end to the inane mouthing of the wind and the tiny particles of sand, as hard as diamond chips, which struck at man and horse.

The bay whinnied.

Thorp pulled his scarf down from his burning eyes. There was a low sandy ridge seen through the swirling sand, and at the base of it was an eroded adobe.

Thorp swung down from the saddle, gripped the reins, and led the bay toward the adobe.

There was a moment's respite as they passed behind the house, and then Thorp stopped short. A horse and a burro stood in an alcove behind the house, with their heads bent away from the searching wind.

Thorp tethered the bay to a post and drew Porter's Winchester from its scabbard. He levered a round into the chamber, then walked toward the rear door. It was slightly ajar.

He eased open the door, cursing the gritty sound as it scraped the ground. The wind howled about the adobe. It was dark inside the big kitchen.

Thorp padded across the kitchen to a doorway that must lead into the living room; then, he stopped short. There was another sound intermingled with the moaning of the wind and the rattling of particles of sand.

He stood to one side of the doorway and peered into the next room. There was a curious huddled mass in one corner of the room, beside a smoke-stained beehive fireplace. A fire was burning low, and the tempting odor of coffee drifted to Thorp.

The figure moved. Someone had a blanket pulled up over the head as protection against the sand, which trickled into the room. Then Thorp heard the tinny sound of a guitar, out of tune. The figure moved again, the blanket fell back, and a man sat there, raising his head as he struck a chord. "Have courage, my boy, to say NO!" howled the man.

Thorp walked into the room.

The man turned quickly, and his jaw dropped.

"Take it easy, *amigo*," said Thorp in cowpen Spanish.

The man stood up, revealing a gnomelike figure clad in tight-fitting Mex *calzones* and worn half-boots which had once been beautifully carved. The man's face seemed carved from mahogany by a master hand which etched every line and wrinkle into the tight skin until there was hardly a smooth place to be seen.

A ragged beard covered the lower part of the face, and the long hair of the head hung down over the greasy collar of a velveteen jacket. But it was the eyes that held Thorp's attention. They were the hardest-looking green he had ever seen outside of that of an emerald.

The eyes flicked down to the Winchester.

"I won't hurt you, old one," said Thorp in Spanish.

"For Chrissakes, speak English," said the man. He spat to one side. "And don't call me old, brother."

Then Thorp saw the worn butt of the six-shooter, which was tucked behind the *faja*, or wide cloth band he wore about his lean middle.

The man leaned against the wall and idly excavated a front tooth with a dirty fingernail. "You want trouble or coffee?" he asked.

Thorp grinned. "Coffee."

"Fair enough."

The man turned and squatted beside the fire. He rooted two tin cups out of a bag lying beside the hearth and filled them with the steaming brew. "Squat, *amigo*," he said over his shoulder.

Thorp let down the hammer of his Winchester and leaned the weapon against the wall, on his side. "Some storm," he said casually.

"Yeh. Ain't as bad as a blue norther, though." The green eyes studied Thorp. "You want to sweeten this stuff up?"

"A little sugar if you have any."

The man grinned. "By the nails of Christ," he said. He took a square black bottle from the bag. "Mezcal," he said. "Traded a bag of cow horn powder for it."

"Cow horn powder?"

The man spat. "Told the Mex it was rhinoceros horn."

"So?"

The green eyes squinted as the man poured a shot into each cup. "Rhinoceros horn is good for what ails a man who ain't making time with the ladies."

"You think he'll know the difference?"

"Hellsfire! He don't even know what a rhinoceros looks like."

They squatted in front of the fireplace. The coffee was strong and hot, and the mezcal lacing gave it the right touch to take some of the weariness out of Thorpe.

"The name is Chusco Barnes," the man said suddenly.

"Howdy."

Thorp drained his cup. Barnes refilled it. "Ain't no use bucking this storm. Might as well sit it out. You want to play cards, shake dice or play the coffeepot?"

"The last is all right, Chusco."

The little man leaned against the wall. "I didn't get the name," he said quietly.

"I didn't give it."

"Running, son?"

Thorp drained his cup and stood up. "Thanks for the jamoke," he said.

Barnes grinned. "I ain't no law man. Ain't none of my business what your handle is, but I always feel like an ass talking to a man when I don't know his name."

"My first name is Thorp. My friends call me Kid."

Chusco eyed Thorp. "Kid? I'd like to see how big *they* was."

"Where you heading, Chusco?"

"North a way."

"Me too."

"Listen to that wind!"

Thorp picked up his Winchester.

"Where you going, Thorp?"

"To take my horse into the kitchen."

The little man nodded. He stood up and followed Thorp into the kitchen and then outside. They brought the animals into the kitchen. Thorp unsaddled the bay and rubbed it down.

Chusco Barnes had two fine-looking animals. The horse was a sorrel gelding with a good-looking Mex saddle on it. A rifle hung in a figured leather scabbard beside the saddle.

Chusco leaned against the wall and rolled a cigarette. He lighted it and blew smoke rings toward Thorp. "Nice-looking horse," he observed.

Thorp nodded.

"Got blood on his back. Blood on the saddle, too."

Thorp turned. "What big eyes you have, grandma."

"You come from yan side of the *rio?*"

"Maybe."

Chusco inspected his cigarette as though it was something of a rarity. "Well, if you didn't, and the *rurales* are jumping dust after you, I'd say you were safe enough here until the storm blows over."

"Who's chasing you, Chusco?"

The little man grinned. "Nobody, excepting my conscience."

They walked into the other room. The wind had quieted a little, but it was still too rough to leave.

"You know where you are?" asked Chusco.

"I think so."

"You're near Hueso, which ain't much except a few 'dobes and jacales, with a rundown cantina thrown in for good measure."

"How far from Juarez?"

"Eighty-five, maybe ninety miles."

Chusco filled the cups again. "I'm heading that way. You got a mind to want company?"

"No."

Chusco shrugged. He squinted up at Thorp. "Just as you say. Might tell you that this country is as full of *bandidos* as a cow pond is of wrigglers. Most of them would kill you for a pack of makings or just to see a gringo kick."

"How come they didn't get you?"

Chusco grinned. "I got ways of getting around. The odds are you *might* make it to Juarez if you threw in with me for the trip. I need a handy man with a gun."

"Now it shapes up."

"What do you say?"

"Fair enough."

Chusco sat down on his blanket and picked up his scarred guitar. He began to pick out a few chords. Then he looked up at Thorp. "I seem to have seen you somewheres before."

"Ain't likely."

The man played on a plaintive little Mexican tune. "There was a man I knew once in Arizona. Tough hombre. Hard case. Used two guns like most men try to use one. Looked a lot like you. Same eyes. Same build."

"So?"

The eyes flicked down to the tied-down, holstered Colt. "Nice piece of hand artillery, Thorp."

"Thanks."

Thorp got up and walked toward the kitchen to get a blanket.

"Travis Barrett!" called out Chusco.

Thorp whirled, and the Colt leaped into his hand.

Chusco was tuning the guitar. "You find the Fountain of Youth, Barrett?" he asked.

"Travis was my brother," said Thorp softly.

The green eyes flicked up. *"Was?"*

"He died yesterday, across the *rio,* near the Sierra Vieja."

Chusco leaned back against the wall. "I knowed you wasn't Travis, and I didn't know you was kin. Don't surprise me none he's dead. It was bound to happen. It always does with his kind."

"You talk too much."

"No offense."

Thorp got the blanket and placed it on the floor on the opposite side of the fireplace from the strange little man. "Where did you know my brother?" he asked quietly.

Chusco held out his hands and waggled them. "*Quien sabe?* Yuma maybe." he grinned. "The *town,* not the *pen.* Gila Bend. Tucson." He rubbed his thin jaw. "No, 'twas Globe. I mind it now. I went up there to see Isobel."

"Isobel?"

"Yep. *Isobel.* Speak with reverence, brother. What a lady. You note I say *lady* instead of woman?"

"Yes."

"Always refer to Isobel as a lady, son, and we'll get along."

Thorp sipped at his coffee, listening to the frenzied moaning of the wind and the rattling of the sand particles down the chimney.

"You're fast with a cutter," said Chusco suddenly.

"Gracias."

"Fast enough, I guess, but you ain't anywheres near as fast as Travis was."

"Whoever was?"

Chusco shrugged. "There's *always* a faster gun, Kid." he looked up. "Travis, teach you?"

"Yes."

Chusco nodded. "Good teacher. Maybe he should have let you stay on the ranch, Kid."

"I said you talked too much!"

Chusco picked at the guitar. He cocked his head to listen to the wind and then began to play, and it seemed to Thorp Barrett that some of the vague mouthings of the wind had settled in the man's voice. An eerie feeling came over him. It would be a long wait before they could leave for Juarez, and Thorp wasn't so sure he was going to like it.

CHAPTER FOUR

J uarez dozed under the late afternoon sun. The Moorish bell tower of Mission Nuestra Senora De Guadalupe De El Paso rose above the flat dirt roofs of the town like the finger of God, and the sun shone on it warmly. Bluish smoke rose from the chimneys, and the mingled odors of chili, beans, and meat cooking in hundreds of pots throughout the town met the two dusty travelers who stopped at the end of town.

Chusco Barnes shifted his chew and rested his thread-bare elbows on the pie-plate pommel of his heavy Mexican saddle. "Now you're here," he said out of the side of his mouth, "what do you aim to do?"

Thorp Barrett slanted his hat low over his eyes and looked beyond the town to where he could see the Franklin Mountains and the crumbling face of Comanche Peak beneath which El Paso lay. It seemed so close, and there was only Juarez and the Rio Grande between him and it, but there was one unseen barrier between him and the United States. He was an outlaw in Texas and New Mexico, and if he crossed the bridge into El Paso, he might be seen and recognized. He looked back over his shoulder into Chihuahua.

Chusco spat, and the sound of the juice striking the ground made his sorrel shy a little. "Hell of a note," said Chusco. "How old did you say you was?"

"I didn't."

"Seventeen, eighteen, no more, eh?"

"You're doing the talking... you usually are."

"Well, pardon me all to hell!"

Thorp grinned. The little man was a fascinating companion, filled with all sorts of lore and legend, a veritable fountain of misinformation, but when the thoughts were weeded out, there were some surprising ideas to be found.

Chusco jerked a thumb toward the town. "This is as far as you can go, *amigo*. Less you want to stick your neck into a noose."

It was as though the little man had read Thorp's thoughts, and the thoughts weren't good. Seventeen years old and barred from the country of his birth. There was always Mexico. The country was full of *Americanos* who had fled from their own country. Rustlers, horse thieves, murderers, and even those unreconstructed Confederates who'd rather live and die in an alien country than swear allegiance to the flag they had fought so well against for four long years.

A *paisano* padded past them in the dust, hardly noticing Thorp, but he noted Chusco, and he smiled broadly. "Good day to him of God, Senor Barnes," he said.

Chusco raised his Mexican steeple hat, heavy with coin silver. "And to you, Tomasito, little friend of my heart!"

Tomas stopped and rubbed his jaw. "It is plain to see your *burrito* is heavily laden, Senor Chusco."

"You have sharp eyes, Tomasito."

The man looked toward the town. "It is yet light. The police have been very busy today." He turned, and his liquid eyes studied Chusco. "I would not let a friend of mine go into town if I thought the police might be interested in him."

Chusco glanced at Thorp.

"Comprende, amigo?" asked Tomas.

"Yo comprendo, amigo." Chusco felt in his pocket and then tossed the man a coin.

Tomas deftly caught the bit of spinning metal and then doffed his dusty hat. He padded off down the road.

Chusco spat again. "You know where to find this *amigo* of yours, Thorp?"

"I'll find him."

Chusco nodded. He looked up at the sky and then at Thorp. "Then I guess it's the end of the trail for us, Thorp."

"Nice knowing you, Chusco."

"Likewise."

Chusco thrust out his hard little hand, and the strength in it was enough to make a man wince. *"Vaya con Dios, compañero."*

Chusco spurred his sorrel and led his burro toward the west. He turned when he was fifty feet away. "You stay out of El Paso, Kid."

"Gracias."

Chusco scratched in his beard. "You get into any trouble in Juarez; you just ask for Chusco Barnes. *Comprende?"*

"Yo comprendo, compañero."

Thorp watched the little man ride off. Chusco looked back several times as though expecting Thorp to call out to him, but Thorp sat his saddle without moving until the man was out of sight in the thick brush which encroached on the town.

Thorp touched the bay with his spurs and rode along the first street he saw. The odors of the food, hot and spicy, reminded him that he had not eaten since early that morning.

Dogs and chickens rooted in the piles of rotting

garbage left on the gutter-less streets. Barefooted children played directly in the path of the big gringo horse,
scuttling to cover at the last possible moment. Little men
leaned against house fronts, swathed in the usual big hat
and gay serape, and their dark eyes studied the young
gringo who rode such a fine *caballo* and carried such fine
weapons.

There were girls too, hardly in their teens, who wore
low-cut dingy white blouses and flowing skirts. Their
bare legs showed freely, and their eyes boldly studied the
gringo through the cigarette smoke they blew from
nostrils and mouths. And always, the little silver cruci-
fixes dangled above their full brown breasts.

Dusk covered the town when he found a man who
knew Bernardo Parillo. The house was at the edge of
town, close to the river, isolated from the nearest house
by trees and brush.

Thorp swung down from the tired bay, loosened his
Colt in its holster, then rapped on the door.

"*Quién* es?" a harsh voice called out.

"A friend to Bernardo Parillo."

"So?" Feet shuffled on the floor. "Perhaps I have no
friends?"

"That is unfortunate, Bernardo."

"Your voice sounds familiar."

"Open the door then."

The door yawned open, and a thick-bodied man stood
there with his hand resting on his knife hilt. "Mother of
God!" the man said quickly. He peered more closely.

"I'm not Travis Barrett," said Thorp quietly.

"Who then?"

"His brother."

"He has no brother."

"Then I've been mistaken all these years."

Bernardo studied Thorp. "Where is he? Where did
you last see him?"

"He is dead, *amigo.*"

"You lie!"

Thorp slowly lowered his hand to his brother's Colt. "Look at this gun," he said quietly.

The Mexican took the splendid weapon. He nodded. "It is his." He shot a wary glance at Thorp. "How did you get it?"

"We were trapped in a 'dobe near the Sierra Vieja. My brother died helping me to escape."

"Madre de Dios!"

Bernardo shook his head. He handed the Colt back to Thorp. "Come in. My house is yours."

A pot sat in the coals of the fireplace, and the room was thick with the pungent odor of chili and beans. A candle guttered in the neck of a bottle. The room was hung with serapes, bridles, holsters, belts, saddles, and weapons. A carved wooden *santo* was in a wall niche, and before the figure, a candle glowed in a red glass cup.

Parillo turned, and the light shone full on his dark face, etched by a white scar on the right cheekbone. "The rest of his men?"

"All dead."

"All?"

Thorpe nodded. "Clay Farrar, Jim Finley, Porter Angus, and my brother."

"It is not possible."

"But it so."

"Yes... I should have known they would all die together."

The dark eyes lifted. "They were close those *caballeros.* It is fitting that those who rode so close together in life should do so in death."

Thorp dropped into a chair.

The Mexican opened a bottle and placed it and a glass beside Thorp. "There will be food soon. I will take care of your horse."

Thorp poured a drink. His brother hadn't been much of a drinker. He had always said it dulled the eye and slowed the reflexes, and too many men had died because of it. But the liquor seemed to fill a gap in him. Something had been torn from him that night near the Sierra Vieja, and he had slowly been replacing some of the missing parts, but he knew as long as he lived, the gap would never be completely filled until Doug Scott died under the flaming muzzle of the gun Thorp carried at his side, his brother's legacy.

Bernardo came in and began to fill plates from the pot. He placed the plates and crisp tortillas on the table. "Eat, *amigo,*" he said. "I know you enough to know that you speak the truth."

"So?"

Bernardo smiled. "The bay. It was once mine. I lost it to Porter Angus in a dice game. The bay knew me."

When they had finished, they shoved back the plates, and Bernardo rolled corn husk cigarettes for both of them. They sat in front of the fire.

"And now... what of you?" asked the Mexican.

Thorp shrugged. "I can't go back across the *rio,* Bernardo."

"That is so. You have money?"

"Nothing."

Bernardo smiled. "I thought so. How do you *Americanos* say it? Easy it comes in; easy it goes out?"

"Something like that."

Bernardo placed a hand on Thorp's knee. "There is a box here. Left by your brother into my care. He and I rode together many times. Once, he saved my life from the *rurales* in Sonora. Once I saved him from the Yaquis near the Rio de Bavispe."

The Mexican left the room and soon came back with a japanned metal box. He placed it on Thorp's lap. "The box and what is in it are now yours."

"What is in it?"

Bernardo shot a hard glance at him, and then his face softened. *"Quién sabe?* It is not locked, nor did it matter."

"I apologize, *amigo."*

"It is nothing." Bernardo waved a hand. "I have the hot pride, you understand?"

"I understand."

"I will leave the room while you look."

"No."

Bernardo stood up. "I will clean the dishes then."

Thorp opened the box. In it was a thick wad of bills bound together with an elastic band, a gold repeater watch, a handful of gold coins, and an exquisite silver-mounted derringer.

Bernardo placed the plates into a pan, then leaned against the wall. "Then you have money?"

"Yes."

"It did not matter. What I have is yours, and I am not a poor man."

"Gracias."

"It is nothing."

Bernardo lighted another candle and sat down in front of the fire. "I am traveling south within a matter of days. I have business down there, which will keep me busy for some months. Perhaps you would like to ride with me?"

"I have other plans."

"You do not mean to go back to your country?"

Thorp slowly rubbed the butt of his brother's Colt. "There is a man I have to see."

"So?"

Thorp looked at him. "Do you know Marshal Doug Scott?"

"Yes."

"He killed my brother."

"He is a dangerous man for a young cockerel like you to challenge."

The gray eyes lifted and held the dark eyes of the Mexican. "It doesn't matter," said Thorp coldly.

Bernardo slowly formed a cigarette. "He will not come to Mexico; therefore, you must go to the United States to find him. Where does he stay?"

"Sometimes in Las Cruces. Sometimes in El Paso."

"Bueno! I will help you. I have friends. Stay here with me for a few days. My friends will ask questions. Discreetly, you understand. Then perhaps you can work out a plan. Meanwhile, here is *aguardiente* and food in plenty. There are many pretty girls in Juarez who would like to meet a young man such as you. Eh?"

"Perhaps. Bernardo, do you know a man by the name of Chusco Barnes?"

"Si. What of him?"

"What does he do?"

Bernardo grinned. "He is a smuggler and a very good one too. I have done business with him. Always the *rurales,* the police, and the customs officers are looking for him and they can never find him. He has many friends here in Chihuahua."

"He rode with me from near Hueso."

The dark eyes studied Thorp. "Perhaps it was just as well. This is dangerous country for a young *Americano* traveling alone. You are lucky having two friends, such as Chusco Barnes and myself here in Juarez, *amigo."*

"Gracias, Bernardo."

The Mexican stood up. "I must go into town. Stay here. It is your home as well as mine."

Bernardo swung a gun belt about his waist and buckled it. He put on his hat and stopped beside the door. "You are determined to kill this man Scott?"

"Yes."

The Mexican shrugged. He closed the door behind him, and then Thorp heard the steady beating of hoofs on the hard earth.

Thorp picked up the box which had been left to him by his brother. There was enough money in it to keep him for quite a spell. Enough money to buy a small ranch or business. Enough money to keep him until he found and killed Doug Scott.

CHAPTER FIVE

Thorp Barrett sat in a chair which he had tilted back against the front wall of Bernardo's house. It was dusk. Three days had drifted past since Bernardo had set his spies to work across the *rio*. No news had come as yet.

Thorp rolled a cigarette and lighted it. From somewhere down the dusty road came the faint strains of music. A warm wind crept over the town, swaying the dusty leaves of the trees.

A horseman showed on the road, and a moment later, Bernardo guided his horse into the yard and dropped from the saddle. "There is news, *amigo,*" he said quietly. "Yes?"

Bernardo squatted in front of Thorp and rolled a cigarette. Thorp lighted it for him.

"The man you seek is now in El Paso."

Thorp leaned forward. The front legs of the chair struck the hard earth.

"Wait! There is more!"

"Go on."

"He was badly wounded in the left thigh. The bone was smashed. His men brought him to El Paso. He lost much blood. It is doubtful whether he will live or not, *amigo.*"

"He won't!"

The dark eyes half closed. "You would kill a man in that condition?"

"My brother was riddled with slugs when Scott shot him to death."

Bernardo inspected his cigarette. "He stays in a small hotel. There is a nurse in constant attendance. It is said his men stay close to the hotel waiting to see what happens."

Thorp stood up.

"You will still go?"

"Yes."

Bernardo stood up and flipped the cigarette away. "I have a man who will get you across the *rio.* Do not try to cross by the bridge. There are always lawmen waiting on the other side. They say sooner or later; a wanted man will cross that bridge. They are not often wrong."

The Mexican waited.

"Get the man," said Thorp quietly.

Bernardo shrugged. "Just as you say."

The night was dark. The small boat grounded on the American side of the Rio Grande and Thorp Barrett stepped out onto the soft bank. The Mexican shoved off the boat and looked back. "You will be back?" he asked.

"I don't know."

"Go with God then, friend."

The boat faded into the darkness.

Thorp walked up the bank. The bridge was far up the river to his left, and he could see the lights reflected on the dark running waters.

There were a few adobes and jacales dotting the banks. He passed them and found a narrow, wandering street, which he followed until he reached the more settled part of the town. He had been there several times before the Barrett Corrida had been run out of New Mexico and into the Sierra Vieja for their last stand.

The town was booming and had been doing so for quite some time since the Southern Pacific, and the Santa Fe had reached there. The "run" of the town was San Antonio Street west from the Acme Saloon to El Paso Street, thence south for a few blocks. It was this area Thorp had to avoid, for there might be men there, both friendly and unfriendly, who would know a member of the Barrett Corrida by sight. Barrett Corrida, the words meant little now, a bit of passing history, to be forgotten in time, for there was one man left of that lawless organization, and after this night was over, he'd either be dead as the others were or be running south into Chihuahua under an assumed name.

The hotel was on a quiet side street to the north of San Antonio Street. Bernardo's informant had said it was of two stories, built of adobe and painted yellow and blue. Thorp could hardly miss it.

He walked steadily to the east until he could cross San Antonio Street blocks away from the thriving nightlife center of the town, but even at that distance, he could hear the tinny music and the murmuring of many voices.

There was no moon as he picked his way through narrow streets, at times treading through garbage and trash piles. There were no lights, and the small, secretive windows were shuttered tightly.

He saw the hotel before he realized he was close to it. It was a curious amalgamation of adobe and wood. The second story was encircled by a wooden porch, which was roofed, and the flooring of the porch formed a roof over the wooden boardwalk which ran in front of the hotel. There were lights in the lower story, but only one room was lighted on the second floor.

Thorp looked up and down the deserted street before he crossed it and padded his way to the rear of the hotel.

He scaled a crumbling adobe wall and found himself in a littered courtyard in the center of which was a dying tree.

He loosened his Colt in its sheath and crossed the yard to the rear door. He eased it open and looked down a dim hallway. There was a light in the front room of the hotel, and a man dozed behind a counter. That meant trouble, for the stairs leading up to the second floor, must be at the front of the hotel.

Thorp closed the door and stepped back. The second-floor porch had no stairway leading up to it from the yard.

Thorp walked to the end of the building. A tree hugged the scabby wall. Thorp looked back. There was no one to be seen. He climbed the tree and dropped a leg over the rickety railing of the porch. The boards creaked beneath his weight as he walked toward the doorway.

He opened the door softly and looked into a hallway, dimly lit by several lamps which guttered a little in the draft from the opened doorway.

He walked along the hallway. He tested several doors and found them all locked. The door on the left side of the hallway, at the front of the hotel, opened easily to his touch.

The lamp on the marble-topped table glowed with a soft, steady light. Beyond the table was a bed with a high board back and a lower foot. There was someone in the bed, but he could not see who it was. On a small table beside the bed was a pitcher and a glass, some bottles of medicine, and a basin.

Thorp looked back over his shoulder toward the dark stairwell. It was quiet in the hotel. It seemed as though there was no one in the building other than the dozing clerk, the person in the bed, and Thorp.

Thorp stepped softly into the room. A coat hung from a wall peg, and the light shone on a badge. Thorp wet his lips. He moved forward and looked down at the person in the bed. It was a man. A tall man with graying hair. His lean face was pale and drawn, and the place where his left thigh should be mounded high as though splinted and bandaged. The man was Scott, all right.

It had been so damned easy. Almost too easy.

Thorp looked down at the man who had killed Travis. For a moment, his courage failed him, and then he remembered the taut, grinning face of his brother when he had faced Doug Scott in the yard of the adobe house at Sierra Vieja, with one gun gone and the other empty, while Scott had poured half a dozen slugs into him as though he had been killing a rattlesnake instead of a brave man.

Thorp drew out his brother's Colt. He looked about the room. A revolver hung in a holster near the black coat with the badge pinned to it. Thorp looked at Scott again. Did he have the strength to hold a gun steady in his hand and face the brother of the man who had died at Sierra Vieja?

What would Travis Barrett do in such a case?

Thorp wiped the sweat from his face. He raised the Colt and cocked it.

The wind blew through the open window and ruffled the damp hair of the wounded man.

Thorp turned quickly. There was someone on the stairs. He let down the hammer of the Colt and then sheathed the weapon. He walked to the door and stepped out into the hallway, drawing the door closed behind him. He had just time to get ten feet from the room when he saw someone step into the hallway from the stairwell.

It was a young woman, or a girl, carrying a tray. She glanced at Thorp and smiled. "Thank Heaven there's someone here," she said.

Thorp took off his hat. She was young and pretty too. The soft light of the hall lamps gave a luster to her light brown hair. "Can I help you?" he asked.

"You can open that door for me." She indicated Scott's room with a nod of her head.

Thorp touched his lower lip with his tongue. He glanced down the stairwell. He walked to the door and held it open for her, and as she passed, she smiled up at him. Her eyes were dark blue. "Thanks," she said.

She placed the tray on the marble-topped table. "You can do something else for me," she said.

"Yes, ma'am."

"Help me to raise him so that he can eat."

"Looks like he's asleep!"

She walked to the bed. "He must eat to keep up his strength."

Thorp cursed mentally. As long as she was there, he had no chance of doing what he had come there to do.

He walked to the side of the bed opposite her. Together they slid their arms under Scott's broad shoulders, and Thorp felt her soft small hands in his. The marshal opened his eyes. "Time to eat, Emily?" he asked weakly.

"Yes."

They lifted him, and the girl placed pillows behind his back. The marshal looked at Thorp. "Thanks," he said.

Thorp stepped back, and his hand brushed the Colt. There was no recognition in the man's eyes, but then Thorp's face was shaded by his low-pulled hat.

She placed the tray on his lap. "Can you manage?" she asked.

"Yes."

"I have to go up on San Antonio Street for your medicine."

He shook his head. "It's too rough up there. Wait until one of the boys gets here."

Thorp walked to the door. "Good evening," he said.

"Wait a moment!" she called.

He stopped in the hallway.

She came out and closed the door behind her. "Are you going to your room?"

"No."

"Then you must be going up town?"

"Yes."

She smiled and tilted her shapely head to one side. "Good!" she said. "You can escort me. I'm not afraid, but he gets nervous when I walk out of here alone at night."

"I'm sorry," he said.

She took him by the arm. "I'm Emily Thurlow."

"Tom Barnes," he said. The name would do as well as any other.

"Are you from El Paso, Mister Barnes?"

"No."

They reached the bottom of the stairs. She stopped to awaken the clerk. "I'm going up town, Mister Pascoe," she said. She looked up at the ceiling. "He's eating now. Just drop in on him for a moment in about half an hour. I won't be gone much longer than that."

"Yes, Miss Thurlow."

They walked out into the dark street.

"You're his nurse?" asked Thorp.

"Yes. He was badly wounded in a fight with outlaws near the Sierra Vieja. It's a wonder he survived the wagon ride here. But he's tough. All steel and whang leather, his men say."

"Yes."

Thorp looked ahead. They were walking directly toward the most populated section of the town, where the bright lights illuminated every face. What was it Bernardo had said? *There are always lawmen waiting on the other side. They say sooner or later; a wanted man will cross that bridge. They are not often wrong.*

"Why did you say you were sorry back there?"

He flushed. "I hadn't intended to come up here."

She glanced up at him. "You didn't tell me where you came from."

"Globe, Arizona."

She smiled. "I know it well. My father used to work there."

"Where do you have to go now?" he interrupted.

"The pharmacy is just a block up the street."

The street was crowded. Monte, poker, chuck-a-luck, and faro games were booming as usual. Thorp pulled his hat a little lower. At any other time, he would have been more than proud and eager to walk the street with such a girl as Emily Thurlow, but this wasn't the night he would have picked.

"Here's the pharmacy," she said. She turned to look up into his face. "Thanks, Mister Barnes."

"Emily!" a man called out.

She turned. "Hello, Jed."

"How's Doug?"

Thorp stepped back. The man wore a badge. He glanced quickly at Thorp, but Thorp had walked into the crowd. "Wait, you!" he called out.

Thorp stepped behind a group of men who were watching a street hawker. He stepped into the street and walked quickly to the far side, glancing back as he did so. The man with the badge had left Emily and was forcing his way through the crowd.

Thorp darted behind a wagon.

"Billy!" yelled Jed. "Stop that kid with the black hat."

Thorp glanced to one side. A short, bench-legged man started toward him. Thorp jumped into an alley and freed his Colt. As Billy stepped in after him, Thorp swung the Colt, felt it strike hard against Billy's head, then he started to run.

"Halt damn you! You men here! Give me a hand! That's Thorp Barrett!"

Thorp reached the next street. Jed was fifty feet behind him. The officer drew his pistol and fired. Thorp turned, raised his Colt, and fired once. Jed pitched face downward in the muck, and then Thorp darted across the street, swung up over a fence, ran across a yard, scaled another fence, and dropped into the filth of an alleyway.

Men yelled to each other in the street. Thorp sprinted down the alley. He was about five or six blocks from the *hotel,* as close as he could figure.

The trouble was that he was in a maze of winding side streets and alleyways and wasn't quite sure where the river was.

Five minutes drifted past, and he thought he was getting closer to the river when he heard the beating of hoofs on the street behind him. He stepped into a doorway.

Three horsemen came past. "He's heading for the river," said one of them.

"He won't get across the bridge," said another. "Some of the boys are heading that way now."

"They saw it was one of the Barrett boys."

"Can't be Travis. Scott killed him at Sierra Vieja."

"Must be the kid then."

"He's almost as good as his brother then. He killed Jed Martin with one shot."

Jesus God... thought Thorp.

He stepped out into the street. Two Mexicans seemed to materialize out of the darkness. "Which way to the *rio?*" asked Thorp.

"For why do you want to know?" asked the taller of the two.

Thorp brushed past them, and one of them reached for his arm, but the Colt came out and hit him full across his mouth. He grunted in pain and went down, spitting blood and teeth. His companion drew a knife, but Thorp kicked him in the groin and followed through by hitting him on top of his steeple hat with the Colt, driving down through the thick felt to crash against the skull, dropping him beside his cursing friend.

Thorp ran down the street. Then he could smell the *rio.* He looked back. Horsemen had turned into the street. Thorp plunged through the brush and felt the water at his feet. He pulled off his boots and waded in, striking out as his feet left the bottom. The current carried him swiftly along, and then his feet hit bottom on the Mexican side of the river. He crawled into the brush and dropped flat, and his breathing was harsh in his throat. The fat was in the fire now. There was only one thing to do. Get to Bernardo Parillo and go with him deep in Chihuahua, where the people didn't give a *centavo* whether or not a gringo lawman lay dead in the mucky El Paso streets.

Strangely enough, as he got to his feet and walked toward Bernardo's house, he wasn't thinking so much about the death of Jed Martin as he was about the deep blue eyes of Emily Thurlow, Doug Scott's young nurse.

CHAPTER SIX

The hard hand shook Thorp awake. He looked up into the dark face of Bernardo Parillo. *"Es de dia!"* said Bernardo.

Thorp sat up. Light was coming in through the little window.

The Mexican handed him a cigarette and lighted it. "Body of God," he said. "El Paso is swarming with men looking for you! Even here in Juarez, there are hard-eyed men walking up and down the streets eyeing every gringo they see."

Thorp drew in on the cigarette. "I'll pull out," he said. "I don't want to give you any trouble."

Bernardo rubbed his jaw. "It is time I left myself. You are willing to go with me?"

"No. Let me go alone. I don't want to get you mixed up in this."

"Listen, *Querido, amigo!* There is a price on your head! Enough money to make a poor *paisano* well-to-do for the rest of his life. You would not get five miles from here. Dead or alive, they say, and it is easier to kill a man than to try to bring him in alive. They talk of you now like they talked about your brother."

Thorp stood up. Bernardo handed him a pair of

boots. "You must stay here with me until it is dark. We will be warned if anyone comes looking for you. Mother of God! Why did you not kill the marshal?"

"The man was helpless, Bernardo."

The dark eyes hardened. "Then it would have been easier, eh?"

"Yes."

"And you did not do so! Why?"

"I wanted him to have a gun in his hand."

"No dene razón? Have you reason? Do you know what happens now?"

"I don't give a damn!"

Bernardo gripped him by the shirt front. "This Scott, when he is able to get about, will follow you to the ends of the earth. He knows you want to kill him because he killed your brother. Now you have killed one of his best friends. It would have been better to kill Scott and then flee across the river. But *you* have to be a caballero! A man of honor. *Dios en Cielo."*

Thorp sat down and pulled on the excellent boots. "Let's eat," he said quietly.

Bernardo held out his hands, palms upward, and looked imploringly at the ceiling; then, he walked into the other room. In a little while, Thorp could smell the coffee. He grinned.

———

THE NIGHT WAS DARK, with a faint touch of moonlight to the east. Bernardo looked back over his shoulder. "I think we are safe enough now."

There was a scattered collection of adobes ahead of them. "Quatro Jacales," said Bernardo. "I have friends here."

The Mexican dismounted in front of a cantina. They had ridden twenty miles since dusk. Thorp swung down and eased his crotch. He followed Bernardo into the cantina.

The bartender placed a bottle and glasses on the zinc-topped bar. "Good evening, Bernardo," he said.

"They are here, Eusebio?"

The dark eyes flicked at Thorp.

Bernardo placed a hand on Thorp's shoulder. *"compañero,"* he said.

"I will get them then."

Bernardo filled the glasses as Eusebio walked into another room.

Three men walked quietly into the barroom. Thorp glanced at them. Two of them were Mexicans, and from the looks of them, a man wouldn't want to turn his back on them. The third man was an American, wearing a battered Mex hat. His pistol was hung at his left side, butt forward.

"Porfirio Estrella, and Juan Vaca," said Bernardo, indicating the two Mexicans. "This Yanqui is Deuce," he said with a smile.

The two Mexicans nodded. The American eyed Thorp up and down.

"Just a kid, Bernardo," he said with a sly grin.

"He is all right."

Deuce spat. "How do we know?"

"Because I say so!"

"Thorp, his first name or his last name?"

"My first name," said Thorp. "The last name is Barrett."

"Thorp Barrett? Any relation to Travis Barrett?"

"My brother."

The sly eyes flicked up. Deuce reached for the bottle and filled a glass. He tossed the liquor down. "Pretty fancy hogleg you got hanging there."

"It was my brother's gun."

"Was!"

Bernardo stepped in between them. "Travis Barrett is dead," he said quickly.

Deuce spat on the floor. "Him? He was just a tinhorn compared to me. He thought he was pretty fancy with a cutter, but I've killed eleven men, kid."

Bernardo glanced into the fly-specked mirror behind the bar, and there was a warning in his eyes as he looked at Thorp.

Deuce emptied his glass and refilled it. He emptied it again. The three Mexicans watched him. Then he took out his pistol and placed it on the bar. It was pitted and battered, altogether a sorry-looking specimen of a Colt, but there were eleven notches cut into the walnut grips.

Deuce looked at Thorp. "I'll trade you even, gun for gun, kid."

Estrella and Vaca moved back a little. Bernardo wet his lips. "Talk about it some other time, Deuce," he suggested.

"Shut up!"

Bernardo paled a little. His hand brushed the haft of his knife. The bartender had come into the room, and he stood at the end of the bar.

"You hear me, kid?" asked Deuce.

"I hear you, Deuce," said Thorp quietly. Cold sweat was running down his sides.

"Give out then."

"*No.*"

The man turned, and Bernardo stepped hastily backward. Deuce took his gun in his hand. "Give," he said softly.

Then Thorp knew his tactics. His gun was in his hand, ready for action, while Thorp's Colt was still holstered. He had been tricked.

Their eyes met. They could hear the breathing of the other men.

The Deuce made his move, but the flicker in his eyes gave him away. Thorp snapped his left hand up to his hat brim, flipping the hat from his head toward the puffy face of Deuce, and as the hat struck Deuce across the bridge of the nose, Thorp had his Colt out. He crowded close as he fired. The blast of the heavy powder charge drove Deuce back even as the slug struck him in the navel.

Deuce clawed at the edge of the bar with his left hand. His Colt hit the floor. His eyes glazed, and then he fell heavily.

The smoke rifted as the draft blew through the room.

"Los Dulces Nombres," said Porfirio Estrella. He crossed himself swiftly.

Bernardo filled the glasses. "Here," he said quickly. "Drink up and let us ride. Eusebio! Close the door after us and bar it. Get rid of the *bazofa* on the floor." He threw some money onto the bar. His hard eyes met those of the bartender. "You saw nothing. You know nothing. Understand?" Bernardo drew the edge of his hand across his throat.

"Sí, Bernardo," said Eusebio. His eyes were on the money.

The four of them walked to the door when they had finished drinking. Estrella and Vaca walked outside first, looked up and down the road, and then nodded.

They rode south on the Chihuahua Road.

It was full moonlight when they stopped to breathe the horses. Porfirio took a bottle from his saddlebag. "Deuce was fast. But *his* gun was out! The *muchacho* drew and fired before Deuce could pull the trigger. This one is like the *viboras cascabeles!* He strikes like the rattlesnake! What will he be like when he is a man?"

Bernardo shrugged. "He is a man now."

Juan Vaca rolled a cigarette. "Is this the first man you have killed, Thorp?"

"No."

Bernardo took the bottle from Porfirio and raised it to his lips. He drank deeply. He lowered the bottle and handed it to Thorp. "Your brother killed nine, it is said. He started at seventeen. How old are you, *amigo?*"

"Seventeen."

The three Mexicans looked at each other, and there was a little fear in their eyes. Each of them had killed his man, but this boy had slain so quickly and skillfully that it had put the fear into them. What they did not know was that Thorp had never practiced the hat trick before he had killed Deuce. He had heard some of the Barrett Corrida talk about it; that was all. The fear Deuce had instilled in Thorp had been burned out in the swift action which had resulted in the death of the man.

Two men, in two nights, thought Thorp. *Where do I go from here?*

CHAPTER SEVEN

The sun-splashed *plazita* was a good place for a man to stay. The thought was Thorp Barrett's as he lounged beneath the cottonwoods near the spring. Beyond the little town were bronze-red hills with green clouds of trees and brush mantling them. It was a sleepy, out of the way place, where a man could be happy the rest of his days if there wasn't a driving ambition within him.

Thorp eased his back against the tree and rolled a cigarette. Bernardo Parillo, Porfirio Estrella, and some others had ridden to Juarez on some of Bernardo's usual and very profitable business. It was a place Thorp had avoided during the year he had ridden with Bernardo's *corrida*.

Juan Vaca had died with a slug in his back during a fight in the Chisos Mountains. But Bernardo and his men had gotten clear of the *rurales* and had made a handsome profit on the cattle they had driven across the Rio Grande.

Others of Thorp's temporary *compañeros* had died in the way of their kind. Some of them had been killed in cantina brawls; others had died under the bullets of the *rurales;* two of them had been caught by Yaquis, and it wasn't pleasant to think of what Bernardo and his men had found left of them.

The *plazita* seemed a long way from the violence Thorp had become accustomed to since he had left home. Now that seemed so long ago, although it had only been two years.

He had seen the bloody Rio Grande from El Paso Del Norte clear down the three hundred miles to the Big Bend country. It was a land of canyons, mountains, and mesas stippled with chino grass, tornillo brush, grease-wood, and cactus. It was a vast silent land usually haunted only by javelinas, deer, panthers, and bears. The gun smoke of *rurales* and Texas Rangers had drifted after Bernardo and his *corrida* in forgotten canyons and along unnamed water courses. They had split the brush in wild escapes from posses and had traded slugs with angry ranchers on both sides of the *rio*.

Thorp looked to the north toward the dead mesas of purple lava beyond which lay his own country.

"You are lonely again, Thorp?"

The soft voice, with the quaint pronunciation of his name, came from behind him. He turned quickly, and his hand instinctively dropped to the butt of his Colt.

It was Teresa, standing there with a water olla balanced on one slim hip. She was just a kid, thought Thorp, fifteen, or at the most, sixteen years old, daughter of Orlando Campos, the drunken *alcalde* of the *plazita*.

Thorp shoved back his hat and watched her as she knelt to fill the olla.

"You did not answer me, Thorp," she said.

"I was thinking of my own country," he admitted.

He had been in the *plazita* for two weeks now, recovering from a bout of fever, and the girl had been kind to him. Orlando, in one of his drunken stages of extreme confidence, had signified his willingness to let Thorp have the girl for fifty dollars in gold.

She placed the olla on the bank and turned to face

him, resting her slim hands on the ground behind her. The action brought out the soft line of her young breasts. "Why do you not go back?" she asked.

He shrugged. "I like it here, Teresa."

"For why?"

He took a chance. "Because of you, little one."

Her liquid eyes studied him. The sun glinted from the comb in her thick dark hair and from the crucifix between her breasts, *always* the crucifix. It always bothered Thorp when he made free with the village girls, as though he was doing something sacrilegious.

"Do you mean that?" she asked.

He stood up and flipped away his cigarette. He walked toward her and looked down at her, and she looked up at him with no fear in her eyes. Thorp was more like Travis now. The same height, the same weight, the same catlike stride, and too, the same hardened look in his gray eyes.

"Yes," he said softly.

She stood up and placed her hand on his shoulders. He drew her close and lifted her, for she was almost a foot shorter than he was. For a moment, she clung to him, and then she fought free, snatched up the olla, and darted up the pathway. She turned at the rise and stood there with her breasts heaving. "My father has gone to Tres Montes," she said breathlessly. "He will not be back for several days... and nights." Then she was gone.

Thorp slowly rolled a cigarette.

"Nice work," a dry voice said from the far side of the spring.

It was the second time Thorp had been surprised within a matter of minutes. He whirled, cleared leather, and crouched, weaving a little as his eyes probed into the brush.

"Not bad, son, but you're getting careless." This time the voice seemed to come from a place closer to Thorp.

Thorp wet his lips. "Show yourself, damn you!" he said.

"Don't lose your temper, son. Travis never did."

"Chusco Barnes!"

The grinning little man stepped out of the brush. "Guess a man has to dillydally a little bit, but for God's sake, Thorp, do it at the right time and the right place."

Thorp sheathed his Colt. "This place is like the end of the world. Nothing ever happens here."

Chusco held out his hand, and as Thorp gripped it, he said, "You'd better not bet on that, son. I've got news for you about your *compañeros*."

Thorp looked closely at Chusco. "Yes?"

"Bernardo told me to tell you to pull foot as quick as you got my message."

"Why?"

Chusco rubbed his jaw and looked away. "The *rurales* trapped him and his boys at Zaragoza. I had a chance to talk to him before they stood him up against a wall and shot him."

"Good God!"

"I came down here on business. I'm heading north but not to Juarez. The *rurales* are getting too rough, so I'm heading northwest to cross the border into Arizona. Aim to hit Globe."

"Isobel?"

Chusco quickly doffed his dusty steeple hat. "Yes," he said reverently.

Thorp grinned. "An old goat like you."

Chusco looked pained. "She never mentioned that, Kid."

"The name is Thorp!"

"Yeh... Thorp!" Chusco put on his hat. "Bernardo suggested I find you, warn you, then take you with me up north."

"No."

"Why not?"

"I'm not ready to go. When I am, I figure on finding Doug Scott."

"Won't be easy. They say he left the government job he had. Crippled from that broken thigh your brother gave him."

"Where is he?"

"Quien sabe?"

"Let's get on the trail then, Thorp. I'm getting too itchy in this country. Maybe they got a place for my peculiar talents, as they say, up in Arizona."

Thorp looked toward the *plazita,* and the thought of Teresa was strong in him. "Later, maybe," he said quietly.

"Damn it, *hombre!* You got no time to be sitting around here like a bitch in heat!"

"You always did talk too much."

Chusco spat. He padded into the brush and then led forth his horse and burro. "Mind me when I say it was ten days ago when they wiped out Bernardo and his boys. I got down to Chihuahua, then come north again, figuring I'd find you here. Maybe some of Bernardo's boys talked. Maybe the rurales know you're here. If they do, they won't be missing long, Thorp."

"I'll take that chance."

Chusco studied him. "Getting to be quite the he-coon, ain't you?"

"I get by."

Chusco waved a hand in anger. "I'll get some food in the *plaza.* Hire a *muchacho* to keep an eye on the road for me. I aim to leave here after dark and keep moving until I hit the Rio Escondido."

"Nice trip."

Chusco spat.

Thorp walked to the burro and took the guitar from its back. He fiddled with it.

"Take it easy!" snapped Chusco.

Thorp grinned. He tuned it; then softly began to play a little *verso* he had learned from Juan Vaca.

"Not bad," admitted Chusco.

"Let me borrow it for tonight," said Thorp.

"You sure you're going to stay?"

Thorp winked. "For a while, *amigo.*"

"Damned idjit!"

The smuggler led his animals up the pathway. The sun was low over the Sierra Madres. Thorp rolled another cigarette and looked to the northeast. Bernardo had been his *amigo*. His last thought had been to warn Thorp. It came to all of them. It was the second time Thorp had been the last survivor of an outlaw *corrida,* both of them good in their time.

———

THE MOON WAS low in the eastern sky over the Sierra Del Nido. The adobe of Orlando Campos was a good two hundred yards from the rest of the town. In the old days, there had been many houses in between the adobe of the *alcalde* and that of the remaining houses, but Apache raids, *bandido* forays, and time had leveled most of them to low humps in the greasewood. Now and then, a foot trod on earthenware or kicked a bleached bone out of the way.

Thorp paused near the adobe. It was dark. His bay horse was tethered in a hollow fifty yards away. It was a lesson he had learned from Bernardo. The night was quiet. Chusco Barnes had spent most of the evening in the cantina and was there even now, but he had also picketed his animals out in the brush beyond the town.

Thorp looked to the east. There had been no dust on the road all evening. Chusco's muchacho was still out there, squatting in the brush, dreaming of the riches he would buy with the silver Chusco had promised him.

Thorp padded to the rear of the house and tapped on the door. There was no answer. He walked to the side of the house. Teresa's room was there, with a low courtyard, once a little haven of peace and beauty, with flowers and shade trees, but now a dusty, trampled litter, beyond the shuttered window.

Thorp pushed aside the sagging gate and walked to the window. He tapped on it, but the house seemed as silent as the grave. Thorp shoved back his hat. He took the guitar from its sling, grinning a little at the silliness of the whole business, then began to play softly.

It seemed a long time before one of the shutters swung open, and he could see her there in the dimness, dressed in white. Thorp pretended he did not see her as he sang, softly and well, hoping the sound would not reach the *plazita*. Even if it did, it really didn't matter. Everyone in town knew how Orlando Campos had offered his girl to the tall young gringo for gold.

He stopped playing and walked toward the window.

"It is late," she said shyly.

"The moon is just up."

"I am not dressed to come outside."

"Then I will come in."

"No. What would people say?"

He leaned against the side of the deep window and smiled at her. He could see the contrast her dark hair made against the white of her gown.

"It is said you will leave soon, Thorp."

"Who knows? I can't stay here forever."

"Why not?"

He shrugged. "I am a gringo. What would I do here?"

"There is good land. Land for farming and grazing."

"It's not my line of work, Teresa."

She studied him in the dimness. "What is?"

"*Quien sabe?*"

He came closer to her, and she retreated a little. He placed a long leg over the window ledge and stepped into the dark room. The aura of perfume and candle grease hung in the air.

She stood near the wide bed, a slim figure in white,

with her long hair hanging down her back, and he knew now why she had been so hesitant in coming outside. She wore her thin nightdress.

He placed the guitar on a chair and unbuckled his gun belt.

"Please, Thorp," she said quickly. "My father might return."

"You know he won't!"

"Perhaps he will."

He grinned. "Supposing he did?"

"What do you mean?"

"You know, *mi vida.*"

She stepped back a little, and her hand went to her throat. "Why did you not agree?"

"I don't like to buy my women."

"You have bought them before?"

He grinned again. "In a way... yes."

He walked to her and drew her close, feeling her soft warmth beneath the filmy gown. He kissed her and felt her hands go about his neck. She looked up into his face. "When will we be married?" she asked.

"Soon," he said. His hands reached out, and she drew back.

"Go now," she said.

"Are you joking, *querida?*"

She pulled away from him, and the backs of her legs met the edge of the bed, and then she was on her back with him bending over her. She looked up at him, and there was no fear in her dark eyes. Then he noticed the wetness on her cheeks. "What is it, *mi chula?*" he asked.

"Please go, *mi vida.*"

He stared at her. Her warm body was there for the taking. She had allowed him in when she wore nothing but her nightdress after assuring him that very afternoon that her father would be gone.

The wind crept into the room and dried the perspiration on his lean face. Suddenly he thought of Orlando

Campos, with his damned goat's face and his perpetual drunken leer. He was so different from the daughter he had somehow bred.

He looked down at her. She was all mixed up, wanting him to come, leading him on, and then pulling a typical feminine turnabout. Thorp suddenly raised his head.

"What is it, Thorp?"

A cold shaft of thought lanced through his rising passion. He turned to look toward the door.

"Thorp?" she cried. She clung to him, wanting him now, with all her soul and body.

He stood up and snatched his gun belt from the chair, swinging it about his lean hips with practiced ease, buckling it and settling it.

She was behind him, trying to imprison him with her slender arms. He thrust her from him, feeling her wince as hard hands met soft flesh.

He turned toward the window, and then he heard the muttering of voices outside the door. He cleared the window and stood in the cold moonlight. Something moved in the dusty shrubbery, and he saw a steeple hat rising. The moon shone dully on the metal of a rifle.

The door burst open. "Where is he?" yelled Orlando Campos.

Thorp ran for the wall. The man in the shrubbery raised his rifle, but the Colt was out and flaming, and the man never knew what hit him.

The girl screamed, and Thorp turned to see her just outside the window, fighting with her little strength to hold back two men. "Run, *mi vidal*," she screamed.

A gun flamed close to the girl, and she went down. Thorp swung over the wall, glanced back, and saw the red stain spreading on the white gown, just below her breasts. He turned and dropped into the yard again. Two men charged him.

He went into a crouch, right elbow in the hollow above the right hip bone, lower arm extended, with the

Colt even with his line of vision, and he did not seem to sight as he fired twice. Smoke rifted in the yard. One man went down with a sobbing cry while the other ran forward with odd little dancing steps to fall heavily at Thorp's feet.

Thorp started for the girl, then turned and swung up and over the wall. As he hit the ground, a rifle spat from the greasewood, and a sledge seemed to smash hard against his right shoulder, spinning him about. He did the border shift, feeling the butt of the Colt smack into his left hand, and he emptied the heavy weapon into the yelling Mexican who stood up in the greasewood.

Then Thorp ran, staggering like a drunk, with the hot blood flowing down his side and his belly and the fires of hell beginning to rage in his throat.

The town was alert. Men yelled, and doors banged. Thorp reached his bay. It shied and blew at the odor of blood, but he managed to get into the saddle and ride to the north.

A man appeared in the brush, running like a deer. Thorp raised his empty pistol.

"Thorp!" the man yelled. It was Chusco.

"I'm hit, *amigo!*"

There was a crackling of gunfire near the Campos' adobe. Chusco came to Thorp and looked up into his pale face. "Jesus," he said. He took the reins and led the bay to the hollow where he kept his own animals.

Two Mexicans ran toward them. Thorp cursed. He was helpless, and Chusco was worse than useless in a fight.

Chusco slapped the bay on the rump and turned to face the two men. He drew his Colt and fired from waist level, and the first man went down. The revolver misfired, and the second Mexican raised a large-bored *escopeta.*

The knife seemed to flash from nowhere. It struck the Mexican in the throat. He gagged and went down.

Chusco stepped in close, whipped the knife from the dying man's throat, wiped the blade clean on the dirty *pantalones,* then sheathed the blade.

Without a word, he raced to his animals, freed them, mounted the sorrel, and led the burro toward Thorp. "Can you ride?" asked Chusco.

Thorp grinned. "I'll have to, or they'll make a *capon* out of me if they catch me.

The little man led the way, riding swiftly, leading the burro and Thorp's bay, and as he rode, he cursed in a fluent stream of English, Spanish and Indian.

The moon was up high, and it silvered the slopes they traversed. Far behind them, they could see yellow lights in the aroused *plazita.*

"There's hell to pay and no pitch hot," said Chusco Barnes.

"Rurales?" asked Thorp. He knew those hard-riding straight-shooting lawmen, many of whom were pardoned criminals who had taken to a life of upholding the law as well as they had once been known for breaking the law.

They'd track him down to the gates of hell if they had to and then charge hell with a bucket of water to get a prisoner.

"No," said Chusco, "and lucky for you, they ain't!" Campos rigged the deal. Rounded up some of the local hard cases to try and get you and turn you over to the *rurales* for a reward. Used Teresa as bait, and did it work? Ask yourself, *amigo,* just ask yourself."

There was sickness within Thorp Barrett, and not all of it came from the piece of lead in his shoulder. He looked back. Perhaps she *had* been the lure, but in the end, she had tried to help him.

He looked ahead. Nothing but mountains and Apache, with their kin the Yaquis. But there was no going back. He knew he was through in Mexico as he had once been through in Texas. He began to feel as he knew his brother must have felt. He was on a one-way trail and at the end of it was the law, in one form or another. Texas Rangers, US marshals, sheriffs, town marshals, and *rurales.* They'd get him. He knew it as well as he knew he had a bullet in his shoulder. There was one thing he meant to do before they got him, and that was to find Doug Scott and kill him.

CHAPTER EIGHT

He was back in the drab, walled yard of the old adobe back of the Sierra Vieja in that tense moment before the torch sailed over the wall to reveal Travis Barrett, catfooting it toward the arroyo. The lefthanded Colt rapped, and it seemed as though the one shot triggered half a dozen guns along the wall top. Travis leaned forward as though facing a strong wind, and the dust puffed from his clothing as the heavy slugs slammed home into his body.

Then it was the wounded marshal again, down on one knee, with his Winchester in his hands, firing shot after shot at Travis Barrett, who lay there grinning even as he died.

"Travis!" yelled Thorp Barrett.

A hard hand crushed down on Thorp's mouth. He opened his eyes and looked up into the shadowy face of Chusco Barnes.

"God, son," breathed Chusco, "have silent nightmares."

The pain throbbed through Thorp's right shoulder again, and the agony of it reminded him of where he was. Somewhere along the Rio Escondido, in the Sierra Vallecillos, with the Apache prowling through the jumbled hills for the two white men they had seen late on the afternoon of the day before.

They were still in darkness, and as they listened, with the drum-thudding of their hearts interfering with their hearing, it seemed as though another silent presence moved in with them and squatted down near the entrance of the cave to wait patiently until both men were under his control, and his name was Fear.

Chusco moved softly, bellying toward the cave entrance. Thorp dropped his left hand down to the hard, reassuring butt of his brother's Colt.

Chusco took off his hat and squirmed between the rocks. He squinted his eyes and looked out into the darkness, and it seemed to him that the night was peopled with unseen beings created from his racing imagination.

Thorp felt the warm blood run down his right side. It seemed to ease the battering pain.

Thorp wet his dry lips. They had one canteen between them, and it was only half full. He knew well enough that Chusco Barnes had given up his share more than once to try and ease the raging thirst in Thorp.

Chusco had picketed the two horses and the burro a good half a mile from the cave in the hope that the Apache would not find them. If they did well, it was almost a hundred miles to the border, and a man in good condition, on foot, *might* make it if luck was with him.

Something moved beyond the cave entrance. Thorp raised his left hand, and his thumb rested on the hammer spur of the Colt. It moved again, and the Colt hammer snicked back.

"Thorp?" It was Chusco's hoarse voice.

Thorp let down the hammer.

Chusco crawled into the cave. He looked back over his shoulder. "Quiet," he said. "Nothing out there but the wind rustling the brush. Once more, you get one of them nightmares, boy, and I'll have to gag you."

"It's the fever, Chusco."

"Yen," said Chusco dryly. "The fever that damned brother of yours left with you."

Thorp bit his lip. Chusco had done more than his share.

The little man squatted beside Thorp. "Far as I know, they ain't found the animals. We got hardly enough water for another day. But, in order to get beyond the, *no* into safer country, we've got to get out of here within the next five or six hours, ride like mad until just before dawn and then hole up."

"So?"

Thorp could feel the hard green eyes on him as though Chusco was plain to see.

"There's one of two things we can do, *amigo mio,* either we ride with you carrying that slug in your shoulder, or I cut it out, here and now."

The unseen presence seemed to move closer to the two silent men.

Thorp closed his eyes. His shoulder was a raging hell again. Riding that way would be pure agony, and he might become delirious and begin shouting and yelling. If the slug was removed by the untrained hands of Chusco Barnes, the man might do more damage than good, and even so, if he succeeded, there was still that torturous ride through the blazing hill country with hardly enough water to wet a geranium. Either way....

"Well, *amigo?*" asked Chusco quietly.

Thorp eased his shoulder. "There's one other thing you can do, Chusco."

"So?"

"Pull foot out of here and leave me be."

Chusco stood up, and his head almost touched the rough roof of the cave. He looked down at Thorp. "Which do we do? Cut or ride?"

It would have been easy for Chusco.

Pull out and leave Thorp to his death. No one would be the wiser. Thorp knew well enough that Chusco was no humanitarian. The little man was as hard as the country in which he had lived most of his life. Thorp had doubted the little man's ability until he had seen him face those two Mexicans the night they had trailed Thorp from the *plazita.* In a matter of seconds, both of them had died, hardly knowing what and who had killed them.

"We cut," said Chusco with an air of finality.

"No light, Chusco."

"The cave goes deep, and there are a few turns in it. I can shield the light with a blanket. Can't make a fire. Those bastards would smell it like a beagle smells out a rabbit. I can sterilize the knife with *aguardiente,* although I hate the thought of wasting good likker."

Thorp leaned back against the side of the cave. In all his time riding with the Barrett Corrida and with the Parillo's bunch, he had never been wounded. He had been cut a little, and once he had been creased, but this was the first time metal had been driven into him seeking for his life.

Chusco bustled about. In time he arranged his operating room around a bend in the cave, carefully shielding the candlelight with blankets, a shirt, and several gaudy bandanas.

Thorp was helped to the blankets Chusco had spread on a fairly level stretch of the cave floor. He lay flat on his back, listening to the *wheet-wheet wheet* of steel against stone as Chusco honed his *cuchillo.* The cave was hot, and the aura of sweaty clothing hung in it. Thorp felt nausea in his belly and the green bile taste in his throat. None of this type of experience had been told to him by Travis. Nor had Travis ever mentioned more than casually the sort of end that would come to the men of the Barrett Corrida. Travis had been a curious amalgamation of the romanticist and the practical, hard-headed killer. Now he lay in a filthy blanket beside the forgotten adobe in the gaunt shadows of the Sierra Vieja, with slugs of misshapen lead still in his rotting body and his once handsome face battered into something inhuman by the slugs from Doug Scott's Winchester.

"Ready?" asked Chusco.

"As much as I ever will be."

"Here."

Thorp took the bottle and drank deeply. For a moment, his stomach rebelled, and he thought he'd spew the good *aguardiente* all over Chusco, but he kept it under control and looked up at Chusco with a wan smile on his face.

"Hog," said Chusco as he took the bottle and gauged the contents of it against the light.

Thorp felt his senses waver, lift and reel as the liquor took hold. He hardly noticed Chusco kneeling beside him with the crude implements with which he meant to extract the bullet.

Thorp looked away as he felt Chusco remove the blood-stained bandage. The cloth stuck a little, and he winced in pain. He felt naked to the world in the guttering yellow candlelight as he waited for Chusco to cut.

The touch of the knife made him tauten his muscles and nerves.

"Easy, Kid," said Chusco.

Something warm dropped on Thorp's neck, and he realized it was Chusco's sweat. Which one of them would sweat the most within the next ten or fifteen minutes? It took seconds for the steel to probe down in the swollen flesh about the puckered mouth of the bullet hole.

He could see Teresa standing there in the moonlight with the shape of her legs revealed against the sheer material of her thin gown and her brown breasts swinging free with the crucifix glinting in the cold light of the moon. *Always the crucifix.*

"Ah... Jesus..." said Thorp softly.

"Easy, Kid."

"Damn you! The name is Thorp."

"You ain't in no condition to correct me, brother."

The hot blood was flowing now as the steel went deeper and deeper. Was there no end to it? It seemed as though the knife tip was probing into his belly by now. Then it touched something, whether bone or lead, he never knew because the grating agony of it finally made him lose his senses...

It was the girl in the hotel. Her dark blue eyes studied him through a smoky veil. What was her name? Ethel? Evelyn? "Emily!" he said loudly.

The caustic voice came from close to his right ear. "Emily? Before God, *amigo,* I thought it was Teresa."

Thorp opened his eyes. The candlelight danced on the rough roof of the cave, plunging parts of it into shadow while other parts were illuminated, only to change again and again until it seemed as though he was looking into a stampeding kaleidoscope.

"Look," said Chusco.

Thorp turned. The little man held a misshapen chunk of something on the tip of his knife, and the knife glittered redly in the candlelight. "Beauty, ain't it?"

"Yeh..."

Chusco pursed his lips. ".56/50," he said. "Spencer, maybe. They got a wallop."

"I know."

Chusco grinned. "Want it?"

Thorp shook his head.

The slug thudded against the floor.

The fresh bandage was tight and warm, warm with the fresh flow of blood.

Chusco handed him the bottle, and Thorp drank deeply.

"How you feel, Thorp?"

Thorp tried to focus his eyes. "Let's ride, amigo," he said weakly.

Chusco nodded. He cleared the materials from his improvised operating room after he extinguished the

candle. In a little while, he was back, and he helped
Thorp to the mouth of the cave. He turned Thorp's gun
belt so that the holster was at his left side, with Colt butt
forward for a twist draw with his left hand. It wasn't
good, but it was better than standing defenselessly in the
open with a gaggle of Apache coming down on him with
liquid hell in their brown eyes.

They went down the loose talus slope like a pair of
ballet dancers practicing intricate glissades, and their
eyes constantly turned from side to side to look toward
the brush on each side of them, half expecting to see the
Apache rise from the brush and close in on them before
they had a chance to draw and fire.

The bottom of the canyon was deep in shadow. The
cold sweat dripped from their faces as they stood there
with their arms about each other's shoulders.

Then they went on, feeling each step, and each step
was a bloody agony to Thorp Barrett.

When they reached the animals, they waited a long
time with their guns in their hands, probing the night
with their eyes.

"I'll get the gear," said Chusco.

Thorp leaned against his horse. "Jesus," he said.

"I've got to get the water, Kid."

Thorp did not answer.

The little man faded into the darkness like a shadow
itself.

Thorp swayed drunkenly. His Colt was loose in his
left hand, and he knew he didn't have the strength to
raise and fire it. The blood was seeping gradually down
his side, and the wound throbbed like the summer
thunder in the hills.

Chusco whistled softly. He came close on silent feet
and fastened the gear to his saddle. He turned and gave
Thorp a leg up into the saddle. Thorp looked down at the
wizened face of his friend. "Too much noise to ride," he
managed to say.

"Gawd damn!" snapped Chusco. "I know! But I can't lead two hosses, a burro and a jackass all at once!"

Thorp couldn't help but grin. "Well, pardon me all to hell," he said.

They rode to the north, toward the meeting place of the Rio Escondido and the Rio de Bavispe, through a suburb of hell.

The wind shifted and brought with it the warm odor of some spice-odored brush.

Thorp's head sagged a little, and his hands gripped the pommel.

"Think of Emily," suggested Chusco.

Thorp shook his head. She had almost caused him to be trapped in the crowded streets of El Paso, and a man had died because of it.

"Think of Teresa," said Chusco.

Thorp shook his head. Something had been torn from his soul that night back in the plazita when Teresa had first betrayed him and then had died for him.

"That leaves Isobel," said Chusco. He wet his thin lips and looked up at the dark hills.

Thorp nodded.

"Nothing suggestive," said Chusco.

"No."

"Always refer to Isobel as a lady, son, and we'll get along."

"I will, Chusco."

The tone of his voice seemed far away. Chusco looked quickly at him.

Thorp rode straight-backed in the saddle, and the knuckles of his big hands were white from the pressure with which he gripped the pommel. But his eyes were wide, and yet it seemed as though he did not see the dim trail ahead of them.

Chusco shook his head. He looked behind them. There was no sign of life. He looked at Thorp again. He had seen men ride that way before until they had died in the saddle. There was nothing else to do but ride, and if death chose to close upon them, whether by using the hands of the Apache or by draining the lifeblood from the Kid drop by drop, there was nothing Chusco Barnes could do to stop it.

CHAPTER NINE

Thorp Barrett stood in the dry wash, which ran behind the old adobe. The sun glittered on the six tin cans which he had placed on a sagging fence rail the height of a man's belly. He drew the last of the smoke from his cigarette, then flipped it to one side. For a few seconds, he stood there, and then, seemingly at a silent command, his left hand shot down to the butt of his Colt, and it cleared leather and roared into action.

The six shattering reports echoed along the wash, and seconds later, the tin cans struck the gravelly bottom of the wash, each of them neatly punctured by a soft-nosed forty-four.

He stood there, looking through the wreathing smoke, and it seemed as though Travis Barrett had come back from the shadows to walk the dry earth of the Southwest once more.

Thorp opened the loading gate of the engraved Colt with his thumb and began to feed cartridges into the hot cylinder from the loops on his cartridge belt. There seemed to be a little stiffness in his right shoulder as he moved.

There was an empty holster at his right side, low, tied down to his thigh. When the Colt was reloaded, he slid it into the formed leather sheath and settled it. He rolled a cigarette and lighted it, and his eyes were on the scattered tin cans. He walked to them and gathered them up, placing them on the fence rail. He walked back to his firing position.

The sun was low over the mountains. His eyes were shaded by the black hat, but the nose and the mouth could be seen, and the lips were tightly drawn.

The cigarette was flipped away. The silent command came again, and the Colt leaped into the right hand, but the action was fractions of a second slower. The Colt shook out its load, and once more, the echoes drifted along the dusty wash. When the smoke cleared, four of the tin cans had been driven from the fence, while two of them still sat there, glinting in the sun.

Thorp reloaded the Colt and slid it into the left-hand sheath. He walked partway up the side of the draw, and then suddenly, from an awkward angle, he drew and fired twice, and the two tin cans clattered along the wash.

There was dust on the road as he stopped in front of the adobe. He stepped into the house and took a Winchester from behind the door, levering a round into the chamber.

He stood within the doorway, watching the dust as it gained in volume and height.

A man appeared, riding a blocky sorrel. His steeple hat seemed to shine in the sun from the ornate, coin silver ornaments which encrusted it.

Thorp grinned. He took a bottle from a cabinet and placed it on the table with two glasses.

The rider drew up in a cloud of dust. "Time to move on, Thorp!" he yelled.

"Why, Chusco?"

The man looked back over his shoulder. "I cut up a man in Benson."

Thorp wasted no time. The two men worked swiftly, snatching up their few belongings. Chusco saddled

Thorp's bay. Neither of them spoke. There was no need to speak. Evidently, there was hell to pay and no pitch hot.

They were on their horses, with saddle and cantle packs in place, before Thorp spoke. "Which way, Chusco?"

The little man wet his lips. He took the bottle from inside his jacket and drank deeply. "Tombstone?"

"They'll be looking for you there."

"Tucson?"

"Fair enough... for a start."

Chusco suddenly grinned. "It's either there or Yuma, and I mean the part of Yuma on the hill... the pen."

They cut down the wash, turned behind a lone hill, rode hard along a rocky flat, then plunged into the thick brush along a wide dry wash.

They eased the horses when they were undercover.

"What started it this time, Chusco?" asked Thorp.

"He cheated."

"You never do."

Chusco grinned.

"How bad was it, Chusco?"

The little man looked back over his shoulder. "Don't see no dust," he said.

"How bad was it?"

"Forget it."

The hard right hand closed on Chusco's left wrist. "You heard me, *amigo!*

Chusco swallowed a little. "Seems to me you got no right to get waspy, Thorp."

Thorp released his grip. "You killed him then?"

Chusco nodded.

"Damn you to everlasting hell!"

"Don't talk that way to me!"

The look in Thorp's eyes was too much for Chusco. It had been that way for the past three months, ever since Thorp had begun to exercise his crippled shoulder. In the

past year, they had drifted from Nogales to Tucson and
Tucson to Gila Bend. From Gila Bend to Yuma, thence
back to Tucson again. Every week the Kid had become
more bitter. *Kid!* He was as much like Travis as Travis had
been like himself. It was the bad shoulder that plagued
him, for he wouldn't continue his search for Marshal
Doug Scott until his shooting hand was as good as it
ever was.

Chusco felt inside his jacket and brought out a wad of
greenbacks. "They's enough here for a few more months
of living high on the hog, Thorp," he said.

"With blood on it."

Chusco reined in short, and this time his eyes were as
hard as emeralds. "Damn *you* to everlasting hell," he said
softly. "Sitting on your rump back there in the 'dobe
while I forage for greenbacks. You ain't done a lick of
work in months whilst you baby that bad wing of yours.
Nothing but eat, drink, practice fancy draws and burn up
a few hundred dollars' worth of cartridges. Gawd
dammit! I feel like I been keeping a woman who's too
damned lazy to wash a pot or make a bed!"

They eyed each other.

Thorp shoved back his hat. "You know well enough I
won't stand for any more trouble. You keep up this way,
and they'll run us out of Arizona. I can't go to Texas,
New Mexico, or Chihuahua. If this job of yours runs us
out of Arizona as well, it'll take me years before I can
find Scott."

Chusco drew rein and hooked his right leg about the
pommel of his Mex saddle. "You listen to me, Thorp. It's
been two years since Travis was killed. You're still young
enough and smart enough to make something out of
yourself."

"Like you?"

There was hardly a movement of the wrinkled face,
but Thorp knew he had hit home. He was instantly sorry
for what he had said. Without Chusco's help, he would

have been shot to tatters back in the *plazita* in Chihuahua, or his bones would be whitening in that lost cave in the Sierra Vallecillos. Then too, Chusco had practically supported Thorp, in whatever way he could, legally or illegally in the long year which had just passed. And in all that time, Thorp, because of his bitterness at being incapacitated by his wound, had given the tough little boot nothing but trouble.

Chusco slowly dropped his leg from the pommel and felt for the stirrup with his foot. "We'd best pull foot," he said.

It wasn't in Thorp to apologize. Not right now anyway. He watched Chusco ride on, hunched in his preposterous saddle. The little man did not look back.

Thorp touched the bay with his heels and followed Chusco. He looked back over his shoulder. Dust was raveled against the sky to the southeast. Whoever was chasing Chusco was heading the wrong way.

———

THE SUN WAS DYING in the west in a magnificent display of intermingled rose and gold when Chusco drew rein at the juncture of two roads. He had been riding fifty yards ahead of Thorp all afternoon.

He did not look back as Thorp approached and drew rein.

Thorp eyed the two roads. One led almost due north to meet the Tucson road some twenty-five miles away. The other trended southwest through the foothills of the Santa Rita's toward the Santa Cruz River, about thirty miles off.

Thorp reached for the makings and slowly rolled a cigarette. He snapped a match on his thumbnail and lighted the cigarette.

"Which way?" asked Chusco.

Thorp drew in on the smoke. The older man was

heading for more trouble. In the past year, Chusco had become irascible and waspy, picking fights, careless of the outcome. It wouldn't be long before the whole territory would be alerted to look for him if they weren't looking for him right at that very moment.

"Well?" asked the little man. He bent his head sideways and eyed Thorp speculatively, like a bird eyeing a fat worm.

"Which way do you want to go, Chusco?"

Chusco jerked a thumb. "North."

"Bueno!"

"Let's ride then. I got a hankering to see Isobel."

Thorp shook his head. "Not together, Chusco."

"Then I'll ride south with you."

"No."

The sun was gone now, and the fanged mountains stood etched against the sunset sky. A cold wind blew up out of nowhere, and scattered dust and brush along the flats.

"What you mean?" asked Chusco softly.

"You go your way; I'll go mine."

"So it's come to that?"

"It has."

It wasn't in Chusco to soften now or to tell Thorp what he had done for him. The little man knew well enough what had happened, yet he had tried many times to straighten out Thorp Barrett. But he knew now he had done nothing more than to help Thorp along the trail he had picked for himself.

Chusco spat. "Stay away from Scott," he said.

Thorp touched his right shoulder. "I'll go my own way, Chusco."

"Yeh... you will," Chusco shifted. "How you fixed for *dinero?"*

"I've got enough."

Chusco scratched his lean jaws. He jerked his chin once. "So long, Kid."

"So long, Chusco."

Thorp kneed the bay away from the little man. He touched the bay with his heels and started down the road.

"Thorp!"

Thorp turned in his saddle. Chusco beckoned to him. "It's no use, Chusco," said Thorp.

The little man reached and took his cased guitar from where it was slung from the cantle pack. "Parting gift," he said. "Isobel never did like my playing anyways."

Thorp rode back and took the guitar. "Why?" he asked.

Chusco grinned. "What the hell else you know how to do except steal cows and shoot straight?"

Thorp passed a hand along the case. The guitar was a good one. Chusco had stolen it from a drunken Mexican in Naco.

"Go on, Kid." Chusco spurred his horse forward. He did not look back.

Thorp attached the case to his cantle pack. He rode south.

A half a mile north, Chusco reined in his horse. He could just about see Thorp moving south. Chusco sat there until the darkness came, as though expecting to see Thorp, but there was nothing but the sighing of the wind through the brush.

CHAPTER TEN

The late fall rain was slanting down on Wickenburg, and the Hassayampa was making noises like a real big river. The rain darkened the warped wood of the false-fronted buildings and stained the sagging adobes. Now and then, a slickered horseman splashed his way along Center Street, in a hurry to get into a warm and dry saloon.

The barroom near the stage station was quiet except for the soft tones of the Mex guitar being played by the lean young man who sat in a chair tilted back against the rear wall of the saloon. A full whisky glass stood on the table beside him, and there was a bottle next to the glass.

The bartender stood at the streaked front window, looking out toward Tegner Street.

A drummer carefully brushed the nap on his derby hat. "When does that stage get in?" he asked.

The bartender shrugged. "Usually, it's half an hour to an hour late. With this rain, it may be later than that."

"Will it go on this afternoon?"

"*Quién sabe?* It'd be better if it stayed here until morning. Otherwise, you might have to spend the night at a swing station, and that ain't exactly like staying at the Hotel Astor, mister."

The drummer turned irritably. "Can't you play anything but those mournful Mex tunes, you?"

Thorp Barrett raised his head. "I like them," he said quietly.

The drummer laughed. "Listen to him! You get paid for playing, don't you?"

"Sometimes."

The drummer took a silver eagle from his pocket and threw it at Thorp. Thorp picked it out of the air with his left hand.

"Play something else. Anything else!" snapped the drummer.

The bartender turned and rested his elbows on the bar. "Take it easy, mister," he said.

"Why? Bad enough I've got to be stuck in this hole without having to listen to that damned Mex stuff."

"I said to take it easy!"

The man filled his glass and downed it. His face was a little flushed. "You Westerners think you're God Almighty," he said. "Got to act polite to a damned guitar-picking bum."

The heels hit the floor. Thorp Barrett rested his lean hands atop the guitar.

"Ho, Jesus," said the bartender softly.

The drummer glanced quickly at Thorp. He could see there was no gun holstered at the young man's side. "I paid you to play," he said quickly. He was a big man, rather soft in the paunch, but still a big man with muscles. The young man didn't look as though he'd want trouble. Besides, if he was really a man, he wouldn't be sitting in a third-rate saloon picking out uncertain Mex tunes on a guitar.

For a moment, Thorp eyed the man; then, he looked at the bartender. The bartender jerked a thumb at the drummer. "He's a little nervous, Kid," he said.

"Thorp!"

"Thorp then!"

Thorp rested the chair back against the wall. For a few seconds, he looked at the drummer, and then he began to play. The bartender grinned.

"What's that tune?" asked the drummer.

"*What Was Your Name In The States?*"

The drummer flushed.

"Lay off him," said the bartender.

The door swung open, and a short, bench-legged cowpoke came in. He swung his hat, scattering the raindrops from it. "Howdy, Virg," he said to the bartender. "Seen the stage up the road. Got a weak thorough brace. Jim is tightening it with some Mormon buckskin. Says he'll be in 'bout half an hour from now. Howdy, Thorp!"

Thorp nodded. "Shorty," he said.

"Will the stage go on tonight?" asked the drummer.

Shorty squinted wisely. "Doubt it, mister."

"Damn!"

Shorty grinned. "Jim asked me to ask you if you could feed the passengers, Virg."

Virg flickered a heavy hand toward the free lunch. "All I got."

Thorp reached for his drink and downed it. For two weeks now, he had been thinking of leaving Wickenburg. It had been over a year since he had left Chusco Barnes on the Tucson Road. In that time, he had drifted to Nogales, thence to Tucson, but he had not seen nor heard about Chusco being there. Thorp had gone up to Prescott and driven a freight wagon from Prescott to Flagstaff. From there, he had drifted west to Kingman and then down the Colorado to Yuma. He had tried his hand at swinging a double-jack, had pearl-dived in a greasy spoon, swamped in a saloon, and had ended up by playing his way through another dozen saloons and Mex cantinas.

Shorty took his glass to the table near Thorp, kicked a chair between his legs, and then sat down with his arms resting on the chair back. "How's it go, Thorp?"

"Slow."

Shorty looked back over his shoulder. "Doug Scott is in Globe," he said softly.

The eyes hardly flickered. "Thanks, Shorty."

Shorty downed his drink and then refilled his glass from Thorp's bottle. "You still aim to go there?"

"Yes."

"You're loco!"

Thorp began to play *Old Rosin the Beau.*

Shorty hitched his chair a little closer. "You ain't fooling me, Thorp. You ain't a saloon musician no more than I'm a cowpoke working for a few measly bucks and found a month. I still think you ought to throw in with me. I got big ideas, Thorp."

"You sure have."

"I can get plenty of good boys to ride along with me. Trouble is they ain't brains like you have, Kid."

"Thorp!"

"Dammit, Thorp then!"

Thorp rubbed his jaw. He was sick of Wickenburg, of the saloon, of guitar-playing, and of Shorty's grandiose schemes to make a killing and then pull out for Mexico or South America to live like kings thereafter.

"How about it, Thorp?"

Thorp looked toward the streaked window at the front of the saloon. He had been lonely ever since he had pulled away from Chusco Barnes and Shorty Leclerc was a poor substitute.

"You want my brains or my guns, Shorty?" asked Thorp.

"Both!"

Thorp shook his head. "I've got a job to do," he said.

"Forget Scott."

"I can't."

Shorty's face darkened. "Listen! I been fooling around with you for weeks. I got a job lined up. A real heist! I need you, and you'd better pitch in with me."

Thorp eyed the short man. "What are you driving at?"

"I know you killed that soldier at Kingman this spring."

Thorp stopped playing.

Shorty leaned closer. "You got drunk one night and talked about it, Kid."

"The man was a deserter. On the run for murdering his sergeant."

"That don't cut no ice."

"He drew on me, Shorty."

"Who was there to see who drew first on who?"

"I'm telling you how it was."

Shorty emptied his glass and refilled it. "I was in Ehrenburg two days ago. They got a wanted poster out for you. It don't say anything about you shooting in self-defense. It just says you're wanted for *murder,* Kid."

The bartender looked out of the window. "Here comes the stage," he said.

Shorty moved to look back over his shoulder, but the cold voice made him turn. He stared at Thorp.

"You keep your mouth shut, Shorty. I'm pulling out of here on that stage. You open your mouth, and I'll find you and shut it permanently."

"You don't scare me."

Thorp stood up.

Shorty had his Colt in its holster, and there was no sign of a gun about Thorp Barrett, but the older man swallowed hard. "All right, Kid," he said hastily.

"Thorp!"

Shorty nodded weakly.

The stage drew up in front of the saloon. A man opened the door, and Jim Conroy, the driver, ushered in three passengers. One of them was a young woman. She glanced uncertainly about her.

Jim waved an expansive hand. "Best we can do for food," he said. "Restaurant burned down yesterday, and the hotel don't serve this late."

The drummer eyed the young woman. He tipped his hat, but she looked away from him.

Jim led his three charges to a table near the front of the saloon, and the bartender brought trays of food to the table.

The drummer turned. "Play, damn you!" he called to Thorp.

Shorty swallowed a little.

Thorp picked up the guitar and began to play, very softly, *La Raza de Bronce Que Sabe Morir.*

The drummer stiffened, and he turned slowly to look at Thorp. "I said I didn't want any of that Mex stuff," he said thickly.

Thorp looked up. "Just stand there, brother, and drink all you like, but don't tell me what to play."

The drummer walked back toward Thorp. Shorty stood up and walked to one side. The drummer looked down at Thorp. "What was that you said?"

Thorp placed the guitar carefully on the table and stood up. "Go on back," he said softly.

For a moment, the big man eyed him, and then he turned and walked back to the bar.

Shorty whistled softly.

Thorp leaned against the wall and rolled a cigarette. He lighted it. The young woman was glancing curiously at him. Another of the passengers was a broad-shouldered man wearing a dark suit. He ate carefully and slowly, with great deliberation, and from the way he held his head and used his hands, Thorp suddenly realized the man was drunk as a lord. The other passenger was a thin, bespectacled man who glanced nervously about him as he ate.

The drummer was holding his temper back. It had been sharpened by the long delay in the arrival of the stagecoach, and the whiskey and Thorp Barrett had honed it to a razor edge. He drank steadily, and now and then, he watched Thorp through the fly-specked bar mirror.

Thorp played steadily as the passengers ate. Shorty eyed the drummer. "Jesus," he said softly, "he's got an edge on for you, Thorp."

Thorp nodded. He looked at the young woman, and then he stiffened. She sat at the table with the man who was a little the worse for wear with drink. The other passenger had vanished into the rainy night.

Jim, the stagecoach driver, emptied his glass and wiped his mouth. "I'll check with the agent and see if he wants me to go on," he said.

"You'd better," said the drummer. "I won't stay in this hole another night."

Jim shrugged and then walked out of the saloon. The rain drummed steadily against the thin walls, and a slow, monotonous dripping began from the center of a stained patch on the sagging ceiling.

Thorp got up and went into the back room where his gear lay beside the cot he slept in at night. He filled his war bag and got his possibles together. There wasn't much. He swung his gun belt about his waist and settled it after he buckled it. He still wore it on the left side. Hours of practice had helped him in developing the speed of his right hand again, but there was always the feeling that it would let him down at a crucial moment. Maybe it was all in his mind, but it was a cinch; he really believed his left hand was faster than his right, which was more than Travis Barrett could have said.

Thorp put on his dark coat and took his slicker from a hook. He walked into the saloon and placed his gear on a chair. Shorty sat at a table near the sidewall, and the little man was rapidly getting drunk. Virg stood at the window, looking out into the wet evening. The drummer leaned against the bar, and he looked uncertainly at Thorp.

The big man at the table looked at Virg. "You got rooms?" he asked.

"Hotel next door."

The man nodded. He looked down at the woman. "How about you, missy?"

"I had hoped to go on," she said.

The man waved a hand. "Never mind. I'll take you around tonight, missy. Ellis Walters is a real sport."

Thorp picked up his guitar. He was about to put it into its case when the drummer turned. "Play," he said.

Thorp looked at him.

"Play, damn you!"

Thorp began to tune the guitar, but he wasn't thinking of the drunken drummer. It was the big man, Ellis Walters, who was bothering him.

The young woman walked toward the door, but Walters took her by an arm. "Let me buy you a drink, missy," he suggested.

She shook her head. Thorp looked closely at her. Her face was shaded a little by the hat she wore, but there was something familiar about her.

"Let the lady alone," said Virg.

Walters turned slowly. "You shut your mouth, bar critter," he said quietly.

The drummer hiccupped. Shorty raised his head, took another drink, then leaned back against the wall.

"I'll wait for the stage at the hotel," said the woman.

"You'll wait here," said Walters.

Thorp placed the guitar on the table and walked forward.

Walters bent his head. "You going to take that drink with me?" he demanded.

Thorp stopped ten feet from the man. "Let the lady alone," he said.

Ellis Walters turned slowly. "Who asked you to butt in?"

"I'm dealing myself in."

Virg wet his lips and glanced uncertainly from one to the other of them. "He's been drinking, Thorp," he said.

"So?"

Ellis Walters wasn't as drunk as he had pretended to be. Thorp knew it as soon as he looked into the man's hard eyes. "Listen, sonny," he said quietly. "You go on back and play that cheap guitar."

Shorty's feet hit the floor. He stood up and walked slowly toward the rear door.

"Stay where you are," said Walters to Shorty.

"I was just leaving, mister."

"You won't get a chance to work around to the front of this place and come in behind me."

Virg swallowed hard. "Tell you what," he said hoarsely, "let's all have a drink together."

Jim Conroy came in and shook the rain from his hat. "The agent says I got to go on. We can make the next station in three or four hours. How about it?" He stared at Walters and Thorp Barrett. His eyes widened. Jim Conroy had been around long enough to recognize two rutting stags ready to lock horns.

The drummer waved a hand. He grinned at Walters. "Don't be afraid of him, mister," he said thickly.

"Shut up," said Walters. He glanced down at Thorp's right side. Then deliberately, he looked at the young woman. "You going to have that drink with me or not?"

Thorp moved forward. Walters swept back his coat and slapped his right hand down for a draw, but Thorp was too fast. He crossed over his right hand, clamped it on Walter's gun wrist, and almost instantly, his own Colt was jabbed against Walter's lower belly, just above the crotch. Walters grunted in fear and pain. He blinked his eyes. "Sorry, Kid," he said.

Thorp stepped back and sheathed the Colt. Walters raised his right hand to wipe the sweat from his face, but instead, he gripped his hat brim and flipped the hat toward Thorp at the same time as he drew a double-barreled derringer from his left coat pocket and fired it.

Thorp Barrett had dropped to the gritty floor, drawing and firing as the hat sailed over him. The smoke billowed about the two men, and then Ellis Walters fell heavily on top of the man he had tried to kill. Thorp rolled him away and stood up, with his brother's engraved Colt in his hand, smoke wreathing from the muzzle.

"I know you now," said the young woman.

Thorp seemed to shake his mind free from what he had just done. He looked at her with bleak eyes. It was Emily Thurlow, the girl he had been escorting along San Antonio Street that night so long ago in El Paso when he had shot Jed Martin to death.

The drummer stared at Thorp and then at Ellis Walters. He fumbled for a glass, then shoved it back. "Jesus," he said thickly. "I never saw anything like that before. And I was going to brace him sometime this evening."

Virg climbed over the bar. "You got more luck than brains, *hombre.*"

Virg knelt beside Walters. He fumbled inside the man's coat. "Thank God," he said. "He's alive."

"I could have told you that," said Thorp.

Shorty came to Virg, and the two of them carried the man back to the rear room and placed him on Thorp's old cot. "Get the doc," said Virg.

Thorp sheathed his Colt and picked up the neat little derringer. He slid it into a pocket. "Let's go, Jim," he said.

Conroy stared at him. "There'll likely be an investigation of this, Kid."

"Let's go!"

"All right. All right!"

Thorp got his gear and walked toward the door. Emily stood under the dripping porch roof. She looked up at him as he came outside. "Thanks," she said.

"He asked for it."

"I thought I knew you from somewhere."

"I thought I knew you, too."

She looked through the streaked window. "Will he be all right?"

"Yes."

"You've changed."

"It's been a long time."

The stagecoach drew up in front of the stage station. The thin little man scuttled into it. Thorp took her by the arm and helped her into the coach. He placed his gear in the rear boot and got into the coach. Jim's whip popped soggily, and the Abbott-Downing lurched uneasily on its great leather-thorough braces as it moved east along Tegner Street.

Thorp sat beside the girl. The other passenger had draped a blanket about him and was already seemingly asleep.

She glanced at Thorp. "They're still looking for you in Texas and New Mexico," she said quietly.

"I know. Chihuahua and Sonora, too."

"You're riding the wrong way then."

He looked down at her. "Where are you bound?"

"Globe."

"To see Doug Scott?"

"Yes."

"Why?"

"He's my stepfather."

There was no expression on his lean face.

"Get out at the next stop," she said. "I won't say I saw you."

"No."

"But why?"

He leaned back against the rear cushions. "I was going to Globe anyway."

"To find my stepfather?"

"Yes."

She stared at him. "But you can't just ride into Globe and try to kill him!" She placed a hand on his arm. "I can wire ahead and warn him."

"Go ahead."

"You wouldn't have a chance!"

He shoved back his hat. "I'm sick of running. Sick of stalling. For these past few years, I've done little but think about the day I'll face Doug Scott in the street and shoot to kill. Even up. One man against another."

The coach lurched into a rut and threw her against him. His arm was as hard as steel beneath his coat. She eyed him. "You're no longer Thorp Barrett," she said quietly.

"So?"

"You're Travis Barrett. A ghost haunting this earth to kill a good man who was only doing his duty."

The horses picked up speed as they reached the end of town. The rain slashed down steadily. The hoofs thudded steadily against the road, and the coach swayed easily in a slow rhythm. There were many miles between Wickenburg and Globe. Miles in which anything could happen, but somehow Emily Thurlow knew Thorp Barrett would reach Globe safely in order to do what he thought he had to do.

CHAPTER ELEVEN

Globe was booming. The Old Dominion Mine was the Copper King of Arizona Territory. There were still Apache haunting the Pinal and Apache Mountains, skulking in close at night to watch and wait for stray citizens of Globe. The Apache had hated the White-Eyes for taking Besh-Ba-Gowah, the Metal Village, from them. It was silver that had started the mining activities at Globe, but copper had made the raw town boom. Mules and burros climbed through the hills, and ox teams brought in merchandise from Silver City in New Mexico, for the nearest railhead to Globe was one hundred and twenty miles away.

The Globe stage plowed its way through the muddy streets, making a furrow through red-shirted miners, bearded prospectors, soldiers, cattlemen, and drifters. Broad Street had followed the winding course of Pinal Creek, and tinny music blared out from at least half a hundred saloons and hurdy-gurdy houses which lined Broad Street. The red-light district shacks lined the creek bed along North Broad Street.

The stage stopped in front of the station, and Thorp Barrett opened the door and dropped to the street, into three inches of thick mud. Emily Thurlow stood on the step, and Thorp lifted her easily from the step to the wooden sidewalk. The thin man who had ridden with them from Wickenburg through several changes in stage routs hesitated on the step, and Thorp gave him a hand. In all that time, he had said little other than that his name was Eben Piatt.

Thorp took his gear from the rear boot and placed it on the walk; then, he dug out Emily's luggage and that of Eben Piatt.

Piatt looked up at Thorp as he stepped up on the walk. "Listen to what the young lady says," he said quietly.

Thorp shoved back his hat. "You've got a good pair of listening ears, Mister Piatt."

Piatt reddened. "She made sense," he said stubbornly.

"That's up to me to decide."

"She could have wired ahead, and you would have walked into a welcoming committee, Barrett."

Thorp looked up and down the street. "I guess you're right."

Piatt picked up his suitcase, tipped his hat in the direction of Emily, who was looking up the street, then he blended into the throng.

She turned as Thorp placed her luggage beside her. "What happens now?" she asked.

"Who knows?"

"Why did you really come here?"

"We've been over that a number of times."

"You won't change your mind?"

"No."

"There is still time to leave before my father knows you're here."

He looked up and down the street. "I *want him to know I'm here.*"

She studied his tanned face. "Why were you so nice to me on the trip?"

He looked away.

"Why, Thorp?"

He reached down for his bag.

She placed a hand on his arm. "Because you knew if you came here with me, you were sure to find my stepfather, isn't that it, Thorp?"

He did not answer, and he nodded. "I realized that fact just before we got here."

Thorp tipped his hat. "I won't see you again, Miss Emily."

"Not if you can help it, you mean."

"Yes." He stepped into the street. "Goodbye, Miss Emily."

She watched him as he crossed the street and entered a saloon. There was indecision and fear mingled on her face, but she had not been able to send word ahead to Doug Scott. Somehow she thought the whole thing would resolve itself without a killing, but she wasn't at all sure. A cold wind blew down the street, and she shivered, but it wasn't from the searching wind.

———

THE WHISKEY BARREL was loaded to the mines. Thorp stood at the end of the bar farthest from the door, sipping his beer. A half-eaten free lunch sandwich lay on a plate in front of him. He had lost his appetite. He wondered why he had really come to Globe.

Smoke hung thick in the crowded room, and the noise was enough to drive a sober man out into the wet night. Three bartenders worked steadily behind the long bar, and at some places, the bar customers stood three deep.

Thorp leaned against the wall and finished his beer. The bartender hardly paused in his work as he scooped up the empty glass, refilled it, planted it on the bar, picked up the money, and began to make a sangaree.

Thorp raised the glass to his lips and then lowered it.

A man had entered the saloon and now stood just inside the doorway, studying the crowd. There was no mistaking him. It was Doug Scott. A little thinner, a great deal more gray at the temples, with fine lines etched from the base of the nose to the sides of the tight-lipped mouth.

Thorp pulled his hat lower and placed his elbows on the bar, lowering his head so that Scott would not see him.

When Thorp looked up again, the man was gone. "Can I leave my warbag and possibles here?" he asked the nearest bartender.

"Backroom. No one will touch them."

Thorp got rid of his gear and guitar. He left the saloon by the rear door and went up the muddy alleyway beside the saloon. A fine, misty rain drifted in the cold air.

He stood there a long time in the shelter of a doorway. The streets had emptied considerably. Now and then, a slickered or ponchoed rider splashed past. The yellow light from windows made irregular patches on the muddy street.

Thorp rolled a cigarette and lighted it, and as he did so, he saw the man limp out of a saloon directly across the street, look up and down, then set off to the north. He stopped at a cigar store and went in. Thorp crossed the street. He was twenty feet from the cigar store when Scott came out, puffing at a cigar.

Thorp settled his gun belt. He walked slowly toward the man until the half-light from a water-streaked window shone on his face.

Doug Scott stared at Thorp, and then he slowly took the cigar from his mouth.

"By God," he said softly. "It's hard to believe."

"You know me then?"

"Certainly! But for a moment there, I thought I was looking at Travis Barrett."

"The man you killed."

Scott eyed Thorp steadily. "He would have killed me, Barrett. He made a cripple out of me."

A man passed them, and he glanced at them, then his look settled on Thorp. He hesitated for a moment, opened his mouth to speak, and then went on to the corner, where he stopped and looked back at them.

"Emily said you were here, Barrett," said Scott. "I found it hard to believe."

"Why? You knew I'd come someday."

"No. There have been so damned many stories about you, Barrett, no one ever really knew the truth."

"Such as?"

"You died in the Rio Grande escaping from El Paso the night you fought Jed Martin. You were stood up against a wall in Zaragoza and shot by *rurales* with Bernardo Parillo, the *bandido jefe*. You were shot to death by Mexicans in some hassle down near the Sierra Del Nido. You were caught by Apache and tortured to death in the Sierra Vallecillos. Shall I go on?"

"No. You know I'm here. In the flesh."

"To kill me."

"Yes."

Scott shook his head. "Emily said you had no other thought in your mind."

"It's been a long wait, Scott."

The older man looked up and down the street. "Here?" he asked quietly.

"Pick the time and place."

Scott smiled thinly. "You're too generous and a fool, if I may say so. You let me walk away from you now, and maybe you'll never have another chance at me. On the other hand, if I do turn my back on you, I may get a bullet into it."

Thorp flushed, and his hands tightened.

"The Barrett way," said Scott evenly.

"I ought to buffalo you for that. I've never killed a man in cold blood yet."

"How many notches, Thorp?"

"I don't mark notches, Scott."

"Three? Four? Five? How many? As many as Travis had? Nine, wasn't it?"

"I could kill you now, but it isn't my way. I'll walk across the street. When I turn, Scott, you'd better draw and draw fast."

Scott whitened beneath his tan.

"Or are you afraid to face a Barrett who is unwounded?"

"You're a damned fool, Barrett."

Thorp stepped into the street and looked up at Scott; then, he walked across the muddy thoroughfare. He looked up at the muddy sidewalk. A woman stood there. "Thorp," she said quietly.

"Go home, Emily."

"No."

Thorp wanted to turn and clear leather with his Colt. To stand behind the kicking, smoking weapon and know that his soft-nosed forty-fours were ripping the life from Doug Scott as Scott's Winchester had ripped the life from a man who lay helpless in front of him years ago.

Boots sloshed in the mud, and Thorp turned quickly, with his Colt half-drawn, but Doug Scott walked easily, with his empty hands swinging by his sides. "You shouldn't be out in the streets at this time of night, Emily," he said.

Thorp stood to one side.

Scott looked down at the beautiful Colt. Then he looked up at Thorp, and there was a question in his tired eyes.

Thorp jerked his head. "Take her home," he said.

Scott stepped up on the walk. "I might tell you," he said quietly, "that the name of Barrett is a border legend now. Some versions say it was Travis Barrett who escaped from the adobe at Sierra Vieja and left his younger brother Thorp there shot to doll rags. Others say both

Barrett boys died there. Every man along the border had heard one version or another. The story has been set to music in both this country and in Mexico and sung in every cow camp from the Rio Grande to the Canadian."

"Interesting, Scott."

"Yes." The man looked up and down the street. "There's a thought in that for you. Many men think Thorp was killed, and Travis still lives. You shook me a little tonight when you came up to me. I know I killed *Travis*. I *know* you're *Thorp*."

"So?"

"Let me talk to you tomorrow."

"No."

She was looking at Thorp, and he could not meet her gaze.

"Let me talk to you tomorrow," repeated Scott. "Where are you staying?"

"In the hotel across the street from the Whiskey Barrel."

"Bueno! At nine in the morning?"

"Come and see."

He tipped his hat as they walked away. It was hard to believe that a man as hard case as Doug Scott had softened, that he could love and be loved. Thorp rolled a cigarette and lighted it. He needed a drink. The words of Scott came back to him as Thorp walked toward the saloon. What was Scott driving at? Sure, Thorp looked like Travis, but he had never heard any stories about Travis still being alive and Thorp being buried in a forgotten grave at Sierra Vieja. Either way, both Barrett boys were still wanted in New Mexico and Texas for crimes committed before the Barrett Corrida had died in its own blood.

Thorp stopped outside of the saloon. If it wasn't for the girl, Scott would be dead in the center of the street by now. It was the second time she had saved his life by being there at just the right instant. Thorp shook his head. Scott couldn't butter his way out of the debt he owed Thorp Barrett, no matter how fluently and convincingly he talked in the morning.

CHAPTER TWELVE

The rapping at the door made Thorp turn from the window where he had been watching the morning life of Broad Street. He took out his repeater watch and glanced at it. Exactly nine a.m. "Come in," he said.

Scott opened the door and limped in. "Morning," he said.

Thorp gestured toward a bottle and glasses on top of a marble surface table.

"This early?" asked Scott.

"You may need it."

Scott nodded.

Thorp filled the glasses and handed one to Scott. "Sit down," he said.

Scott glanced down at Thorp's waist. There was no gun belt there. "First," said Scott quietly, "thanks for holding off last night."

"It was for her, Scott."

"Yes." The tired eyes studied Thorp. "She likes you, Kid."

"The name is Thorp."

"Yes. Why do you really want to kill me, Thorp?"

Thorp stared at him. "I'll be damned," he blurted out.

"Yes. I killed Travis. But maybe he was dying already. The light was poor. He had a dozen slugs in his body when we buried him."

"It was the way you finished him off, Scott."

"I wasn't sure who it was. Can you remember details in a gunfight? The light was bad. I knew as long as that man had a gun in his hand, he'd shoot and shoot to kill. I had my men to worry about." Scott rubbed his left thigh. "Travis damned near got me, Thorp."

"Too bad he didn't."

Scott flushed. He raised his head. "All right. I'll talk to you in the only way you might understand. I don't want to be killed by you, nor do I want to kill you. But you're forcing my hand, Barrett.

Now put up or shut up! Draw and be damned to you!"

Thorp grinned. "I'm in no hurry."

"I thought you were like your brother. He was a hellion but a clean fighter, just the same. He would have forced a fight the instant he saw me last night, as you saw me in the Whiskey Barrel. Yes, I knew it was you standing there at the end of the bar. I haven't been a lawman most of my life without having developed some faculties of observation."

"What you driving at?"

Scott downed his whiskey. "Maybe I could have talked to Travis easier than I can with you."

"You don't make sense."

The eyes held Thorp's. "I know you for what you are, Thorp. A carbon copy of Travis Barrett! You're just the shadow of a gunman. A man who is rotting in his grave when he might have become something in this country. All he left is a phony legend and a carbon copy of himself to haunt the earth until someone riddles that carbon copy with bullets!"

Thorp wet his lips. "Get out of here," he said thinly. "Take care of your affairs. The next time I see you, I'm drawing, no matter where we are."

Scott hurled the glass into a corner and walked out.

Thorp buckled on his gun belt and settled it. He adjusted his string tie and then took another drink. Just enough to settle himself. He walked downstairs into the lobby. "What do you know about that man who just left here?" he asked the clerk.

"Doug Scott? He's a hard case. Used to be a marshal in New Mexico."

"What's he doing here in Globe?"

The clerk shrugged. "Who knows. There are a lot of men in Globe, and many of them have no business being here that I know of."

"If you have trouble with Scott, leave him alone. He's the man who killed Travis Barrett."

"So? Have you ever seen Travis Barrett?"

"No."

Thorp walked to the door.

The clerk hastily swung the register around and ran a finger down the list of guests. "Room 16," he said. "T. Barrett. Jesus God!"

———

THORP ATE a tasteless breakfast and then walked the streets of Globe. The thought occurred to him that if he did meet and kill Scott, providing that he himself wouldn't be strung up or placed in jail for the shooting, there wasn't any future for him, at least none that he had planned.

He was tired of his aimless drifting, and there was nothing he really knew how to do except shoot, play a guitar, and herd cattle. He leaned against a wall, warmed by the morning sun, and rolled a cigarette. Maybe he should pull out before Scott had him picked up for being a member of the old Barrett Corrida, but maybe Scott had too much pride in himself to let others do his fighting for him.

The batwings swung open in a saloon across the street, and a swamper emptied a bucket of dirty water into the street. There was something familiar about the man. Thorp crossed the street and walked into the saloon. The place was empty except for the swamper and a bartender who stood at the far end of the bar engrossed in a newspaper.

The swamper was singing softly to himself as he swung his huge mop, then he burst into song. "Have courage, my boy, to say no!" he howled.

"For Chrissakes, Chusco!" said the bartender.

Thorp walked toward the little man. "Chusco," he said quietly.

Chusco turned and peered uncertainly at Thorp. "Travis," he said.

"Thorp!"

Chusco leaned on his mop handle. "Don't crap me, son. I know Travis Barrett when I see him."

The bartender looked up quickly.

Thorp eyed Chusco. The man had deteriorated, and it was plain to see his mind was wandering. "What happened to Isobel?" asked Thorp.

Chusco smiled. "There she is," he said. He pointed toward the bar.

Thorp turned. There was an immense oil painting stretched along the back of the bar, above the mirror. A voluptuous woman, with huge breasts and thighs, lying on a bearskin rug, eyeing the big room with bovine eyes.

"Ain't she just something though, Travis?" asked Chusco.

The bartender placed a bottle on the bar. "Have a drink," he said to Thorp. "You too, Chusco."

Chusco shuffled to the bar and filled two glasses. "Thanks, Frank," he said.

Frank eyed Thorp. "He called you Travis Barrett."

"Yes."

"Travis Barrett is dead."

"I didn't say I was Travis Barrett. *He* did."

The heavy-lidded eyes flickered a little. "Yeh... so he did."

Chusco refilled his glass and raised it toward the oil painting. "To Isobel," he said loudly.

"You'd better drink with him, Barrett," said Frank.

Thorp dutifully raised his glass. Chusco looked at Frank. Frank hastily filled a glass, and the three of them stood there. Chusco looked at Thorp. "Your hat," he said.

Thorp whipped off his hat. The three of them solemnly drank to Isobel, then Chusco, without a word, went back to his mopping.

"Is he always like that now?" asked Thorp.

"Yeh."

"How long has he been here?"

"Six months or more. I ain't quite sure."

Frank refilled Thorp's glass. "Travis Barrett, eh."

Thorp remembered what Scott had said. "You ever see Travis Barrett, Frank?"

The bartender grinned. "Yeh."

"When?"

"Five minutes ago."

Thorp looked into the back mirror. He was lean, lacking perhaps a little of the breadth of his brother's shoulders, but he was an inch taller. He affected the same garb Travis had worn. Black trousers, dark blue shirt, and black tie, with black coat and hat. His face was burned by the suns of Chihuahua, Sonora, and Arizona. He spoke as his brother did, with a soft, slow drawl. The eyes were the same, and yet, there was something indefinitely different about them.

What was it Scott had said? *There have been so damned many stories about you, Barrett; no one ever really knew the truth. You died in the Rio Grande escaping from El Paso the night you fought Jed Martin. You were stood up against a wall in Zaragoza and shot by rurales with Bernardo Parillo, the bandido jefe. You were shot to death by Mexicans in some hassle down near the Sierra Del Nido. You were caught by Apache and tortured to death in the Sierra Vallecillos.*

"I'm right, ain't I, Barrett?" asked Frank.

The name of Barrett is a border legend now. Some versions say it was Travis Barrett who escaped from the adobe at Sierra Vieja and left his younger brother Thorp there shot to doll rags. Others say both Barrett boys died there. Every man along the border has heard one version or the other. The story has been set to music in both this country and in Mexico and sung in every cow camp from the Rio Grande to the Canadian.

"Have courage, my boy, to say no!" cried out Chusco as he staggered toward the door with a bucket of filthy water.

Many men think Thorp was killed, and Travis still lives.

"There were two Barrett brothers," said Thorp quietly.

"Yeh... one was a kid, hardly more than twenty-one by now if he was still alive. One thing I know, Barrett. You'll never see twenty-five again."

"Lang Spencer could use you," said Frank.

"Who's he?"

Frank smiled. "You're new to Globe, all right. Spencer owns this place and several others. Has a finger in quite a few pies. Gambling, merchandising, red-light houses. I can go on."

"What's the pitch?"

Frank sucked at a tooth. "Lang Spencer always has use for boys like you. Fast men with a cutter. The pay is good, Barrett."

Thorp refilled his glass and sipped the whiskey. It almost made him ill. He wasn't cut out for a drinking man.

"What do you say?" asked Frank.

"I might not be here too long."

"Trouble?"

"Perhaps."

Frank grinned. "Spencer can take care of that. The

Arizona Territorial Government respects Lang Spencer. He's got friends, has Lang, *big* friends."

Chusco came back in, glanced up at Isobel, then began to mop the floor again.

Thorp placed five dollars on the bar. "Give that to Chusco," he said.

"What will I tell Lang Spencer?"

"I don't know."

"He's back in his office now."

Thorp shrugged. Frank walked to the end of the bar, swung over it, and walked into a back hallway. In a few minutes, he was back. "He'll see you," he said.

Thorp walked past Chusco. There was a little sickness inside of Thorp, and he realized it wasn't from the whiskey but from seeing his old *compañero* like that.

Thorp walked into the hallway. A door was partly open. "Mister Spencer?" he called out.

"In here, Barrett."

Thorp walked into an office. A large, neatly dressed man sat behind an immense desk, with a cigar stuck out of the side of his mouth like a river steamer's jackstaff. Spencer looked up, and his eyes narrowed. "Travis Barrett?" he asked.

"Maybe."

"Sit down."

Spencer shoved a box of cigars toward Thorp as he sat down. Thorp took one and lighted it as Spencer studied him.

"I thought Frank was pulling my leg?" he said.

"So?"

"I heard you were in town, but stories like that drift all over. I've met men who swore up and down they met Wild Bill Hickock and John Wilkes Booth long after they were dead."

Thorp sucked in on the cigar. "I didn't say I was Travis Barrett."

"You don't have to."

"What's your pitch."

"I heard you came here to have a showdown with Doug Scott."

"You hear a lot."

Spencer smiled coldly. "It's part of my business." He relighted his cigar. "Do you know why Doug Scott is in Globe?"

"No."

"One story is that he killed a man in Chamberino, New Mexico, and just got over the state line ahead of a posse."

"Go on."

"I think the whole damned thing is a put-up job. The deal was rigged so that Scott could stay here under a cloud of suspicion."

"You haven't made any sense so far."

"Take it easy! It so happens that a government express rider was murdered in the Pinals a few months ago, and twelve thousand dollars was rifled from his express bags. The story is that it was done by Apache. I think Scott was sent here to find out who actually did it."

"That's possible. I didn't know he was still a marshal."

Spencer blew out a cloud of smoke and watched it drift toward the open transom. "I'll bet this saloon against a good cigar he still is." Spencer eyed Thorp. "That doesn't go any farther than this room, Barrett. Understand?"

"Yes. What does all this have to do with you and me?"

"It's only a matter of time before the law catches up with you, Barrett. New Mexico wants you. Texas wants you. Mexico wants you."

"That may be."

"You know the score, Barrett. There's a reward of one thousand dollars for you posted in New Mexico right now."

"Keep talking."

Lang Spencer took the cigar from his mouth and

leaned forward. "I'll talk business. Doug Scott is a shrewd operator and a damned good actor, but there is one thing that can spoil his game. His stepdaughter."

Thorp took his cigar from his mouth. "What do you mean?"

"Evidently, Emily Thurlow wasn't let in on the plan. She was in California when she heard Scott was in trouble and supposedly hiding out here in Globe. I have a feeling it took some of the wind out of his sails."

Thorp leaned back in his chair. No wonder she hadn't tried to warn Scott. She believed her stepfather was living outside of the law as Thorp was doing.

"Then you drift into town, Barrett, to add to the confusion. I have a feeling that Doug Scott is a very worried man right now." Spencer smiled. "I know you intend to kill Scott, but in a fair fight, if there is such a thing in your line of work."

"Meaning?"

"Scott is a good man with a Colt. I've seen top guns cut down by men who had half of their speed. The odds of the game. The little unknown factors which make yours a risky business."

"We'll see about that, Spencer."

"I'll get to the point then. By killing Scott, you'll be neck deep in trouble again, and it will only be a matter of time before the law catches up with you."

"So?"

"I want to get rid of Scott, and I'm willing to pay for it. My fee to you will be one thousand dollars with a verbal guarantee I'll have you out of Arizona Territory as quickly as possible and on the way to where ever you want to go. California, Canada, South America, you name it, and I'll see that it's done.

"You might as well cash in on this vendetta of yours, Barrett. A slug in the back from a darkened doorway will do the job just as well as one fired in a street fight, and it's a helluva lot more certain.

"Under my plan, you can get rid of Scott to satisfy yourself and then ride out of here with a thousand dollars for a new start."

Thorp leaned back in his chair. "I have a feeling it was you behind that express robbery."

"I didn't say that."

"You didn't have to."

The broad face tightened. "They always said you were hard to get along with."

Thorp stood up.

"Well?"

"Give me a little time to think. I've never been offered blood money before."

"You might as well cash in that fancy Colt of yours. A thousand dollars for one bullet placed in the right spot."

Thorp nodded as he left. Chusco was gathering up the garboons to polish them. *"Adios,* Travis," he said.

"Adios, Chusco."

Chusco looked at Frank. "Knew him well in the old days."

"Yeh."

Thorp walked outside and relighted the cigar Lang Spencer had given him, then he suddenly snatched it from his mouth and hurled it into the gutter.

CHAPTER THIRTEEN

Thorp hired a horse and rode slowly out of town. He needed time to think. He had never thought of killing for money. He had met plenty of men on both sides of the border who would kill a man for a lot less than a thousand dollars. He intended to kill Scott. The thought had never left his mind since that night at the Sierra Vieja when Scott had killed Travis.

Hours of practice had been done with but one goal in mind; to find and kill Doug Scott and let him know who was there to kill him.

It was the young woman who bothered him. She had been with the marshal in El Paso at his bedside. She had come from California to be near his side in what she believed was a time of trouble for him. Maybe he was in trouble. Maybe Lang Spencer was wrong.

Thorp knew now he should have killed Scott the first time he had seen him in Globe, then pulled foot for the border. Lang Spencer was trying to make a hired killer out of him for Spencer's own shadowy ends. There was a little time to think things over. Human bloodhounds would soon be nosing around when they knew Thorp Barrett was in booming Globe. Thorp grinned wryly. There was a price of one thousand dollars on his head in

New Mexico. The same price Lang Spencer had placed on Doug Scott's head. Thorp wondered who would cash in on those dollars.

A woman stood on a rise looking to the east, holding the reins of a horse. Thorp knew her at once. He rode up beside her and dismounted, taking his hat in his hand.

She smiled. "I should say this is a surprise, but it wouldn't be true. I was riding too, saw you ahead of me, and came this way by a short cut to meet you."

"Why?"

She eyed the distant Apache Mountains. "I came to find him last night."

"I knew that."

"Would you have killed him if I hadn't come?"

"Yes."

"Or he would have killed you."

"Perhaps."

"Primitive, isn't it?"

"It's a primitive country, Emily."

"Why didn't you talk with him this morning?"

"He isn't an easy man to talk to."

She eyed him. "Then you don't know him as well as you think you do."

"I didn't agree to talk with him to further our acquaintance, Emily."

"You should have."

He slapped his hat against his thigh. "This is a mad country. Everyone around here is mad. I came here for a showdown with Doug Scott, and he wants to talk with me. You knew why I came, and yet you think I should have talked with him."

Her calm blue eyes met his eyes. "You talked with Lang Spencer too, didn't you?

Can you classify a man like him with my stepfather?"

"My, you have big eyes and ears, grandmother," he said sarcastically.

She placed a hand on his arm. "You'll have to work

out your problem with my stepfather, one way or another, Thorp. Kill or be killed, if necessary, and I hope to God that never comes to pass. But stay away from Lang Spencer."

"Who told you to tell me that?"

"My stepfather."

"I'll be damned!" he blurted out. "I'm sorry, Emily."

She smiled. "You see, Thorp? My stepfather wants to help you."

He leaned against his horse. "Tell him that Lang Spencer wants him killed then. Tell him that Spencer has a standing offer of one thousand dollars to have him shot down one way or another."

She paled a little, and her hand went to her throat. "Why?" she asked quickly.

"The story is that Doug Scott never killed anyone in Chamberino, that he was here to investigate the murder and robbery of that express messenger some months ago. That the Chamberino killing was made up to make it look as your stepfather was on the run, Lang Spencer is sure that is the story. He wants to get rid of your stepfather."

"But why? You haven't told me that yet. Thorp?"

He shrugged. "I think Spencer had something to do with the killing and the robbery. He's afraid of Doug. So long as I hate Doug Scott the way I do and plan to kill him, Spencer, like the skunk he is, thinks I should cash in on it."

She looked away. "How can men be like that?"

"It's easy. You said it is a primitive place, Emily."

"My stepfather didn't tell me why he came here."

"It seems as though you messed things up by coming here."

"Yes... I see that now."

He placed his hat on his head. "I'm going back," he said.

"Let me ride with you."

"No. Spencer thinks I'm considering his offer. If he sees us together, he'll know I don't intend to take his pay for killing Doug."

"I knew somehow you were playing a part, Thorp."

He turned quickly. "What do you mean?"

"The lean and hungry look. The tied-down gun. The hard case reputation. I've heard a great deal about your brother. Are you trying to make him come back to life in your body?"

"We've talked enough," he said quickly.

"My stepfather always said Travis Barrett would have made a great lawman. He had courage and a great heart. He didn't seem to know what fear was, and he died the way he had lived. Perhaps you have copied him more closely than you've realized. You've changed a great deal since that night I met you in El Paso. You've changed in many ways. Somehow I think you've learned to be generous now."

She had a way of probing into his soul as Chusco's knife had probed for the bullet so many long months ago. She seemed to be able to bring to life the half-formed thoughts and ideas he had never been able to fully realize or bring to express himself.

She swung up her arm and pointed to the west. "Why don't you leave now, Thorp?"

"No."

She shrugged. He gave a lift up into the saddle, and his strong, lean hands felt the softness of her. Then she leaned down toward him and kissed him before she spurred the mare toward the town. She drew rein fifty yards from him and turned. "Stop playing a part," she called back. "Don't be the shadow of your dead brother, Thorp. *He* wouldn't have wanted it that way."

He watched her ride down the slope. She confused him. He touched his lips, then looked to the west. Maybe she was right. Maybe he should leave.

———

He was seated on the window sill, idly playing his guitar, when someone rapped at the door. It was dark in the room, for he had not lighted the Argand lamp. "Who is it?" he called.

"Spencer."

"Come in."

The door opened, and the man came in. "Practicing?" he asked sourly.

"No. I like to play and think at the same time."

"You're an odd character, Barrett."

Thorp lighted the lamp and looked across it at Spencer.

"Well?" asked Spencer.

"I haven't yet made up my mind."

"I won't wait much longer, Barrett."

"You'll wait as long as I want you to."

Spencer flushed. "I own a dozen gunmen around this town."

"Then get one of them to do your dirty work."

Lang Spencer took out a silver cigar case and selected a cigar. He clipped the end of it, then jammed it into his wide mouth. "You're not so big you can't be taken care of, Barrett."

"The job will cost you another thousand for that crack."

He lighted his cigar over the lamp and puffed it into life. "No," he said quietly. "There are plenty of men trying to build up a reputation as leather slappers. It would be worth more than money to say they had gunned Travis Barrett."

"That'll be the day."

Lang Spencer walked to the window and looked down into the street. "Come here," he said over his shoulder.

Thorp stood beside the big man.

"You see that man standing there near the water trough?" asked Spencer.

"Yes."

"The tall man near the saloon?"

"Yes."

"The man leaning against the post?"

"Yes, dammit!"

Lang Spencer turned, and his face was inches away from Thorps. "All my boys. I'll give you until ten o'clock tonight to make up your mind, Barrett."

"You make it almost too easy."

The big man walked heavily toward the door. He opened it and walked into the hall. Thorp snatched up his hat and followed the man. Lang Spencer did not look back as he walked down the stairs and crossed the lobby. Two men stood up from their chairs and followed Spencer out into the street.

Thorp rolled a smoke, then walked out into the street. Lang Spencer was gone, but two of his men lounged across the street from the hotel. Thorp was almost tempted to try them, but he knew damned well he'd have the odds against him. Besides, he hadn't come to Globe to tangle with Lang Spencer's hired gun-slicks.

He walked down the street to a restaurant and ordered food, and even as he ate, he saw a tall man watching him through the wide window from across the street.

———

THORP OPENED HIS ROOM DOOR. Doug Scott sat in the armchair, with his stiff leg propped up on another chair.

"Make yourself at home," said Thorp dryly.

Scott nodded. He gestured toward a flask on the table. "Have a drink."

"*Your* liquor?"

"I didn't distill it if that's what you mean."

"Emily told me what you told her this morning."

"So?"

"Thanks for the tip off."

"It doesn't change our position any."

"I didn't expect that," said Scott dryly. "Have a drink."

Thorp poured a drink and sat down on the bed to eye Scott. The big marshal has a brass nerve, and somehow Thorp thought that if they had known each other under different circumstances, they might have been friends.

Scott sipped his liquor. "This is an odd situation."

"Yeah."

The marshal grinned suddenly. "There's a thousand dollars reward for you in New Mexico. There's a thousand dollars reward for the man who brings in the killers of the express messenger. There's a thousand dollars offered to you to get rid of me."

"Everybody wants somebody else," said Thorp softly.

"I could arrest you or kill you and claim that thousand dollars in New Mexico. It states that they want you dead or alive."

"I could kill you and claim that thousand from Lang Spencer."

"True. Are you broke, Barrett?"

"I'm a little strapped," admitted Thorp.

"You won't take Spencer's thousand."

"Why not?"

"You wouldn't have told Emily about it if you had meant to take it."

"True enough."

Scott leaned forward and slowly rubbed his game leg. "I've got an offer for you too, Barrett. That thousand dollars originally offered in New Mexico was for the arrest of any one of, or all of the Barrett Corrida. You were just a kid then. They had nothing specific on you. No killings at any rate."

"What's your offer, Scott?"

"You know damned well I didn't kill any man in

Chamberino. That I'm here to find the man or men who killed that messenger, I'm still a US Marshal, Barrett."

"I might have figured that one out."

"I sent a wire to New Mexico last night after I knew you were in Globe. I have the answer here in my pocket."

"So?"

"The governor of New Mexico is willing to offer you a full pardon if you help me get the killers of that express messenger."

Thorp emptied his glass and refilled it. "Bull crap," he said. "Supposing I do get a pardon from him? There are still a few other counts waiting for me. The killing of Jed Martin in El Paso the night I escaped is one of them."

Scott shook his head. "Jed Martin lived, Kid."

Thorp stared at him.

"I'm sorry you carried that on your conscience all these years, Thorp."

Thorp waved a hand. "Maybe it didn't bother me."

"I can't believe that, Kid."

Scott sipped at his liquor. "We could have run you down that night near the Sierra Viejas. I held my boys back to give you a chance."

"But why?"

The gray eyes studied Thorp. "You were just a kid. I thought then you might come to your senses while you were on the run. You would never have done so in prison. It seems I figured wrong. You copied your brother. You wanted to kill me. This is a chance to clear yourself. The last one you'll ever have. What do you say?"

Thorp got up and walked to the window with his glass in his hand. At first, he didn't see anything clearly, for the face of Emily Thurlow seemed to be between him and the street below him. Then he knew he couldn't hurt *her*, at least. Doug Scott had held out hope to him.

"Well?" asked Scott quietly.

There were men in the street, men watching and

waiting. A sudden hate welled up in Thorp for them and their kind.

"I'll do it," he said as he turned.

"Thank God, Kid!"

"The name is Thorp Barrett!"

"The only information we are sure of is that there were three men in on the death of the messenger, and one of those three men is Buck Norris, Lang Spencer's bodyguard. A prospector saw Norris standing over the body of the messenger, and there were two other men close by, neither of whom the prospector could identify. The prospector passed the information on to a friend and then vanished, afraid of what Norris would do to him. We can't arrest Norris on hearsay."

"Spencer just as much as admitted that he was behind the deal."

"That doesn't mean a thing. We've got to get him to admit it in the presence of a witness who would be willing to testify against him and his boys."

"I haven't told him for sure what I planned to do. I have until ten o'clock tonight, Scott."

"So?"

"Maybe I can have him come here again. I'll try to get him to admit he had something to do with the killing." Thorp jerked a thumb toward a closet. "You can hide in there and listen to us."

Scott stood up. "It's farfetched, Thorp."

"Let me see what I can do."

"What time is it?"

The marshal looked at his watch. "Quarter to seven."

"I have until ten o'clock then."

Scott rubbed his game leg. "Maybe. Lang Spencer doesn't trust anyone, Thorp. He made you a proposition, and he knows now you're hedging on him. Maybe that ten o'clock deadline was a ruse. You might step out into the street and die with a slug in your back any minute from now."

Thorp drained his glass. "I'll go to his saloon."

"You're a damned fool!"

"No. He won't want a killing there. It's too close to home. It's the best place for me to be. If I make the deal with Spencer to come here, I'll get word to you."

"Keno." Scott held out a big hand. "You don't know what this means to me, Thorp."

Thorp ignored the hand. "Get out of here," he said harshly.

CHAPTER FOURTEEN

Lang Spencer's Copper Queen saloon was well patronized when Thorp Barrett walked into it and stopped at the end of the long bar. Those men who weren't too drunk to care eyed the tall figure of the newcomer and then looked hastily away.

"It's him all right," a miner said to a companion.

"Travis Barrett?"

"Yeh. I had seen him once in Silver City."

"Bull crap," said a gambler. "Travis Barrett was killed in the Sierra Vieja a couple of years ago."

"That's bull crap!" snapped the miner. "I know him, I tell you."

Frank, the bartender, leaned close to them. "It's Travis Barrett, all right."

"How do you know?" asked the gambler.

"Chusco called him Travis, and Chusco ought to know."

"I'll copper that," said the miner.

The gambler looked at Thorp again. "Well," he said slowly, "maybe..."

"There's a one way a man could tell," said Frank softly.

"How?" demanded the miner.

Frank grinned slyly. "Force him into a fight. If you're dead before you hit the floor, it's Travis."

"And if it ain't Travis?"

"You might die when you hit the floor. Hawww!"

Thorp looked up at Isobel; then, he looked for Chusco. The little man was seated at a table in the farthest corner of the saloon, with an empty glass in front of him and a dreamy look in his bleary eyes as he contemplated Isobel.

Frank mopped the bar in front of Thorp. "Spencer's got a bug in his butt about you," he breathed as he leaned close to scrub at a tobacco stain.

"So?"

"Christ man! Spencer gives the orders around here. He's got three of his boys back there with him now. Buck Norris, Matt LeMay, and Lon Gifford. All good men with a cutter, and they ain't afraid of Satan himself."

Thorp picked up the bottle and his glass. "Thanks," he said. He walked to Chusco's table, and quite a few pairs of eyes watched him as he did so.

Chusco looked up. "Howdy, Travis," he said.

"Chusco! Have a drink with me?"

"Don't mind if I do."

Thorp filled their glasses. Chusco held his glass up toward Isobel. "To her," he said.

"To her," echoed Thorp.

A man came out of the backroom and stood at the end of the bar. His eyes met those of Thorp, and Thorp saw something in them which carried him back some years to the night he stood in the cantina at Quatro Jacales and faced Deuce. It was the unspoken challenge that one gunfighter threw at another.

"What's your pleasure, Lon?" asked Frank.

It was Lon Gifford, one of Lang Spencer's gun swifts. Thorp glanced about the room and saw a man enter and stop at the end of the bar. Thorp spoke out of the side of his mouth to Chusco. "Who's that man?"

Chusco peered at the newcomer. "Matt LeMay," he said thickly.

Neat, thought Thorp. One at each end of the bar. Where was Buck Norris?

Lon Gifford downed his drink and wiped his mouth with the back of his hand. He had sized up Thorp, and now it was time to make his play.

Thorp sipped his liquor. For some reason, the barroom had quieted down. Frank looked across the room to Thorp, and there was a warning in his eyes.

Lon Gifford moved down the bar and stopped at the center of it, glancing up at the picture of the luscious and voluptuous Isobel. He squinted one eye. "Fat, ain't she?" he said to the man who stood next to him. The man looked away, but Gifford tapped him on the shoulder. "You hear me?" he asked.

"Yes."

"I said she was fat, *real* fat."

Chusco Barnes seemed to come to life. He straightened up in his chair.

"I told Lang Spencer he ought to get a real picture up there," said Gifford loudly. "That fat old bitch spoils the place."

The hackles rose on Chusco.

Then Thorp knew Gifford's play. Rile Chusco and goad Thorp into defending his old friend.

"Sloppy fat," said Gifford.

Chusco was out of the chair and across the room before Thorp could stop him. Chusco ran full on into one of Lon Gifford's elbows. He staggered back. Gifford grinned. "Riled, Chusco?" he asked. He turned a little and drew, and it was damned fast, just about as fast as any man Thorp had seen in action, and that included Travis. The big Colt rapped once, and a hole appeared in Isobel's plump navel.

"You dirty sonofabitch!" yelled Chusco.

Gifford turned and swung up his right arm. The pistol

barrel struck Chusco alongside the head and drove him to his knees. Thorp stood up and started toward the stricken old man.

Gifford swung his body a little, and the muzzle of the Colt entered on Thorp's belly. "Git back you," said Lon Gifford.

Thorp snatched up a chair with his left hand and hurled it toward the gunfighter, and at the same time, he jumped sideways, drew with his left, and fired an instant after Gifford's Colt rapped. The hurtling chair made Gifford jerk, and his slug went wild. Thorp went into a crouch and looked at Matt LeMay as Lon Gifford grunted in savage pain and gripped his right forearm with his left hand. The Colt dropped from nerveless fingers, struck the floor, and exploded, and Chusco Barnes jerked and fell sideways from his knees to lie still.

Smoke swirled up about the big harp lamps, and the saloon was as silent as the grave.

Blood dripped from Gifford's right hand and splotched the floor.

Men looked at Thorp Barrett. This was something they had never seen before. A man, caught with a pistol in holster, under the gun muzzle of a gunslick like Lon Gifford, who had still outplayed him and gunned him into helplessness.

Thorp catfooted forward. Matt LeMay backed toward the door and then disappeared into the night.

"It's Travis Barrett, all right," said the gambler shakily. "No other man moves like that."

Lon Gifford walked toward the rear of the saloon, swaying as he walked. Thorp knelt beside Chusco. The little man opened his eyes. "Hold me up," he said.

Thorp raised him. He looked at the picture. "Lovely," said little Chusco Barnes. *"Adios,* Kid." He slumped in Thorp's arms.

When Thorp stood up, he knew that Chusco had

known all along he was Thorp Barrett rather than his brother. The little man had had a reason.

Lang Spencer came out of the back room, and there were two men behind him. One of them was Matt LeMay, and the other was a shorter, dark-haired man with eyes like chips of gray ice. Lang looked down at Chusco. "Get him out of here," he said. "I'll take care of the burial expenses."

"Thanks," said Thorp.

The cold eyes met Thorp's. "You winged Lon," he said.

"Fair fight," said Frank.

"Shut up, you," said Spencer. "Serve the customers. Give me a bottle."

Spencer gripped the neck of the bottle and poured a drink. "You drinking with me, Barrett?" he asked.

"No."

"When I invite anyone to have a drink, they always have a drink."

Thorp shoved back his hat. "See you later," he said. He walked toward the door, half expecting a slug in the back.

"Barrett!" called out Spencer.

Thorp turned.

The big man raised a glass. "Ten o'clock," he said. "Your room. Be there."

Thorp nodded. He walked out into the street. Men had been peering into the saloon through the big dusty windows. They faded to the sides of the walk as Thorp passed amongst them.

CHAPTER FIFTEEN

Thorp was in his room, looking down at the street, when he heard footsteps in the hall. He turned, drew his Colt, then stepped to one side of the door. It was a little after nine o'clock. "Barrett?" The low voice came through the door.

Thorp opened the door, and Doug Scott came in. "Jesus," said the marshal. "You sure carry your guts with you. I heard about what happened at the Copper Queen."

Thorp nodded. "I don't know whether Gifford was trying me out or meant to kill me. Anyone see you come up here?"

"No. I came up the back way."

"Spencer is due here at ten."

"You think he'll come?" Thorp shrugged. *"Quién sabe?"*

"I don't like this closet business, Thorp."

"There's no one in the next room. There's a door between both rooms. You can open the transom and stand on a chair to hear what is said."

"It's still risky."

Thorp raised his head. "Pull out of it then!"

Scott flushed. "I'm sticking."

Thorp walked to the window. He could see Matt

LeMay standing in a doorway. "I don't know whether Spencer is coming here to try and talk me into killing you or into having me done away with because I might know too much."

"I know."

Thorp rubbed his jaw. "I was lucky in the Copper Queen, Scott."

"Not from what I heard."

Thorp whirled. "Sure, it looked good, but I could have been killed easily enough. How long can a man go on facing odds just because he has a reputation?"

Scott eyed him steadily. "At least you're beginning to think about it."

"Chusco died because of that bastard."

"You could have killed him from what I heard."

"No. I was lucky, Scott. You don't know how lucky I was. If Gifford had killed me, Spencer would have had him cleared. They were trying me, one way or another, and all I did was get in deeper with Spencer."

"I have a good horse. You have time to get out of here. I'll loan you enough money to get to California."

Thorp shook his head. "You'd better leave."

Scott walked to the door which led into the other room. It was locked.

"Wait," said Thorp. He left the room and walked downstairs. The clerk looked sleepily at him.

"I want the room next to mine," said Thorp.

"You don't like the one you have?"

"Sure, but I have a lady coming to see me later on tonight."

The clerk grinned. "I get it. I can have champagne sent up for a little extra on the side."

Thorp winked. "I'll let you know." He signed the register with the name of Mary Williams, took the key, and went back upstairs.

Scott grinned as Thorp told him of what he had done. He unlocked the door and walked into the room. It was a corner room overlooking the two streets. He walked to the window and peered through the curtain. "One of his boys is down there, Kid," he said.

"Matt LeMay."

Scott whistled softly.

Thorp leaned against the side of the doorway. "If anything happens," he said quietly, "you stay out of it."

"I'll back your play, Kid."

"No."

Scott shrugged. He passed a hand beneath his coat and touched his Colt. "Good luck," he said.

"Thanks."

Thorp started to close the door. "You like music?" he asked.

Scott was startled. "Yes. Why do you ask?"

Thorp jerked a thumb at his guitar. "I feel like playing."

Scott studied him. "You're a strange one, Barrett."

"Any preferences?"

Scott flushed. *"Little Footsteps Soft and Gentle?"*

Thorp nodded. He closed the door and walked to the bed to pick up the guitar. He tuned it, sat down on the bed, and began to play softly. After Scott's selection, he went on into *The Eerie Canal, Joe Bowers,* and *Poor Boy.*

Thorp leaned back against the bedpost. Then he heard the heavy footsteps in the hallway. He glanced at the transom between the two rooms, stood up, tapped on the door, then sat down on the bed again.

A heavy hand struck the door. "Barrett?"

"Yes."

"It's almost ten o'clock."

Thorp stood up and walked to the door. He opened it and looked at Lang Spencer. Behind the big man, across the hallway, was Buck Norris, leaning against the wall, rolling a quirley.

Spencer walked into the room and sat down. Thorp

leaned against the wall. Spencer's eyes flicked down to Thorp's Colt. "Put it on the table," he suggested.

Thorp shrugged. He drew the fine weapon and placed it beside the lamp. Spencer eyed it. "You're Travis Barrett, all right," he said. "I've heard of that fancy six-shooter."

Lang Spencer leaned back in the chair. "What's the word?" he asked quietly.

"I'm interested."

"Good."

Thorp rolled a cigarette and lighted it. He studied Lang Spencer through the smoke. "What guarantee do I have you'll pay me the thousand?"

"My word."

Thorp smiled. *"Your* word?"

Spencer colored. "What *do* you want then?"

"Pay me now."

"You think I'm a patsy?"

"Your men are watching me all the time. How far would I get if I pulled foot?"

"I don't know, and I can't afford to lose any of my boys right now."

Thorp studied his cigarette as though he had never seen one quite like it before. "Maybe Scott knows too much already. Maybe he's already turned in a report, Spencer."

Spencer waved a thick hand. "He doesn't know crap!"

"You sure?"

Spencer looked up quickly. "I'll bet on it!"

Thorp grinned. "How much?"

The hard eyes narrowed. "What the hell do you know?"

Thorp leaned forward. "I know Buck Norris was in at the death of that messenger. The other two men were you and Lon Gifford."

"Goddammit! I never was there! It was Norris, Gifford, and Matt LeMay."

"Then what do you have to worry about? They killed him and got the money. Funny thing, though, no one ever found out how those three hombres knew that messenger had that much *dinero* on him and how they knew which *way* he was riding and *when.*"

Spencer wet his lips.

"There was someone with brains behind that deal," said Thorp.

"Meaning?"

Thorp grinned. "The man who wants to hire me to kill Doug Scott."

Spencer sat up straight. "He hasn't got a damned thing on me! Now you listen here, Barrett! You'll get a thousand dollars if you kill Doug Scott, and I don't give a fiddler's damn how you do it."

Thorp flipped his cigarette into the garboon. "Let's have a drink on that," he suggested.

Thorp got the bottle and two glasses, and all the time he moved about the room, he felt Spencer's hard eyes upon him.

Thorp poured the liquor.

Someone tapped at the door. "Boss," said Norris. "They's a filly coming up the stairs."

"Who is it?"

"Scott's daughter."

Spencer stood up between Thorp and his six-shooter.

They heard the clicking of heels in the hallway and then a soft tapping at the door. "Thorp?"

Spencer jerked his head toward the door.

"Yes," said Thorp.

"May I see you?"

Spencer nodded to Thorp. *"Thorp,"* he said in a low voice. "You phony bastard!"

Thorp opened the door. Norris was nowhere in sight. Emily came into the room and then stopped short as she saw Lang Spencer. The big man had drawn back his coat and rested his right hand on his Colt while he reached for Thorp's engraved Colt with his left hand.

"Looking for your father?" asked Lang Spencer coldly.

She looked at Thorp, and there was fear in her eyes. "What have I done?" she asked.

"Buck!" called out Spencer.

The gunman came into the room.

"*Mister* Barrett is going to take a little walk with us," said Spencer.

Thorp glanced at the transom. Surely Scott had heard everything.

"Walk," said Norris.

"Both of you," said Spencer.

Thorp turned. "Let her go," he said quietly.

Spencer smiled, but there was no mirth in his eyes. "Later maybe. After I make a deal with Scott."

Yellow lamplight flickered in the dim hallway.

"Down the back way," said Spencer.

Matt LeMay appeared at the head of the stairs and walked toward them. "What happens now, Boss?" he asked.

"We've got a polecat to kill," said Spencer.

Thorp felt as helpless as a baby. He glanced at the door to the room where Scott was hiding, praying to God he wouldn't come out and start shooting with the girl standing there.

Norris prodded Thorp in the back.

Thorp walked toward the stairway which led down to the rear of the building, past the door of Scott's room. Norris and LeMay were just behind Thorp and Emily while big Lang Spencer led the way.

"Thorp!" the voice rang out in the hall from behind the five of them. It was Doug Scott.

Thorp whirled. Scott stood in the doorway of Thorp's room, and as he stepped into the hallway, Lon Gifford appeared at the head of the stairs. His right arm was in a sling, but he carried his six-shooter in his left hand. Even as Scott raised his Colt, Gifford fired. The marshal staggered forward. Thorp slammed a shoulder against the girl and drove her to the floor.

"Thorp!" called out Scott. He threw the Colt toward Thorp. Thorp jumped high and caught it as the lamplight glinted from the engraved surfaces of it. Scott fell forward on his face.

Thorp turned and crashed the heavy weapon down on the head of Lang Spencer, driving him to his knees. Matt LeMay turned and drew, but Thorp's Colt rapped once, and the slug caught the big man through the breastbone, driving him against Buck Norris. Norris drew and fired, and the slug tore at Thorp's left sleeve, but Thorp's second shot caught Norris in the belly, dumping him down on top of LeMay.

Thorp stood there in the smoke-filled hallway facing Lon Gifford. The man came forward like a cat. Then Gifford jumped to one side and fired, but he had given himself away. Thorp had lunged forward, firing as he did so, and as he hit the floor, he emptied the Colt into Gifford.

Gifford whirled with the impact of the heavy slugs, staggered toward the stairwell, caught at the newel post, then pitched down the stairs and out of sight.

Thorp wiped the cold sweat from his face and pulled the girl to her feet. "Your father," he said.

Doug Scott groaned as they carried him into Thorp's room. "It'll be all right," he said. "The slug gouged my right hip.

Devils are bound to make a permanent cripple out of me." He smiled. "I heard everything, Thorp." He looked down at the gun in Thorp's holster. "Recognize that Colt?"

Thorp drew it out. It was the mate to the one he had carried since the day Travis had been killed at the Sierra Vieja. He looked at Doug Scott. "Thanks," he said quietly.

The marshal closed his eyes. "You can wear both of them now," he said. "Wherever you're heading, they'll know you for being the brother of Travis Barrett and as good a man with a pair of sixguns as he ever was."

Emily looked at Thorp. "Where will you go?" she asked.

Thorp placed the six-shooter on the table. "They say I'm just the shadow of a gunman. They're right. But I like being on the side of the law. If that pardon holds good in New Mexico, I'd like to be a shadow once more. The shadow of the best United States Marshal the Southwest has ever seen."

Doug Scott opened his eyes. "It's a cinch," he said. "Now get me a doc, Kid."

Thorp took her by the arm, and they walked out into the smoky hall of death. She shuddered. "It was so fast," she said. "So *very fast.*"

"We can be out of here in a day or so. Then you can forget all about it."

She looked up at him. "I'd like to be a shadow too, Thorp. Your shadow."

He led her to the rear stairway, and they walked down it to the side street. He took her in his arms before they stepped out into the street and kissed her, knowing the long trail was over and that a new, and better way of life, was open before him at last.

TAKE A LOOK AT BARRANCA AND BLOOD JUSTICE:

Two Full Length Western Novels

Gordon D. Shirreffs, Spur Award and Owen Wister Award winning author, tells the tales of the old west as they were meant to be told—with no holds barred action and adventure.

In *Barranca*, a dying blind man vows to reveal the site of a lost silver mine to two Civil War vets, but only if they will help him see through the quest. He knows he won't live long enough to enjoy the spoils, but he wants to die at least having the knowledge that it was found. The unlikely trio must deal with arid desert heat, hostile forces, crooked Federales, and treacherous cliffs to discover the lost valley where a silver treasure beyond their wildest imaginings awaits.

In *Blood Justice*, Jim Murdock had left Ute Crossing seven years before, with a posse hot on his heels and thirsty for blood. Now, he'd arrived back just in time to see another lynching. The three men who were supposed to have murdered the town's leading citizen were removed from the jail at midnight, taken to a hill, and hanged by their necks until dead. Someone was too anxious to get them out of the way, and Jim Murdock was going to find out why. He was going to track down the truth—and the real killer or killers—even if it meant putting his own neck in a noose...

"The joy of reading Shirreffs' work is in his mastery of pacing and his tough, gritty prose." – **James Reasoner, author of Outlaw Ranger.**

AVAILABLE NOW

ABOUT THE AUTHOR

Gordon D. Shirreffs published more than 80 western novels, 20 of them juvenile books, and John Wayne bought his book title, Rio Bravo, during the 1950s for a motion picture, which Shirreffs said constituted *"the most money I ever earned for two words."* Four of his novels were adapted to motion pictures, and he wrote a Playhouse 90 and the Boots and Saddles TV series pilot in 1957.

A former pulp magazine writer, he survived the transition to western novels without undue trauma, earning the admiration of his peers along the way. The novelist saw life a bit cynically from the edge of his funny bone and described himself as looking like a slightly parboiled owl. Despite his multifarious quips, he was dead serious about the writing profession.

Gordon D. Shirreffs was the 1995 recipient of the Owen Wister Award, given by the Western Writers of America for "a living individual who has made an outstanding contribution to the American West."

He passed in 1996.